BEAUTY AND THE BEASTLY

Johnny figured he was in luck tonight. The knockout he had hit on in the club had followed him into the john. She stood at the threshold, smiling at him. A crimson fingernail touched the throat of her leather jacket, tugging the zipper; its slow, high-pitched snarl was louder than thunder. The black leather parted, revealing white flesh.

Her breasts were perfect, standing full, firm and solid. The nipples were round and pink, like the eyes of a white rabbit. Johnny stared at them, half-hypnotized, as he clung to the sink for support.

The zipper continued its downward track, and Johnny began to suspect he was in for too much of a wild thing. . . .

WILD BLOOD

WILD BLOOD

by

Nancy A. Collins

A ROC BOOK

ROC
Published by the Penguin Group
Penguin Books USA Inc., 375 Hudson Street,
New York, New York 10014, U.S.A.
Penguin Books Ltd, 27 Wrights Lane,
London W8 5TZ, England
Penguin Books Australia Ltd, Ringwood,
Victoria, Australia
Penguin Books Canada Ltd, 10 Alcorn Avenue,
Toronto, Ontario, Canada M4V 3B2
Penguin Books (N.Z.) Ltd, 182–190 Wairau Road,
Auckland 10, New Zealand

Penguin Books Ltd, Registered Offices:
Harmondsworth, Middlesex, England

First published by Roc,
an imprint of Dutton Signet,
a division of Penguin Books USA Inc.

First Printing, September, 1994
10 9 8 7 6 5 4 3 2 1

 REGISTERED TRADEMARK—MARCA REGISTRADA

Printed in the United States of America

To the members of my pack:
Alex, Bill, Joe R., Joe C.,
Phil, Scott, and Stacey.
Let it howl.

ACKNOWLEDGMENTS

The author would like to acknowledge the following books that proved helpful in the creation of this novel: *Homeboy* by Seth Morgan, *A Lycanthropy Reader* by Charlotte Otten, *The Behavior and Ecology of Wolves* by Erich Klinghammer, *The Clever Coyote* by Stanley P. Young & Hartley T. Jackson, and *The Wolf: A Species in Danger* by Erik Zimen.

Chapter One

The fourth period bell rang, marking the time for lunch. Skinner Cade exited Mr. Stowe's math class and joined his fellow students in the halls of Choctaw County Junior High School.

At thirteen, he was somewhat undersized for his age. Slight of chest and narrow of waist, with coal-black hair and an olive complexion, he stood out among the raw-boned, fair-haired sons of the local farmers. But his most unusual features by far were eyes the color of freshly minted gold coins, and unusually long third fingers on both hands.

Skinner fumbled with the combination on his locker, trying hard not to look in the direction of Mary Beth Walchanski, who had the locker two doors down from his.

Mary Beth Walchanski: she of the skintight letter sweater and cheerleader miniskirt. Mary Beth was a year older than Skinner and the clearly marked property of Deke Farley, star quarterback for the Choctaw Braves. Mary Beth was also notorious for provoking Deke's jealousy by rubbing herself against lower classmen.

Still, she *was* amazingly endowed. Her breasts strained against her sweater, permanently warping the big felt "C" stitched on its front, while her buttocks—made rock-hard by a regimen of human pyramids and side-splits—clenched and unclenched like the velvet haunches of a jungle cat as she leaned forward, rooting through the tangle of romance novels, Walkman earphones, and discarded junk jewelry that filled the locker. Skinner wasn't even aware he was staring in her direction until Mary Beth straightened up and smiled at him.

He quickly averted his eyes and pretended to try and find something in his locker, but it was too late.

"Hey, you're kinda cute—for a little guy."

Mary Beth's breath was redolent of Juicy Fruit and Cotton Candy Pink Lip Gloss. One of her breasts brushed his elbow. He jerked his arm back as if burned. He felt the hairs on the back of his neck rise as sweat sprang from his palms.

"You've got really interesting eyes. Has anyone ever told you that?"

"Um—not really, no."

Mary Beth affected a little pout. "What's the matter? Don't you like me?"

"Uh, sure I like you, I guess," he muttered.

"Really?" She giggled, leaning in close and batting her eyelashes.

Before Skinner could answer, there was a hand the size of a catcher's mit clamped on his shoulder, spinning him around.

"What's goin' on here? You tryin' t' put th' moves on my woman, *Piss-Eyes*?"

Deke Farley was as big and mean as they could come in Choctaw County, on or off the schoolyard. Tall, athletic, blond and loutish, Deke was the bane of all those less popular than himself. And you couldn't get more unpopular than Skinner Cade.

"I'm *talkin'* to *you*, space-case! I asked if you was tryin' t' beat my time?!"

Skinner was struck dumb by fear and embarrassment. He couldn't speak even if someone had shoved burning bamboo splinters under his fingernails. He stared up at Deke, who towered over him; a wrathful Adonis tricked out in a letter-jacket and an Ozzy Osbourne t-shirt.

"Wassamatter, *Piss-Eyes*? Cat got your tongue?" Deke slammed the flat of his palm against Skinner's collarbone, knocking him against the lockers, sending textbooks flying. Deke's lips pulled into a sneer. "Maybe it ain't *pussy* you're into. Izzat it, Piss-Eyes? Are you *queer*?"

Deke turned to the crowd that had gathered to observe the ritual scapegoating. "Hey! Ol' Piss-Eyes here is a cock-licker!"

Skinner bit his lower lip to keep it from trembling and bent to retrieve his dropped books. Deke slapped them out of his hands again before he had a chance to straighten up.

"I asked you a *question*, Piss-Eyes. Are you *queer*?"

"No." He all but spat the word.

"Then you *were* tryin' t' make time with my girl."

Skinner shook his head and tried, for a second time, to pick up his books. Deke's kneecap smashed into his face, throwing him onto the floor and causing a geyser of blood to burst from his left nostril.

Dazed, Skinner lay on his side, surrounded by his scattered schoolbooks. He could taste his own blood, hot and coppery, at the back of his throat. Everyone was laughing at him. Especially Deke, who stood with one arm around Mary Beth's waist.

Skinner touched his face and stared at the fresh red wetness smearing his fingers.

And changed.

The fear was gone. In its place was rage. A hot, pulsing rage that made his bones crack and muscles rearrange. The laughter grew higher, shriller, turned into screams without Skinner realizing exactly when. Deke's blandly handsome face grew slack, too stunned to register anything but confusion.

Skinner was on him in a whirlwind of fur, fang, and claw. Deke's letter-jacket shredded under his taloned fingers like tissue paper. As Deke shouted for help, Skinner closed his teeth on his tormentor's larynx, sending Deke's blood and screams leaping into his own mouth.

After he finished with Deke's torn body, he stood on crooked hind legs and fixed Mary Beth with a lambent gaze. The cheerleader was cowering against the lockers, too paralyzed by her terror to flee or even cry out. Skinner approached her, his long, pointed penis extending from its furred pouch.

He took her from behind in the blood-drenched hallway, his hairy thighs slapping against her naked rump, snarling in reply to her whimpers of pain.

As he felt orgasm bearing down on him, it suddenly occurred to Skinner that this wasn't how it had happened at all.

This is a dream, Skinner realized as he climaxed.

He woke up with a dry mouth and a sticky crotch. The dream was still fresh in his mind, complete with its mixture of blood-lust and sexual frenzy. Skinner didn't know whether to be disgusted or worried. Had it been simple wish fulfillment or something worse?

His dream had followed reality to the most agonizing detail. Up to a point. Needless to say, he didn't turn into a furry, sharp-toothed demon, nor did he kill Deke and rape Mary Beth when he was thirteen years old.

However, the sight of his own blood had triggered something deep inside him, driving him into a mindless rage. He'd launched himself at the bigger boy, shrieking invective, and surprised everyone—including himself—with the ferocity of his attack.

He succeeded in bloodying Deke's nose before the quarterback pummeled him into the ground. It resembled the scene in *Cool Hand Luke* where George Kennedy beats Paul Newman into a pulp, except in his case nobody begged Skinner to stay down.

Still, it had marked the last time anyone tried to physically bully him at school. The whipping boy had refused to take his ritual beating, endangering the status quo. A repeat of such behavior would have brought the class structure crashing down, and that could not be risked.

Skinner tossed aside his bedclothes, pausing to listen to the sound of his roomie's snoring from the other murphy bed before getting up. He guessed he should feel lucky Kramer was actually asleep this time and not beating off.

He'd hoped that by attending Arkansas State University in Jonesboro, instead of the University of Arkansas at Monticello, he'd be exposed to a wider selection of people from different places and have a chance to take part in the exchange of ideas and knowledge. With only two semesters behind him, however, it was already shaping up to be another version of the hell he'd endured at Choctaw County High.

His roommate, Kramer, was a fat, near-sighted nerd who, when he wasn't doing things like cooking Campbell's soup in the popcorn popper or watching T.V., was either drinking beer or pulling his pud. As far as Skinner could tell, Kramer didn't attend classes of any kind. He certainly never seemed to leave the dorm. At first Skinner had found his roomie's constant presence aggravating, but over the last few weeks he'd learned to fall asleep to the sound of Kramer's one hand clapping.

Still, this was hardly the intellectual and cultural stimulation he'd expected from college life.

He quickly removed his soiled briefs, stuffing them into the plastic trashbag he kept in his closet for dirty laundry. He looked at the digital clock next to his bed as he tugged on a clean pair. Almost six o'clock. His first class was at nine. He might as well just stay up and do some reading before getting ready for the day. . . .

The knock on the door was loud enough to shake Kramer from his snoring. "Hn? Wha—?"

Skinner opened the door and peered out cautiously into the hall. His and Kramer's room was at the very end of the corridor on the third floor, separated from the common room and showers by a gauntlet of jocks and ROTC gung-hos. Naturally, he and Kramer often ended up the butts of practical jokes, usually involving shaving cream, bags of warm lemon Jell-O, and human excrement.

He was surprised to see Terry Spencer, his floor's dorm rep, standing on the other side of the threshold. Spencer was a senior classman assigned to handle the various disputes amongst the students living on the third floor. He had a corner room with its own private shower and toilet and was rarely glimpsed by anyone else living on the same floor.

"You Cade?"

"Yeah . . ."

"You got a phone call."

He knew it was bad news. His family could barely afford to send him to college, much less splurge for luxuries like a phone in his room. Besides, who would want to talk to him besides his family?

The receiver was sitting off the hook in Spencer's room. The older student was trying not to look put upon but wasn't doing a good job of it.

Skinner picked up the telephone, his guts cinched tighter than a poor man's belt.

"Hello?"

"Skinner, that you, son?" It was his mother's husband's voice.

"Luke? What's wrong?"

"It's your mama, son. She's in a bad way. She had another one of her seizures last night. She's in the hospital over in Lake Village. The doctor says it's only a matter of time. . . ."

"Luke, I'm studying for finals. . . ."

"She's been askin' for you."

Skinner sighed and nodded his head, even though Luke wasn't there to see it. "I understand. I'll get there as soon as I can. I'll take the next bus out—"

"I'll tell her you're on your way."

"Luke—? Tell her I love her, okay? In case—"

"I'll be sure to do that for you."

"Thanks."

Skinner was acutely aware of being stared at. He looked up at Spencer, who was standing over him, arms folded, mild curiosity on his sleepy features.

"So—something happen back on the farm?"

"My mother's dying."

Spencer's features tried to arrange themselves into a generic sympathetic expression. "Really? Sorry to hear that, Cade. . . ."

"Yeah. Thanks for letting me use the phone." Skinner hurried out of the room, not wanting Spencer to see the tears building in the corners of his eyes. When he got back to his room, Kramer was beating off again.

*   *   *

It was nearly noon by the time the bus left Jonesboro. There was no such thing as a direct drive to Choctaw County, unless you had your own car. The Greyhound bus Skinner had to take first went from Jonesboro to Memphis, then looped through rural Mississippi, reentering Arkansas via Greenville, then traveled through the river delta on its way to Little Rock.

As it was, the bus never stopped in Seven Devils unless there was a passenger to pick up or unload. By the time he reached his hometown, it would be midnight. He wasn't going to make it.

Skinner shifted uncomfortably in his seat and stared out the window, watching what passed for scenery on the interstate flash by: cow in pasture; exit sign for West Memphis; burned-out car on shoulder; gas station; cow in pasture.

He hated riding the bus. It stank of cigarettes, even though smoking was supposedly prohibited, and the constant hum of the highway made his teeth ache.

He closed his eyes to the Möbius strip of road kill and gas stations and saw his mother—fragile and pale as a child's china doll—lying on her back in a hospital bed, monitored by machines that crowded around her like vultures watching a gazelle breathe its last. She seemed to be looking at something or someone Skinner couldn't see. Her doctor? Luke? Reverend Cakebread? Whoever it was, she seemed to be arguing with them. Skinner could see her lips moving. Sometimes, if he concentrated real hard, he could almost make out what she was saying.

"No ... Not yet ... I've got to tell him ... he's got to know ... time ... there isn't enough ... please ..."

Then she stopped talking to whoever it was and looked right at Skinner, piercing the time and space and consciousness that divided them, and spoke his name.

He started awake with a brief, anguished cry that made the old lady riding across the aisle from him give him a dirty look. Skinner muttered a lame apology under his breath and hurried to the toilet in the back of the bus. There he locked himself in and sat on the lid of the john, with his head between his knees, and sobbed until his ribcage hurt.

His mother was dead.

"I should have been there when it happened."

"There was nothing you could do about that, Skinner," Luke Blackwell grunted, pulling at the tie cinched against his Adam's apple. "You and I both know that—so did she." He nodded in the direction of the open casket set up at the front of Lovejoy's Funeral Parlor's viewing room.

"Still, I'm her son. Her only child. I *should* have been with her. . . ."

"You're with her now. Seeing that she's said good-bye to proper." Luke was tugging at the cuffs of his jacket again. The off-the-rack suit he'd bought at K-Mart hadn't fit him that well when he got married in it, and the last five years hadn't helped the fit get any better.

Skinner nodded, trying not to look at the big mahogany box and what lay inside it. "I just wish I could have told her ... told her ..." He tried to say the words but his throat was swelling shut around them. He lowered his head so that the tears filling his eyes would drop straight onto his shoes instead of rolling down his cheeks.

Luke's big, work-calloused hand closed on Skinner's shoulder and gave it a comforting squeeze. "She knew, son. She knew." He grimaced and glanced up at the speakers hidden away in the cornucopia sported by the plaster of paris cherubs. "Lord, I hate organ music!"

They sat in the viewing room for another hour, during which time three members of his mother's prayer circle and the Methodist minister's wife, Mrs. Cakebread, stopped by to pay their respects. Finally Mr. Lovejoy, the undertaker, stepped in and told Luke, in the hushed tones reserved for paying mourners, that their time was up.

"Best tell your ma good-bye, Skin."

Edna Cade Blackwell lay with her head on a satin pillow, surrounded by billows of white rayon crepe. She was dressed in her Sunday best, a respectable periwinkle-blue dress, her hands folded carefully atop her motionless bosom. Except for her extreme stillness and the uncharacteristic splotches of color on her lips and cheeks given her by the mortician, she could have been sleeping.

As Skinner leaned into the coffin, Mr. Lovejoy moved behind the curtains and turned off the organ music. Skinner's lips brushed his mother's dead, cold cheek. She smelled of formaldehyde and cosmetics and his lips tasted of face powder.

As he left the viewing room, he glanced back over his shoulder in time to see Mr. Lovejoy shut the lid on what remained of the woman he'd known all of his brief life as his mother.

Chapter Two

It was perfect funeral weather: light drizzle with a biting wind. By the time the mourners reached the grave site, everyone was clutching their umbrellas. Skinner sneaked a glance at his stepfather as his mother's polished mahogany casket was lowered into the fresh grave next to that of her first husband. Luke's jaw might as well have been set in concrete, his lips pressed flat against his teeth. Luke wasn't the kind of man to show his pain, although Skinner knew the farmer's heart must be close to breaking.

Reverend Cakebread finished his prayer and everyone tossed a cold, damp clod of earth into the grave. Skinner lingered for a moment beside Luke, sharing the shelter of his umbrella.

"I reckon she's happy now." The older man sighed. "Or if not happy, then at peace." He smiled at a private memory and shook his head. "I loved that old gal. Had ever since high school, even though I could tell she was head-over-heels with your pa. Not that I held that against either of them. Your pa was a fine man. It's only fittin' she should lie beside him. After all, he'd been with her longer than me."

Luke reached inside his suit jacket and withdrew a crumpled business-sized envelope. "Your mama left this with me when they took her off to the hospital in Lake Village. She said I was to give it to you in case ... in case you didn't make it home in time."

Skinner tucked the envelope into his pocket. "Luke—did she ever talk about my daddy? About what happened?"

A muscle in Luke's cheek jerked. "Only once. And that didn't make no sense. She was in pain at the time and full of pills. We better head on back to the house. Mrs. Cakebread's making sure the guests get seen to, but I reckon we ought to be there all the same."

As after-funeral buffets go, Edna Cade Blackwell's was one of the better ones in Choctaw County that year. There were at least two smoked hams, a nice roast beef courtesy of Luke's cousin, Phelan, at least three Jell-O molds, and a respectable selection of pies and cakes prepared by the Methodist Women's Prayer Circle.

Mrs. Cakebread, the Methodist preacher's wife, bustled about the kitchen, tending the percolator and making sure everyone had coffee. Where Reverend Cakebread was a tall man with a vague, somewhat distracted air about him, Mrs. Cakebread was a short, squat woman composed of equal parts hairspray and nervous energy.

"When's the last time either one of y'all ate?" she said by way of greeting the moment Luke and Skinner stepped inside the house.

Skinner blinked, surprised he actually had to think about that one.

Mrs. Cakebread clucked her tongue and hurried them out of their raincoats, shoving plates heaped with potato salad, deviled eggs, and thick slices of ham into their hands.

"Y'all got to keep up your strength! You're doing Edna no service by starving!"

Skinner stared at the deviled eggs on his plate and felt his stomach barrel-roll.

Luckily, Mrs. Cakebread's attention was diverted by refilling the percolator. If there's one thing Methodists do at after-service gatherings, it's drink coffee.

Skinner wandered into the parlor, still clutching his unwanted repast, and stood beside the fireplace. He felt every bit as wooden as the mantlepiece, if not as useful.

An old man squinted at him as if trying to classify a strange type of insect through his thick bifocals.

"Yer Edna's boy, ain't that right?"

Skinner felt his stomach cinch tighter as he recognized the decrepit figure standing in front of him. It was Enos Stackpole, their former next-door neighbor.

Enos had lived on the property adjacent to the Cades, back when they lived on the farm. The last six years had been far from kind to the old coot; he wore an ill-fitting three-piece powder-blue polyester leisure suit that sagged at the shoulders and crotch, and badly worn cowboy boots with cracked heels. His long, white hair was swept back from his bulging brow and slicked with enough

Vitalis to grease a '57 Buick. Skinner noted Enos was wearing a black string tie and hula girl bolo-clasp. His long, bony fingers looked even larger now that the rest of his body had fallen into decay. Liver spots the size of silver dollars covered the back of his hands.

Enos Stackpole had a reputation as something of an eccentric. To put it bluntly, he was the town loon. But his family had once been powerful—if not omnipotent—in the years before the Civil War, and some of that glamor still clung to Enos, its debased heir. He lived alone in the rotting remains of his great-grandfather's old plantation house on the outskirts of town, his only company a collection of ramshackle hutches filled with rabbits he kept as both pets and food.

As a child, Skinner had felt a strange attraction toward the old man, although most of Seven Devils spurned the half-mad hermit. Enos rarely bathed, never brushed his teeth, and had allowed his ancestral home to fall into such an advanced state of disrepair that the only things holding the walls together were the weeds growing up through the floorboards and the termites holding hands.

Enos grinned suddenly, displaying unnaturally white and even teeth. For a moment Skinner was certain that the old man was going to bite him. Enos regained control of the ill-fitting dentures and cleared his throat.

"I was the one that found your pa! Bet you didn't know that!"

Skinner swallowed. No, he *hadn't* known that. But then Skinner doubted Enos knew that he'd once spied him masturbating with the freshly peeled pelt of a dead rabbit, either.

"Yeah, I was the one that come up on him." Enos' voice had taken on a nostalgic note, as if reminiscing about the good old days. "I was out grubbin' for roots when I seen him lyin' there, all chewed-up like. He was sprawled alongside this here deer carcass. I figgered he must have brought it down himself, cause it was already slit open. Then I hears this sound in the woods, off to one side. I was scared mebbe that whatever it was that chomped on ole Will was still hangin' about, and me with nothin' but a walkin' stick to protect myself! But do you know what it was?"

Skinner shook his head.

"It was your ma! She looks at me an' points at what's left of Will and says: 'You best call the sheriff, Enos. Looks like a bear got hold of my Will. I'm gonna try and find Skinner 'fore it's too late.' Then she picks up Will's deer-rifle and walks off into th' woods—"

"You must be mistaken. I wasn't in the woods that day. I was home sick with the flu."

Enos scowled, his over-magnified eyes making him look like a deranged owl. "Don't go tellin' me what I do an' don't know, you cuckoo's egg!"

"Enos, why don't you help yourself to that roast Phelan brought?" Luke was suddenly looming over the old man. "There's more'n we can possibly eat. I'm sure Mrs. Cakebread will be happy to wrap some up for you."

Enos grunted and shuffled off in the direction

of the kitchen, his anger forgotten with the promise of free eats.

"Hope I didn't interrupt anything, but you looked like you could use some rescuin.' "

"Kind of. I'd almost forgotten about Old Enos."

"Enos ain't one to pass up a free feed, even if he's got to get slicked up." Luke fixed him with a strange look out of the corner of his eye. "You alright?"

"I guess so. He was saying something about Mama being in the woods looking for me the day Daddy got—the day he died."

"I wouldn't pay much heed to anything Enos Stackpole might say, son. The old fool's been out of his head since Roosevelt was in office."

"Luke . . . ?"

"Yeah?"

Skinner shook his head. "Nothing."

He was being paranoid. He was underfed and missing sleep, that's all. Why would Luke have a reason to keep Enos from talking about his father's death except concern for his feelings?

It was four o'clock by the time the last mourners picked up their umbrellas and raincoats and left the survivors alone with their grief. Enos was among the last to go, his coat pockets bulging with roast beef wrapped in aluminum foil.

Luke sat and drank a cup of coffee in the kitchen, his good tie draped over the back of his chair like an empty snake skin, staring at where his wife used to sit. He was still sitting there when Skinner went upstairs to bed.

Skinner shucked himself free of his good jacket and tossed it in the general direction of the bed. It missed and fell on the hooked rug instead. As he bent to retrieve the jacket, his hand closed on the envelope tucked in its pocket.

He stared at the envelope for a long moment before opening it. Inside were several pages of neatly folded loose-leaf paper and what looked like a pre-Xerox era legal document. The writing was shaky and rushed, but he recognized his mother's hand.

> *Son,*
> *If you're reading this, I'm gone. I wanted to tell you these things in person, like I should have done years ago, but I kept putting things off, and now there's no more time. The Good Lord's calling me home to be with your father.*
>
> *I wish there was a better way for me to say this, but at this stage all I can do is give it to you point-blank: I'm not your mother. Leastwise, not the one who carried you for nine months in her belly. Will wasn't your natural father, either. We adopted you when you were still a little baby. You were such a beautiful child! Your father and I fell in love with you the moment we saw you. You reminded us so much of the little boy we lost in '56.*
>
> *We were almost too old to qualify for adoption, and we were scared we wouldn't be able to take you. I was forty-four, Will forty-six, but the people at the orphanage were so nice. They could tell how much we really loved you, bless them.*
>
> *Your father and I always meant to tell you someday. Please believe that. But after Will died, I guess I was afraid to tell you. Afraid you'd try and find the par-*

ents who abandoned you. I should have known better than that. I was afraid of losing your love. I know that sounds silly, but when it comes to how you feel in your heart, common sense doesn't have much power.

I've loved you as much—if not more—than the woman who gave birth to you. She didn't want you, but I did. We both did. You're your father's son, even if you're not the flesh of his flesh. I don't know anything about your birth-parents, except that your natural mother might have been an American Indian. We had to go all the way to Arizona to find you.

The people running the orphanage told us that, normally, white familes are not allowed to adopt babies born on the reservation, but they weren't terribly sure if you actually were of Indian descent.

There was more but he couldn't read it. The words kept blurring and jumping around. He carefully refolded his mother's letter, wiping his eyes with the back of his hand.

Luke looked up from his coffee and nodded at his stepson. "So, you read it?"

"Yeah." The inside of his mouth felt like it was lined with sandpaper. He shuffled over to the percolator and poured the last of Mrs. Cakebread's coffee into his cup.

"She really did mean to tell you."

"I know." Skinner took a sip of the dark, bitter brew and leaned against the counter. "When did she tell you I was adopted?"

"Never had to. Same holds true for the rest of the town. Will and Edna disappeared for awhile and when they came back they had a baby with 'em. What with your coloration, folks figured you for some wetback's kid they bought out West. One thing's for sure: no Cade ever had eyes like yours."

At the mention of his eyes, Skinner looked away from his stepfather. He'd endured the nickname of "Piss-Eyes" as a child and was still sensitive about it.

"It explains things. Like why I never felt welcome here."

Luke sighed and turned his coffee mug idly between his big, rough hands. "Folks hereabouts are suspicious of outsiders and them that's different. It pained your mama to see you treated like a yeller dog, but she knew you were strong enough to take it without becomin' all twisted up inside. She had faith in you, Skinner. She was convinced you'd make something of yourself."

Skinner unfolded the photostat of his adoption papers on the kitchen table. "My daddy used to say that if a man wants to know where he's going, he has to know where he's been."

"Skinner—"

There was something in his stepfather's voice that made Skinner's heart speed up. Luke frowned at his coffee as if by staring into its depths he could read the future.

"Skinner, your mama was convinced that what happened to your father had something to do with your natural parents. I'm not sure what it was— she never would talk to me about it—but she saw *something* in the woods that day."

"What are you getting at?"

"I'm just sayin' that before you go runnin' off lookin' for answers, maybe you better give some thought to the questions."

Later that night, William Cade came to visit his son.

He entered Skinner's dreams as he usually did; emerging from the closet as if its door was directly connected to the Afterlife. He was dressed, as always, in the clothes he died in: a red plaid hunting jacket, khaki pants, lace-up boots, a heavy flannel shirt, and a fluorescent orange hunter's cap.

He stood at the foot of Skinner's bed, pausing to light his pipe. "Evening, son."

Skinner wasn't surprised by his dead father's appearance in his bedroom. For the last seven years, Will Cade had made frequent visits to Skinner's dreams.

"I see your mother finally got around to telling you."

"Why didn't you tell me before? When I was a kid?"

"Does it make any difference? Would you have loved us any less?"

"No. I'll always love you—both of you—no matter what."

"We know that now. But back then—back when we were alive—we were fearful of losing your love. And the fear of losing love makes cowards of us all." Will Cade puffed a cloud of aromatic pipe smoke into the air. "You're going to try and find out who your natural parents are." It wasn't a question.

"Yes."

"Do yourself a favor, son. Leave it alone. Your mother and I were the only real parents you had. Leave it at that."

"I can't, Daddy. You know that."

William Cade nodded and lifted a hand to his face. Blood as dark and thick as maple syrup ran down his arm and splattered against the bare floorboards.

"Be careful, boy. The journey you're about to undertake will be dark and bloody. Seeing how I'm dead, I'm not allowed to go into specifics. All I'm able to do is warn you and give you advice. Whether you'll remember it once you wake up is another thing. But pay heed: whatever happens, whoever the father of your flesh may turn out to be, the important thing is to remember who the father of your heart is."

Skinner wanted to ask his dead father what he meant by that, but Will Cade simply shook his head and moved to return to the closet. The door was open and Skinner could see his mother, dressed in the same periwinkle-blue dress they'd buried her in that afternoon, standing on the threshold. She smiled at her husband. It was the happiest Skinner had seen her since his father had set off on his hunting trip, seven years ago.

Edna Cade opened her arms to welcome her long-lost groom, her wrinkles and gray hair disappearing as his arms encircled her waist. The last Skinner Cade saw of his parents before the closet door shut itself, they were younger than himself and locked in a lovers' embrace.

Chapter Three

The night was warm and sticky—hardly unusual in New Orleans, even during the spring.

Johnny paused to check out his reflection in a nearby storefront. His jacket shoulders were padded to just the right thickness and his lapels narrow. His silk tie swam with dozens of tiny hand-embroidered siamese fighting fish. His charcoal-gray stovepipes sported a razor-sharp crease and he wore patent-leather wing tips.

However, there was a price to be paid for fashion, and Johnny was paying it. His feet ached from the pressure placed on them by his shoes, his shirt was bunching along his back, and his carefully mussed coif was degenerating into the real thing.

At least he wouldn't have to suffer for long; he could already hear the bass thumping from the bar three blocks away. As he leaned against a parked car to retie one of his wing-tips, he caught sight of some graffiti sprayed on the wall of the bank across the street:

VARGR RULE

Arcane messages were hardly uncommon in that part of town, although the word "vargr" was a new one on him. It looked like it was missing a vowel or two. He shrugged, dismissing it from his mind, and walked on.

The bar was located in one of the older commercial districts near the Tulane and Loyola campuses. After dark the street was emptied of housewives and became the province of students out for a good time.

The building to the right of the bar had long since been demolished, providing the neighborhood with an impromptu parking lot and graffiti gallery. The bar itself had changed names and owners several times over the past decade, while remaining a live-music venue.

The evening was already well underway. A handful of blow-dried Tulane students dressed in acid-washed Calvin Kleins and polo shirts stood on the street corner, eyeing a gaggle of skatepunks with elaborately decorated boards and baggy jams as they loitered in the parking lot, smoking unfiltered cigarettes.

Johnny glanced at the graffiti-encrusted wall more out of reflex than genuine interest. Twice a year the landlord whitewashed the exposed firewall under the impression it foiled the spray-can artists. All it did was provide a fresh canvas for creative vandalism.

As far as he could tell, there was nothing new in the gallery: the same old scrawled depositions of teenage love; the inevitable "Class Of" bullshit; the handful of local bands making use of all the free publicity they could get; the familiar "Who" band logo sprayed in an unsure hand; the likeness of a grinning man with a pipe clenched in his teeth. . . .

Same old same old. He did notice, however, among the overlapping conglomeration of slogans, names and insults, the words VARGR RULE in paint the color of blood.

Two surly young men flanked the front door. One sported a bicycle-spoke mohawk, his muscular arms wreathed in cobras and rose thorns. He wore a battered leather jacket with sleeves that looked as if they'd been chewed on by a rather large, unfriendly animal. The tattered remnants of leather and silk lining dangled from his shoulders like strands of gristle from a gnawed bone.

The second punk was shorter but equally muscular, with close-cut dark hair and a forelock the color of bleached bone. His jeans were so ragged the only thing holding them together were the bondage straps encircling his hips. Like the spike-haired thug, he wore a black leather jacket with demolished sleeves.

The shorter man reached out and thumped the flat of his palm against Johnny's shoulder, halting him in mid-stride, and held up three fingers the size of sausages. "Three dollars."

"Whassamatta, Sunder?" rumbled the spike-haired giant. "This guy tryin' t' get outta payin' cover?"

"Naw, I don't think he got th' *cajones* for that, Hew," replied the smaller punk, his dark eyes daring Johnny to challenge his assessment.

Johnny flushed as he handed over a sweat-dampened five-dollar bill. Sunder grunted and transferred it to Hew, who held a welter of crumpled paper money in one tattooed fist. He peeled off a couple of ones from the roll and thrust them at Johnny. Sunder stepped aside, allowing him entrance. Johnny could feel their eyes following him as he went into the club.

The place was dark, the lighting provided by the neon beer signs at the bar and the half-dozen lights that hung over the cramped stage like metal bats. The management claimed that the establishment was air-conditioned, although the press of bodies and the propped-open front door rendered its benefits negligible.

The band was already into its first set, not that Johnny cared. The throb of the bass and the drums threatened to rattle the fillings out of his teeth. His eardrums sealed themselves in self-defense.

The three musicians on stage wore the same ragged leather jackets as the brutes guarding the door. The lead guitarist was of medium height with long milk-white hair and a stainless steel ring through his right nostril. His left arm was encircled by a tatoo of a brightly colored snake, its wedge-shaped head resting on the top of his hand, while the rest of its length wrapped itself around his wrist and biceps.

The bass player's high, wide brow was shaved almost to the middle of his head, like an ancient samurai, while the hair at the back of his head hung past his shoulders, making him look like a punker mandarin.

The drummer was little more than a boy, although he had to be at least eighteen in order to play in a bar where liquor was being served. His head was shaved to the skull, giving him a vulnerable, almost babyish appearance, despite the cigarette dangling from his lower lip.

The drummer flailed at his kit like a wife-beater. The bass drum was decorated with a crudely drawn wolf's head, its mouth open in a snarl, with bicycle reflectors glued over the eyes. Under the wolf's slavering jaws was the word VARGR in staggered, dripping letters.

Johnny headed toward the bar; all he wanted to do was get himself a beer, stake out a place at the rail, and bide his time until a suitable candidate for debauchery showed up.

The bar was crowded and it took a good deal of elbowing to get his beer. As he lifted his drink to his lips, he was jostled from behind, slopping Dixie Beer onto his shirtfront. He turned to curse the person behind him and found himself looking into his own face.

The illusion was brief but distracting enough for the girl wearing mirrored sunglasses and a black leather jacket with chewed-off sleeves to slide past him and breach the bar.

Johnny forgot his drink. He forgot his place at the bar. Even with the mirrored lenses obscuring her eyes, he could tell she was the most beautiful woman he'd ever seen.

Her hair was so pale a blond it was without color. It also looked like it was styled with a Cuisinart. Her lips and fingernails were the color of fresh blood. She wore a low-cut leopard-skin print t-shirt and a pair of leather fetish pants with enough zippers for a motorcycle gang. Her feet were encased in a pair of red stiletto-heel pumps that would have deformed a normal instep. Despite these handicaps, she moved like quicksilver on a plate, not even disturbing the head on her beer as she wove through the gyrating dancers.

She was the One. The target for tonight. No other woman would suffice. It *had* to be *her*. Johnny licked his lips in anticipation. He'd screwed punk sluts before. Despite their cultivated decadence, they were all middle-class Catholic school girls at heart.

The girl returned to a table in the corner, parking her tightly trussed rear on a battered leatherette barstool. She sipped her beer and stared in the general direction of the stage without really looking at it.

Johnny sidled alongside her, then leaned over and whispered in her ear. "Hey, baby . . . how about you and me going somewhere private? I got some primo blow. . . ."

She turned to look at him, reflecting twinned images of his lusting features. She smelled of female. He felt his penis grow hard. Her painted mouth bowed into a smile. It was impossible for Johnny to tell if she was genuinely receptive or simply mocking him. The girl pursed her lips and lifted one hand to stroke his face, the tip of her forefinger resting on his jaw. Still smiling her eyeless smile, the girl tapped the cleft of his chin as if dotting the "i" on a signature.

Confused, Johnny lifted his hand to his face. When he drew his palm away, it was smeared with blood.

Johnny leaned against the sink in the men's room, squinting at the smeared mirror as he dabbed at his chin with a wad of wet toilet paper. Things were getting out of hand.

Normally he would have written off the girl in the leopard-skin shirt as too weird and set his sights on far more predictable prey, but he could not get her out of his mind. He could still smell her and feel the feather-light touch of her hand on his face. He knew he would have to make another try.

The band was still thrashing along, their amplified roar muted to a dull thunder by the bathroom door. The sink rattled in time with the music, vibrating against his hip.

What had happened with the punkette was weird, but not so weird he couldn't bring things back under control. After all, control was his life. He couldn't imagine a situation where things could get so far out of hand he wouldn't be able to bring it back into line. He was confident that he would screw the beauty in mirrored shades. It was all a question of *when.*

He saw himself as hunting particularly crafty prey, and it intrigued him. It had been so long since any of his weekend conquests had played hard to get. He had almost forgotten what it was like to *pursue* a woman.

Johnny smiled at his smudged reflection, his confidence restored. He *would* make her his. And the consummation of the chase would be the fuck to end all fucks.

Something moved behind him in the mirror, catching the corner of his eye. At first he did not trust what he saw: years of neglect had produced a fog of grease on its surface, turning it into something short of a funhouse mirror.

The punk girl stood at the threshold, smiling at him, her leather jacket zippered shut. Johnny gripped the sink but did not turn around. She knew he saw her and she didn't care.

A crimson fingernail touched the throat of her jacket, tugging on the zipper; its slow, high-pitched snarl was louder than thunder. The black leather parted, revealing white flesh. Sometime in the last five minutes she'd disposed of her leopard-skin shirt.

Her breasts were perfect, standing firm and solid. Although full, they did not sag in the least. The nipples were round and pink, like the eyes of a white rabbit. It felt as if Johnny's legs had disappeared and the only thing keeping him from falling down was his hold on the sink.

The zipper continued its downward track, exposing her second set of breasts.

They were located just under the first pair, obscuring the split of her ribs. They were smaller than the first set, more like the tits of a girl in junior high school. The nipples and aureoles, however, were far larger than those found on most seventh-graders.

At first Johnny thought she was wearing a pair of foam rubber "joke" breasts, like the transvestites parading through the streets during Mardi Gras, but he couldn't spot a seam of any kind, and he could have sworn that the nipples had hardened as they were exposed to the air. . . .

Was it possible he'd been drugged? Had her fingernails been dipped in some kind of hallucinogen? That was almost as crazy as having two pairs of tits, but at least it kept him from having to accept the thing in the mirror as being real.

Despite his revulsion, Johnny could not bring himself to look away. The zipper continued downward. Her third and final pair of breasts rested just above her belt buckle. They were smaller than the second set, with most of the surface area taken up by oversized erect nipples.

Now completely exposed, she stood with her hands on her hips and sneered, daring him to turn and face her. Instead, Johnny vomited into the sink and collapsed onto the piss-stained floor.

He came to on his hands and knees, his body racked by muscle spasms. The stink of fresh bile joined the odor of stale urine, making the air even fouler than it had before.

I must be drunker than I thought. She couldn't have been in here.

It sounded realistic, plausible, and soothing.

Yeah, but that she still had six tits, nagged his hindbrain.

Johnny shuddered at the memory.

He left the bathroom and returned to the dance floor. The punkette was still at her table. Her jacket was open and she was wearing her leopard-skin shirt. Although he wasn't certain if she was watching him, he could tell she was smiling.

This was getting just too goddamned weird. All he wanted was to get laid. Was that too much to ask? Johnny looked forward to his weekends and the chance to exert his control over others via silk ties and bedposts. Now that control was being threatened by a bleached blond slut in fuck-me shoes. It didn't make sense.

Johnny pushed his way to the bar, desperate to take the edge off the memory of six nipples pointed in his direction.

Somewhere around his fourth gin and tonic he realized they'd switched bands. The group currently on stage, while as loud as Vargr, was dressed in Spandex and had blow-dried hair. Johnny looked around, searching the bar for sign of the girl with the mirrored eyes.

His shoulders slumped when he realized she was gone. There were plenty of women still hanging around, but as far as Johnny was concerned they might have been invisible. A tall, leggy secretary who looked like she'd stepped out of a music video made her interest in him quite clear while borrowing a light for her cigarette, yet Johnny could not find it in him to respond to her overtures.

You might as well pack it in for the night. You've had it.

He paid for his drinks and headed for the door. The humid night air closed around him like a sweaty palm. He pulled at his tie, loosening the knot, and grimaced as his stomach began a series of queasy barrel rolls.

By the end of the block, he was leaning against a telephone pole studded with rusty staples and the faded tatters of band flyers, wiping the sweat from his upper lip with a shaky hand.

Maybe I shoulda called a cab.

He shook his head, fighting the uneasiness in his guts. He had endured drunks worse than this before. If he could hold out another four blocks, he'd be able to catch either the streetcar or a bus. And then it was off to his apartment and bed—alone.

Christ, I must be getting old! Letting a slut like that get the better of me! I got over that kind of shit back in high school! he thought angrily.

Three blocks from the streetcar stop, he staggered into a nearby alley and puked into an open garbarge can. He stood there for a minute, trying to clear the taste of bile from his mouth. His hands trembled as he wiped at his lips with the back of his hand.

Maybe I'm sick. The flu or something. Maybe I picked up some kind of bug at work.

There was a sudden growl, and Johnny realized he wasn't alone in the alley. He must have surprised one of the quasi-feral dogs that prowled the neighborhood at night, raiding unsecured garbage cans. Johnny peered into the dark, trying to locate the animal. The last thing he needed to do was trip over the damned thing.

He edged toward the street, trying not to make any sudden moves that might frighten the animal and provoke it to attack. The growl suddenly gave way to a pained yelp. Johnny hesitated for a second. Something struck him at knee-level, knocking him into a garbarge can. He could tell by its smell as it passed that he'd been sent sprawling by a dog.

"Goddamn mutt. . . ." he groaned. Johnny looked up as he struggled to his feet and his throat constricted into a dry tube.

There were five of them, their pelts shining

greasily in the dim moonlight. At first he thought they were dogs, then he saw that they had hands. One of the beasts sported a spiked crest down its hackle, while another had a white blaze, and yet another had longish fur that hung from its bunched shoulders like a lion's mane.

Two of the larger creatures restrained a German shepherd bitch while a third wrapped its taloned fingers around her muzzle. They needn't have bothered; the poor beast was too frightened to move, much less bite.

Although he'd never been a horror movie buff, Johnny was certain that the shaggy, crooked-legged creatures surrounding him were werewolves. But that was impossible. Maybe he was hallucinating the whole thing. The possibility that he was actually sprawled unconscious in a deserted alleyway with a severe fever seemed positively upbeat.

One of the things stood upright on its crooked hind legs, grinning evilly. Its fur was the color of spoiled cream, its face a disturbing melange of vulpine and hominid features. A stainless steel ring gleamed in its right nostril. Its foreshortened muzzle allowed the creature to utter a twisted, guttural parody of human speech. "Ripper! Cover!"

Johnny tried to get to his feet, only to be pinned to the ground by one of the pack. It was smaller than the others, but its strength was immense. Its short, pig-like bristles scraped against Johnny's exposed skin.

A long, pointed penis emerged from the furred pouch between the leader's legs. It glistened wetly in the dim light. Something resembling laughter came from the others as the monster mounted the terrified bitch.

Johnny was forced to watch as the werewolves took turns raping the dog. Whenever he tried to look away, the thing perched on his back grabbed his head between its furred claws and pulled on his ears until he reopened his eyes.

After they were finished, the bitch lay on her side, legs twitching, blood bubbling from her flared nostrils. The werewolf with the spoiled-cream fur squatted next to the dying animal, tongue lolling from its mouth in parody of her suffering. The thing on Johnny's back giggled. The werewolf twisted the dog's head sharply to one side, snapping its neck.

The smaller werewolf jerked Johnny to his feet, squeezing his pinned wrists like a vise. When he cried out, one of the larger beasts pulled the silk handkerchief out of Johnny's breast pocket and stuffed it in his mouth.

The cream-colored werewolf fingered Johnny's tie and grinned at him, licking its lips with a long red tongue.

"Nice tie."

The small, bristly werewolf giggled again.

Johnny was certain the thing meant to rip his throat out then and there. Johnny shut his eyes; he didn't want the sight of his own blood to be the last thing he saw. He felt the Windsor knot loosen as the werewolf removed his tie.

"Make sure it's good and tight, Ripper."

The smaller werewolf quickly and expertly fastened Johnny's wrists together. Johnny knew enough about knots to realize that it would be impossible to work himself free in time to escape whatever they had in store for him.

Two of the larger werewolves gnawed at what remained of the shepherd bitch. They grinned at Johnny, exposing sharp, yellow fangs flecked with blood and gristle.

"Hurry up!" growled the leader, kicking the beast with the spiked hackles' hairy shank. Although it was easily twice as heavy, the bigger werewolf yelped like a scalded dog.

Johnny moaned as he was dragged down the alleyway by his captors. Sharp talons pierced his clothes, lacerating the flesh underneath. He swooned as the werewolf called Ripper twisted his arm again.

There were two vans blocking the opposite end of the alley. One was a Volkswagen, the other a Dodge Caravan. The rear door to the Dodge was hanging open. It was too dark to make out the name of the band painted on its side, but Johnny knew what it said. He'd known ever since he saw the ring in the lead werewolf's nose and glimpsed the hint of a snake's head under the fur covering the top of his hand.

The cream-colored werewolf picked Johnny up and tossed him into the back of the van like a bundle of newspapers.

"Sorry, sis," leered the leader of the pack. "The male got away. Hope this'll tide you over."

The thing in the van moved forward, snuffling the air like a bloodhound. A twisted, taloned hand reached out and caressed Johnny's face. The palm was dry and hot and felt like a catcher's mitt he'd once had as a boy. Johnny screamed into the handkerchief.

The werewolf bitch eyed him as she idly fondled her middle tits.

"It'll do."

Johnny tried to pull away from the white-furred creature crouching over him, but it did no good. The van door slammed shut, leaving him in the dark with the werewolf bitch.

The smell of female was strong in the confined space of the minibus, triggering instinctual responses. Johnny choked on the bile rising in his throat as he felt himself stiffen inside his pants. The bitch leaned forward, her breath reeking of old blood, hot against his cheek.

"Relax, baby," she growled as she unzipped his fly. "*Vargr* rule."

Chapter Four

Skinner fidgeted in his seat, trying not to brush up against the obese black woman in the purple polyester knit pants suit beside him. This was easier said than done; she was apparently sound asleep—judging by the snores—clutching a large straw handbag that jutted into Skinner's space a good three or four inches.

His mother's funeral had been a week ago, and now he was once more on the bus—but not headed back in the direction of school. He had decided his education could wait until he had attained self-knowledge.

There had been a few hundred dollars left him by his mother's estate, and he'd used some of the money to buy a bus ticket to Arizona. Luke had tried to talk him into going back to school, but they both knew at the time his stepfather was wasting his breath.

At first he'd felt betrayed and hurt that his mother—or the woman he'd believed to be his mother—had not told him the truth surrounding his birth years ago. But now he saw it as a chance to begin afresh. Last week he had been an orphan. Now that was no longer technically true.

He had a mother and father out there somewhere he'd never known, a family he knew nothing about, a heritage he was ignorant of. There was so much he could discover about himself—things that had nothing to do with the claustrophobic world of Choctaw County. He'd always been an outsider in Seven Devils, and now he had a chance to find out where it was he truly belonged.

For the first time since he'd headed off to school, Skinner felt genuine anticipation and excitement concerning his future. But in order to embrace his new future, he first had to uncover his past.

He unfolded the photostat of his adoption papers and studied the first and only clue he had to this mysterious new family.

The Cades had arranged his adoption through the Beatrice Small Foundling Home in Butter Junction, the only town of any size in tiny, isolated Los Lobos County.

Skinner had looked the place up on the map before leaving his stepfather's house. Los Lobos was practically surrounded by the much larger Pima County. Butter Junction itself existed sixty miles southwest of Tucson, two hundred miles northeast of Nogales, flanked by the Papago Indian Reservation and the smaller San Xavier Reservation, boxed in by the nearby Coyote Mountains. The area hardly looked inviting. In fact, what he'd first mistaken for a national historic monument on the atlas proved to be a U.S. Army gunnery range.

For the better part of five days he'd been riding

the bus, heading westward from Little Rock. He slept fitfully, shaving in bus stop restrooms, his personal hygiene restricted by what he could accomplish with a few squirts of liquid soap and a fistful of paper towels the texture of butcher paper.

He'd watched the greens of Arkansas give way to the earth tones of Oklahoma, Texas, and New Mexico. The landscape became increasingly drier and dustier, the trees more and more sparse the further west they headed. Skinner had read of "the wide-open spaces," but this was the first time in his young life he'd ventured beyond the borders of Arkansas, with its lush grasslands and forests. There was something about the lack of protective greenery that made him feel vulnerable and exposed yet at the same time intrigued him.

The bus finally pulled into Tucson at 4:15 in the morning. Skinner blinked the sleep from his eyes, pulled his one piece of luggage—a scuffed hardshell Samsonite suitcase—from the rack over his seat, lurching off the bus into the air-conditioned depot.

Most of the ticket desks were closed until six that morning, but there was a weary clerk working the information station.

"Excuse me, when does the next Greyhound to Butter Junction leave?"

The information clerk blinked and yawned. "Butter what?"

"Junction. It's in Los Lobos County."

The information clerk grunted and ran his finger down a photocopied timetable that was smudged to the point of being illegible.

"Greyhound doesn't go out there."

"Oh. Who does, then?"

The information clerk shrugged. "Jackrabbit Transportation, Inc. They're a pissant local company. The only people who use it are Indians, mostly. They only make three trips a week. You're in luck, though. There's a bus scheduled to leave at dawn. Gate seven."

Skinner thanked the clerk and headed in the direction of gate seven. There were already a dozen people filling the plastic seats in the waiting area, satchels and shopping bags gathered around and between their feet like roosting chickens. A quick scan told Skinner that half of his fellow passengers were of American Indian heritage. The other half were women of various races. A middle-aged man in a rumpled bus driver's uniform stood in the doorway leading to the buses.

"Uh, excuse me . . . ?"

"What is it, kid?" grunted the bus driver.

"Is this the bus to Butter Junction?"

"Butter Junction. Robles Junction. Quijotoa. Devil's Rectum. And any number of wide spots in the road between."

"I'd like to buy a ticket . . ."

The bus driver gave Skinner a quick, probing look. "You injun?"

"Not that I know of."

"You got a brother in the jug?"

"Beg pardon?"

"That's the only reason anyone ever goes to Los Lobos. Either they're going back to the reservation or they're visiting someone at the prison. There sure as hell ain't anything else out that way."

"I still want a ticket to Butter Junction."

The bus driver shrugged, pulling a receipt book out of his breast pocket. "It's your money, kid. That'll be twenty bucks."

The bus trip to Los Lobos made the ride from Little Rock to Tucson seem like first-class on the Concorde.

Jackrabbit Transportation, Inc. consisted of a de-commissioned school bus painted blood-red with a crudely cartooned rabbit dressed in a cowboy hat and brandishing a six-shooter on either side. There was no air-conditioning nor was there an onboard toilet.

As the bus jolted its way along Highway 86, punishing his kidneys with each jounce, Skinner's anticipation battled with his exhaustion and physical discomfort. He hoped that whatever information he might be able to dig up after all these years would be worth the inconvenience of the trip. If not, he was going to be one unhappy camper.

The bus held another twenty or so passengers, half of which were women of various ages and racial backgrounds, and all of whom seemed to be wearing what passed for their best clothes and makeup. These he assumed to be the wives, girlfriends, and mothers of the prisoners at Los Lobos. A couple of the women had small children with them, who whined and complained of being bored and uncomfortable on the hot, dusty bus. Skinner could sympathize.

An hour out of Tucson, the bus stopped at what looked to be no more than a wide spot in the road marked by a large metal sign, pock-marked by motoring sharp-shooters, that read: *Los Lobos County Correctional Facility: Beware of Hitch-hikers.*

A white minibus was parked in the shadow cast by the sign, a man dressed in a prison guard's uniform and mirrored sunglasses seated behind the wheel.

About a mile in the distance—maybe farther, it was hard to judge distances in the desert—Skinner glimpsed the white-washed concrete walls and metal fences of the prison. It didn't look like a place he'd like to visit.

The prison wives disembarked, taking their children with them. The bus started up again and lurched into gear. This time the voices around him were either speaking Spanish or an unrecognizable language he assumed to be either Papago or Navajo. No one offered to bring him into a conversation, which was fine by him.

Twenty minutes later, the bus pulled into Butter Junction. Skinner was the only person to get off the bus.

"Remember, if you plan on getting back to Tucson today, you better be waiting right here at six o'clock this evening, kid," the bus driver told him as he levered the doors shut behind him. "I don't make another run out this way until Tuesday—and this here's Saturday."

Standing in the dust kicked up by the bus's passing, Skinner scanned the surrounding buildings of downtown Butter Junction.

In many ways it was remarkably reminiscent of Seven Devils; half the storefronts were boarded over, while the other half were grimed with so much dust it nearly obscured the wretched array of dry goods and hardware on display.

Main Street was a huge double-wide boulevard, designed for horizontal parking. No doubt, back before the railroad disappeared, the local farmers and Indian tribes had come here in their buckboards to buy and sell their wares on weekends. The handful of battered pickup trucks and jeeps occupying the spaces made the street look twice as big and empty.

Skinner espied what looked to be a café across the street and headed in its direction.

There are diners tucked away in isolated pockets of America that delight a weary traveler with some of the finest of down-home delicacies: platonic potato salad; apple pie to kill for; fried chicken of the gods. Lulu's Eats was not one of these places.

To call Lulu's Eats a greasy spoon would be lavishing it with praise. But what Lulu's Eats *did* have going for it was that it was the only game in town.

"Whatcha having?" grunted the burly Hispanic behind the counter. Skinner didn't see anyone who might possibly be "Lulu" washing dishes or working the grill. "Today's special's chili."

"I'll try that."

The cook shrugged and dipped a ladle into a twenty-gallon steel pot simmering on the stove's front burner, slopping a portion of steaming, reddish-brown substance into a cracked plastic bowl. A couple of individually wrapped packages of saltines—already crumbled—accompanied the order.

"I'd like some iced tea, please."

The cook grunted again and produced a smudged glass filled with tea so weak Skinner could read a newspaper through it, a couple of rapidly dissolving slivers of ice bobbing on the surface.

The cook dropped the lid back on the simmering chili with a clang. "You ain't from around here." It wasn't a question.

Skinner smiled nervously. "That's right. I was wondering if you might be able to help me with some information. . . ."

The cook turned to stare at him, beefy arms folded atop his wide stomach. He looked like a Buddha with a chip on his shoulder. "Like what?"

"Uh, I was wondering if you knew where the Beatrice Small Foundling Home might be. . . ."

The cook's posture relaxed somewhat, but he still looked somewhat suspicious. "It don't exist no more. Old Lady Small died six, seven years ago."

That news, combined with the chili, was enough to knot Skinner's guts into a sheepshank. *All this way . . . for nothing.*

"You could talk to her daughter, though. Miss Small. She's still alive. She helped her mother with the business."

"Does she still live here?"

"Sure. Over on Cottonwood Street. Hey, don't you want to finish your chili?"

"No, thanks! Why don't you take care of it for me?"

The cook watched Skinner hurry out of the

diner, shrugged, and dumped the uneaten chili back into the serving pot.

"Who is it?"

The woman peering out from the dark interior of the little clapboard house at 1327 Cottonwood Street looked to be in her late sixties. With her wispy cloud of white hair and cat's-eye harlequin glasses, she looked like everyone's first-grade teacher.

"Mrs. Small?"

"No. That was my mother. I'm *Miss* Small. Who are you and what do you want?" Whether her thin voice wavered out of irritation or anxiety was hard to tell.

"My name is Skinner Cade, Miss Small. I . . . want to talk to you . . . about the home."

Something flashed in her eyes. "You're one of ours, aren't you? One of our babies."

"Yes, ma'am. . . ."

"Come in! Come in, my dear!" Miss Small beamed, opening the door wide enough for him to enter. Skinner slipped inside, glad to be out of the heat. "Make yourself comfortable in the front parlor! I'll fetch you some lemonade."

"That's alright, ma'am. You don't have to go to all that trouble. . . ."

"Nonsense! It's no trouble at all! I rarely get a chance to see any of our babies all grown up!"

Skinner sat on an over-stuffed Victorian sofa in the parlor, which also hosted an antique player piano, a rolltop desk, and several dead animals trapped under belljars. The room was dominated by a huge oil portrait of a stern, matronly woman dressed in a high-collared blouse and wearing a pince-nez.

Miss Small returned with a pitcher of lemonade and two glasses on a tray. "I see you've noticed Mother."

"Huh? Oh, you mean the picture?"

"Mother was an amazing woman, rest her soul. She passed away six years ago this August, at the age of ninety-seven. She kept operating the home until the very end. Although, what with the advances they've made in contraception in the last decade or two and the legalization of abortion, the turnover wasn't as brisk as it had once been. . . ."

"Miss Small . . . I was wondering if you might help me in locating my natural parents."

Miss Small frowned. "Mother was very much against our babies trying to find their birth-parents. She believed that there were some things people were happier off not knowing. What about your parents, Mr. Cade? The ones who adopted you?"

"They're both dead."

"I see. And now that they've passed on, you'd like to find out more about yourself, it that it?"

"That's right. Do you still have records from when the home was in business?"

"Gracious, yes! Mother was quite particular when it came to keeping records."

Skinner unfolded the photostat and handed it to her. "According to this document, I was born in 1972 and adopted in 1973 at the age of six weeks."

Miss Small frowned and tapped her chin with her index finger. "Cade . . . Cade . . . The name *does* sound familiar. But there were *so* many of you over the years! I won't be able to tell you much until I look at your file. . . ."

"And where do you keep your records? In the desk?"

"Heavens, no!" Miss Small laughed. "Mother ran the home from 1929 until 1986! That's a lot of paperwork . . . and I keep most of it in the attic. You're welcome to go upstairs and look through the boxes."

The thought of sitting in a closed attic in the middle of the Arizona desert, sifting through fifty-seven years, worth of documentation, was enough to make Skinner's butt pucker.

"Which way to the stairs, ma'am?"

It took him three hours and five pitchers of lemonade to finally locate the box containing the documentation for 1973, the year of his adoption.

Skinner entered Miss Small's kitchen with his t-shirt plastered to his back and his hair full of dust and cobwebs, grinning as he hoisted the cardboard file box over his head in triumph.

"I found it!"

He carefully set the box on the kitchen table, rubbing his palms against his thighs to wipe the sweat and grime off. Miss Small opened the container's folding wings, running her arthritic fingers over the yellowed file folders within.

"Let's see now . . . Cade . . . Cade . . . Here we are!" She plucked a sheaf of papers free, flipping through the yellowed documents with the efficiency of an executive secretary.

"Adopting parents, one William Henry and Edna Marie Cade of Seven Devils, Arkansas. . . .

Oh yes, I remember them now! Delightful couple. Normally they would have been too old to adopt. That's how they found their way to us. We dealt with couples the state-funded orphanages turned down . . . mostly those deemed too 'old.'

"Sometimes childless couples over a certain age become set in their ways and have a hard time adjusting to the demands a small child can make. Mother could tell they were good folk, though. She had an eye for character."

Miss Small nodded her head slowly as she read. "Yes, it's coming back to me now. I remember your father—Mr. Cade—most distinctly. Fine figure of a man. Very much the Southern gentleman. You have some of his way about you."

"Is there anything in there about my birthmother? Who she was? What her name was?"

Miss Small handed him the folder. "See for yourself, dear."

The papers felt as brittle as papyrus under his trembling fingertips. 1973. Twenty years ago. So why did he feel like he was handling something as old and important as the Constitution or the Magna Carta?

There were some medical charts documenting the six weeks he spent in the home as an infant—records of his weight, length, blood-type, and other such information—stapled to a piece of paper that bore two tiny purplish smudges that, on closer inspection, turned out to be imprints of baby-sized feet.

There was also something else.

"Hey, what's this? It looks like a birth certificate—" Skinner's frown deepened as he began to read the document. "I don't understand . . . the birth date is the same as mine . . . December 29th, 1972. But in the boxes marked "Father and mother's names" it says 'Unknown.' And this is the real birth certificate, not a photostat. Aren't these things supposed to be registered with the state or something?"

Miss Small looked embarrassed. "Normally, yes, that would be the procedure. But Mother— well, a lot of the women who came to Mother were from the reservation. A lot of them worked as women of the evening in Tucson and Nogales, and they'd come back to the reservation when their time came to deliver. The law is that orphaned Indian children must be handed over to the tribal council, who make sure they are placed with families in the tribe.

"However, many of the natural mothers—well, they wanted their children to have a chance at something better. Mother never filed the birth certificates of babies of Indian heritage—or those she believed to be of Indian blood. That must have been your case."

"What's this? Where it says "Physician or midwife in attendance" someone typed in 'Root Woman.' What does that mean?"

"Oh! That's a midwife who used to supply Mother with the reservation babies. Most of them didn't come into town to give birth, for fear it would get back to the elders. So they trusted Root Woman to deliver the babies to Mother. Since she doesn't technically live on the reservation, everyone involved turned a blind eye to what she was doing. Probably still do."

"You mean she's still alive?"

"Oh my, yes! Root Woman probably delivers half the babies on the reservation, not to mention those belonging to the Mexicans and other poor folk out in the mountains. I haven't seen her since Mother's funeral, but from what I hear, she's still in business."

"Do you think she might know who my birth-mother was?"

"It's possible. She's an old lady, but still has her wits about her. She was much like Mother in that regard. Funny, by my estimation she should be close to a hundred by now. Mother insisted Root Woman was a good twenty years older than her, but I'm sure she was confusing her with her mother."

"Her mother?"

"There have been Root Women serving as mid-wives and shamans in this territory before there were white folk. You see, it's not just a name—it's a job description. Root Woman—well, I'm a God-fearing Christian lady, but I'll admit that she's done a sight more with herbs and folk reme-dies than most doctors have done with needles and pills."

"Where can I find her?"

"She lives off Highway 86, about three miles from the reservation. Her shack's a good mile or two down a dirt road. There's a post with a bleached cow skull and ribbons tied to it, so folks will know where to turn. You're not thinking of going out there, are you?"

"Yes, I am. Maybe she can tell me who my mother was—whether I'm part-Indian, or Mexican, or whatever. But at least I know where my adoptive parents got my name from now."

"Beg pardon?"

"I always thought 'Skinner' was such a weird name for them to pick, y'know? All the other kids where I grew up had names like 'Carlton,' 'Horace,' 'Jethro' . . . they were hick names, but they were at least real first names.

"I remember asking my mama why they'd picked 'Skinner' and she said because—because it was a family name. But there weren't any Skinners on either side of the family that I knew of.

"But now I realize they'd kept the name my real mother gave me—or at least part of it. The one that's printed here, on my birth certificate . . .

"Skinwalker."

Chapter Five

It was mid-afternoon by the time Skinner hitched a ride in the direction of Root Woman's home, perched on the tailgate of a Papago farmer's truck, alongside a bale of hay and a wire cage containing a piglet. The driver, an old man dressed in filthy dungarees and a battered Stetson, had been unwilling to take on a passenger until Skinner mentioned Root Woman's name and handed him a couple of dollars.

By the time they reached the turnoff marked with the beribboned cow's skull, Skinner's butt was aching, he reeked of baby pig, and he was grateful for the sunglasses he'd bought before leaving Little Rock. As the truck came to something resembling a halt, the driver stuck his head out of the window and yelled that it was time for him to get out. Skinner hopped off the back of the truck, waving as the old man left him behind in a cloud of heat and dust.

Skinner hoisted his travel bag and trudged down the dirt road in the direction of Root Woman's shack. He wasn't sure how he was going to go about asking the old woman about what she knew—and if she was as old as Miss Small had suggested, it was possible she might not be able to remember anything that could be of use to him, anyway. Surely she'd delivered hundreds of babies during her career. Why should she remember one particular birth out of the scores she had attended?

You're thinking negative thoughts again, his conscience chided. It was funny, but the inner voice that he always connected with his better self sounded just like his dead father. Maybe it wasn't so funny, once he thought about it.

Miss Small remembered your adoption once she had the proper memory cues. Don't be so quick to assume the worst. Besides, if you thought there wasn't a chance of anything coming out of this, you wouldn't be sweating your butt off and risking sunstroke.

He spotted the midwife's shack from atop a small rise—it was little more than a two-room shanty with tarpaper sides and a corrugated tin roof covered with loose gravel. There didn't seem to be any electricity, and an old-fashioned hand-pump was located a few steps from the rickety front door. No doubt there was an equally old-fashioned outhouse in the backyard, as well.

The area surrounding the shanty was littered with leaning posts, sticks, and other pieces of salvaged wood, each holding up a circular shield. As Skinner drew closer, he could tell the shields were made of animal skins stretched over carefully bent sticks, the outer rims decorated with bits of metal, crystal, feathers, and what looked like bits of tooth and bone. Some of the shields had designs painted on their faces, others were blank. For some absurd reason, Skinner was reminded of the aluminum pie-plate mobiles his mother used to hang in her garden to keep away the crows.

As he wound his way through the field of spirit-shields, there was a sudden movement at the corner of his eye. Skinner turned in time to see what he first thought to be a large dog watching him from behind a small cottonwood tree. Then he saw its cautious, yellow eyes and recognized its pointed snout.

The coyote moved fast, running close and tight to the ground like a cat. It zipped past him and headed around the far corner of the shack. Skinner stood and watched it go, his heart suddenly beating faster than it had a minute ago. He was experiencing the same weird sense of exhilaration he felt whenever he had a chance encounter with something wild.

"You looking for me, stranger?"

Skinner jumped at the sound of the old woman's voice. He turned around and found himself staring down at what, at first, looked to be a walking, talking apple doll.

Root Woman was the oldest living human Skinner had ever seen in his short life. She stood no more than five feet tall and was covered with skin the color and texture of a well-used catcher's mitt. Eyes the color of black glass watched him from within a spider's web of wrinkles. Her snow-white hair was parted down the middle and pulled into two tight braids that hung down to her waist. She wore a loose-fitting long-sleeved floral print dress, a pair of broken-in cowboy boots, and a Dodgers baseball cap, along with a bear claw necklace.

"Are you Root Woman?"

"I reckon I am. Who wants to know?"

"My name is Skinner Cade. . . ."

"That right? Well, come sit in the shade, Skinner Cade, before you boil away what little sense you got."

Root Woman may have looked like a stick figure wrapped in leather, but she moved with the speed and agility of a young girl. She led him around the back of her shack to a shade porch erected outside the back door, the exposed rafters decorated with bundles of dried herbs and roots, but at least they were out of the sun.

Root Woman seated herself on a bentwood rocker, motioning for Skinner to seat himself on a knock-kneed kitchen stool, and produced a briar pipe from the pocket of her dress. "What do you want, Mr. Cade?" she asked, eyeing him as she stuffed the bowl with mixture from a pouch on a small table. "No one comes out this way unless they need something from me."

"I was told by Miss Small that you might have some information concerning me."

Root Woman stopped rocking but continued puffing on her pipe. The smoke that issued from its bowl smelled distinctly of marijuana. "Is that so?"

"I was adopted twenty years ago from the Smalls' foundling home. Miss Small claims that you were the one who placed me there, and that I was little more than a day or two old at the time. None of the documents I found in their records said anything about who my birth-parents might be, but it's assumed one, if not both, were American Indians. I came all the way out here to see if you remembered anything about my natural mother."

"Mr. Cade, I am a *very* old woman. I have delivered more babies, Indian and otherwise, than there are hairs on your head."

"I was born December 29, 1972. Is that any help?"

Root Woman shook her head. "You're wasting your time. I keep no records except those inside my head, and I'm afraid I've become forgetful in my old age."

"The name given to me on my birth certificate is 'Skinwalker.' That's an Indian name, isn't it?"

Root Woman became silent as a stone, staring at Skinner as if he'd just announced he was Jesus Christ reborn. The only proof she was still breathing was the increase in pipe smoke.

"Take off your sunglasses."

Skinner obeyed. When she saw his eyes, the old medicine woman stiffened.

"Now show me your hands."

When she saw his third fingers, she hissed something under her breath.

"You *do* know who my mother is, don't you?" Skinner could barely control the eagerness in his voice as he slid his sunglasses back on.

"You best be leaving now." The old woman's voice was as sharp as a flint arrowhead.

"Why won't you tell me who she is?"

"I don't know what you're going on about. I don't know anything about you. I've never seen you before in my life."

"But—"

"Grandmother? Is there something wrong? Is this man bothering you?"

Skinner turned to face the new voice and found himself staring at the most beautiful woman he'd ever seen.

She wore a faded denim shirt and matching work pants, a battered straw cowboy hat pushed back from her forehead. She was roughly his age, with skin the color of cappucino coffee, her long black hair pulled into two tightly bound braids that hung down to her breasts. She was lean and yet well-rounded in the right places, like a championship thoroughbred. And her eyes were a familiar golden hue. She also had a narrow-gauge shotgun tucked under one slender arm.

"There's no need to get upset, Rosie," Root Woman said. "Mr. Cade was just leaving."

The younger woman fixed Skinner with a suspicious glare as she moved to peck her grandmother on the cheek. "I just got back from checking on the Ortega family's twins. They're both doing fine, now that the mother's taking your remedy before nursing."

Root Woman nodded to herself. "I knew it was milk-fever. I could have called that one in my sleep."

"Please, won't you reconsider? I've come all the way from Arkansas to find out the truth about myself. . . ."

"I'm sorry to hear you've come all this way for nothing, Mr. Cade, but I'm telling you the truth: I don't know anything about you or your parents."

"But—"

The sound of the shotgun being cocked shut

him up. "You heard my grandmother, mister. She doesn't know anything. So why don't you get going?"

Skinner got to his feet, working hard to keep the anger knotted inside him from exploding. He'd worked so hard, come so far ... only to be frustrated by a wizened crone and her shotgun-toting grandchild.

"Perhaps you'll reconsider ..."

"Git!" The shotgun came up in one smooth, menacing motion.

"Okay! Okay! I'm leaving!" Skinner raised his hands and backed away. After taking six steps backward, he turned around and stalked off in the direction he'd first come from.

Root Woman's granddaughter lowered her weapon and frowned at her kinswoman. "What was all that about?"

"He wanted to know who his real mother was."

"Did you deliver him? Was he one of the babies you handed over to Mrs. Small?"

"Oh, yes."

"Granny, I *know* you. You know the names and circumstances of all the women you've ever seen to, plus those of the babies they bore. Why'd you lie to that man?"

"Because I didn't get to this age, Rosie, without realizing sometimes you're better off remembering to forget."

Skinner hadn't exactly been in the best of moods when he left Root Woman's place, and trudging along the side of the road back into town in 90-

plus heat wasn't doing anything to sweeten his disposition.

To get so close to finding out the truth about himself and then run smack into a brick wall—a hundred-year-old wall wearing cowboy boots and a baseball cap, at that—was frustrating enough to drive him to drink. But what was he supposed to do? Force the old lady to tell him what she knew at gunpoint? He sure as hell didn't have enough money left to be able to spare any of it as a bribe. . . .

As he wiped at the sweat rolling down his brow, he spotted an adobe building about a mile up the road. There were a couple of dusty pickups and a Harley-Davidson motorcycle parked outside. Skinner grinned and picked up his pace. Maybe he could get a ride into town from one of the locals.

As he drew closer, he could make out a neon beer sign flickering in the establishment's single plate-glass window and hear muffled country and western music coming from inside. The bar didn't seem to have a name, but there was a hand-lettered notice tacked onto the front door: NO DOGS OR INDIANS ALLOWED.

Skinner stepped inside, cautiously scanning his surroundings. There was a full bar at the back of the building, a couple of well-worn pool tables toward the door, and a vintage Pac-Man squatted in one corner. Hank Williams, Jr. was playing from the jukebox. A couple of locals were shooting pool, while what looked like the owner of the Harley drank at the bar. It was hardly the kind of place Skinner usually picked to hang out, but it felt good to get out of the heat and, come to think of it, he could use a beer.

The bartender looked at him funny as he pulled up a stool and sat down. "I'd like a beer."

The bartender hesitated for a moment, as if trying to decide whether to card him or not, then grunted, producing a bottle of beer from behind the counter. Skinner handed over a couple of crumpled dollars and sat back to enjoy his drink.

Funny how he'd left a dead-end, inbred town stuck out in the Southern bayou country in order to discover his roots, only to find himself in an equally moribund community isolated in the desert. Perhaps his parents had done him a favor, after all, taking him to Arkansas. If anything, Los Lobos was even more depressing than Choctaw County. At least the landscape surrounding Seven Devils looked alive.

He had to admit to himself, however, that the nearby Coyote Mountains were awesome—rising from the desert floor like the hackles of an angered beast. Where he'd grown up the surrounding scenery was flatter than a pancake, with the levee being the closest thing to a hill he'd ever known. However, close proximity to such breathtaking vistas didn't seem to have much of an effect on the denizens of Los Lobos County, as far as he could tell.

Skinner was on his second beer when he felt a meaty finger prod his shoulder.

"Hey—hey *you*."

It was the biker. He was dressed in a pair of grease-stained jeans, an equally dirty Grateful Dead t-shirt, and a pair of steel-toed leather boots.

His beer belly hung over the top of his jeans, exposing several inches of hairy midriff. That and the mustaches hanging down from either side of his nose made him look like a walrus. He reeked of grease, gasoline, whiskey, and b.o. that could knock a buzzard off a shit wagon.

"What's fuckin' wrong with you? Can't you fuckin' *read*?"

Skinner looked at the bartender, whose eyes were fixed on some point up and to the left of the Pac-Man game. "I beg your pardon?"

"Don't you get fuckin' cute with *me*, asshole!" snarled the biker, leaning even further into Skinner's face. His teeth were a grayish yellow color. "You saw the sign on the fuckin' door, didn't ya?"

"Well, I— Uh—"

"Are you a fuckin' injun?"

"No." He said it without even thinking. It wasn't really a lie, because he wasn't consciously lying. It was an automatic response from twenty years spent thinking of himself as a White Anglo-Saxon Protestant.

"Then you must be a fuckin' dog!" laughed the biker, catching Skinner on the jaw with his fist and knocking him onto the floor.

Skinner lay on the sawdust-covered floor for a heartbeat, too dazed by the sucker-punch to do anything except stare up at his attacker with goggled eyes. The biker turned and took Skinner's half-finished beer from where he'd left it sitting on the bar and up-ended it over his victim's head.

"You shouldn't be messin' with the fuckin' firewater, man! You know that ain't allowed! Now

get your lousy red ass back to the reservation before I kick it back *for* you!''

The two locals had taken time out from their
game of pool to watch what was going on, leaning
silently on their cues. The jukebox switched from
Hank Williams, Jr. to Patsy Cline. The bartender
was still looking at the invisible point in the corner
as he dried the glasses.

''You fuckin' deaf, man? I said *git!*'' The biker
leaned down and grabbed Skinner's shoulder.

Maybe it was a combination of the frustration
and stress from the last two weeks—of having lost
his mother, traveled so far for so little, being de-
nied knowledge of his past—or perhaps he'd simply had enough of being treated like shit.
Whatever the reason, Skinner snapped. He didn't
care if the bastard outweighed him by sixty
pounds and could flatten him like a sack of over-
ripe tomatoes.

He came up on the balls of his feet like a jack-
in-the-box, butting the biker square in the gut and
knocking the wind out of him. The biker doubled
over, clutching his beer belly as he gasped for air.
Skinner brought his knee into his opponent's face
as hard as he could. The biker fell to the floor,
clutching his nose with both hands. Blood gushed
from between his cupped hands onto the sawdust.

Before Skinner could turn away from where the
biker was sprawled, swearing through blood and
broken teeth, there was a sound from behind, and
the blunt end of a pool cue landed on the back of
his head.

*   *   *

". . . to remain silent. Anything you say can and will be held against you in a court of law."

The next thing Skinner knew he was lying face-down in a mixture of sawdust, blood, piss, and spilt beer with his arms pinned behind him and someone's knee wedged into the small of his back.

"Wh-what's going on? Where . . . ?"

Judging from the pain that radiated from every part of his body, his attackers had worked him over pretty good while he was unconscious. Judging from the smell, they'd also pissed on him for good measure. He wondered if he'd sustained any internal injuries.

"Come on, buddy. It's time you went and paid the judge a little visit." The deputy helped Skinner to his feet by yanking on his cuffed wrists. It was all he could do to keep from shrieking in pain.

"Am I being arrested?"

The deputy and the bartender shared a smirk. "Catches on pretty quick, don't he?"

"What's the charge?" It was difficult to sound like an indignant taxpayer with his hands cuffed behind his back and reeking of urine, but he tried.

"Drunk and disorderly."

"But I didn't start it—"

"Tell it to the judge, kid."

The deputy led Skinner to the waiting cruiser parked outside the bar. There was no sign of the Harley or the two pickup trucks parked there earlier. It was twilight, the sky rapidly turning purple as the sun sank behind the nearby mountain range. The deputy pushed Skinner's head down and forward as he climbed into the back seat. Somewhere in the gathering dark a coyote chorus took up its song. It sounded like the laughter of hysterical women.

Los Lobos County's jail was tiny. After being booked at the front desk, Skinner was released into a holding tank and told to wait. His only other companion in the cell was an elderly Navajo who was so drunk Skinner had to look twice to make sure he was breathing. After twenty minutes, the deputy who'd arrested him appeared.

"Okay, Cade. Time for your phone call."

He unlocked the holding tank and Skinner shuffled out. "Do I see a doctor, too?"

The deputy gave him a cursory glance. "You don't look that bad off."

Skinner had to admit that, outside of a dull ache here and there, most of his earlier pain had disappeared. He'd always healed fast as a child and had rarely taken ill, even when the measles and mumps had swept through the Choctaw County public school system like wildfire.

The deputy walked Skinner to what looked like a waiting room and motioned to a pay phone on the wall. "Here's your quarter. Knock yourself out, kid."

Skinner hesitated for a long moment, turning the coin over between his fingers, then slid it into the slot.

"Operator, I'd like to make a collect call to Lucas Blackwell, area code 504-555-2431."

He hated calling up Luke this way. Skinner knew his stepfather had been upset over his leaving so soon after his mother's death, but what else was there for him to do? Still, he was the closest thing to family Skinner had left. He didn't really expect Luke to be able to make his bail; he just wanted someone to know where he was.

The phone rang five times, then six. On the seventh ring, someone picked up the receiver.

"Hello?" The voice was distorted by distance and static, but it sounded familiar.

The long-distance operator came on the line. "This is Southwestern Telephone. I have a long-distance person-to-person call for Lucas Blackwell. Will you accept the charges?"

"Hello, Luke? Is that you?"

"Sir, will you accept the charges?"

"No, this is Phelan, Luke's cousin. Skinner, is that you?"

"Yes, it's me! Phelan, would you put Luke on the line?"

There was a long pause, then the operator came on the line again. "Sir, will you accept the charges?"

"For God's sake, Phelan! Say yes!"

"Okay. I'll accept the charges."

"Thank you for using Southwestern Telephone."

"Phelan, where's Luke?"

Again the uncomfortable silence.

"Phelan?"

"I thought you'd heard. I thought that was why you were callin'. . . ."

"Heard? Heard about what? Phelan, what's happened? Where's Luke?"

"He's dead, son."

Skinner stared at the receiver as if he could see Phelan's cow-eyed, slablike face in the earpiece.

"Dead? How? How did it happen?"

"He shot himself. We found him yesterday evening, stretched out on the bed, dressed in the suit he married your mama in. He stuck the shotgun in his mouth and— Well, you get the picture. Anyways, there was a note. Seems he was lonely, what with Edna gone. We're burying him Saturday. Can you make it back in time for the service, Skinner? Skinner? Hello?"

Skinner hung up the phone without another word.

Chapter Six

The buzz of the after-hours check-in bell woke Leon Sykes out of a sound sleep. Not that he didn't expect it. He'd been working the night shift at the Bide-A-Wee Motel, situated on one of Houston's busier hooker drags, for nearly six years. He couldn't remember the last time he'd slept the whole night through.

He emerged from his apartment and stumped toward the night registry, a small cubicle that resembled a drive-up bank teller's booth that faced the parking lot. He rubbed his eyes and peered through the bullet-proof glass at the couple waiting for him.

Sykes knew they were trash. Hell, all you had to do was look at 'em to know they were up to no good. Especially the guy. If anything with hair that long could be called a "guy." The woman wore a skintight red sheath that stopped just short of flashing beaver and enough makeup to hide any number of flaws. She was giggling and wiggling up against her companion, a young punk with waist-length hair and what looked like a ring in his nose. Sykes wasn't sure, but in the illumination cast by the security lights, the man's hair looked white.

"We'd like a room." The punk's voice was distorted by the speaker set into the booth's face, transforming it into something close to an animal's snarl.

Sykes put a registration card and ballpoint pen into the hopper on his side and punched a button. "That'll be nineteen dollars plus a five-dollar key deposit. Twenty-four dollars total. Please fill out the card."

The punk fished inside his leather jacket for some money and Sykes noticed that the sleeves ended at the shoulder, as if roughly cut away by a serrated knife . . . or chewed off by a damn big dog. The punk withdrew a fistful of wadded bills and tossed it into the hopper, scribbling a signature on the card. Sykes retrieved the money and passed a key back through the machine. Meanwhile the bimbo was rubbing herself against the punk like she was trying to start a fire without matches.

"You have room number four-ten. It's on the fourth tier, second door to the left. Check-out's at nine A.M."

The punk grunted something and headed in the direction of the motel units, his bimbo in tow. Sykes watched them go, trying to decide whether what he felt was envy, lust, or simple disgust. His last thought before he fell asleep again was that he was getting too old for this job. Maybe it was time to quit and let a Pakistani family take over the business.

He forgot about the punk and his lady friend until ten o'clock the next morning, when Juanita, the maid, came rushing into the front office, babbling hysterically in Spanish. Once he got her calmed down enough to understand what she was trying to say, he locked the office behind him and hurried to check out Room 410.

The door stood wide open and Juanita's linen cart stood outside, right where she'd left it. Swallowing hard, Sykes steeled himself for what he'd find inside.

In the six years he'd spent running a hot sheets motel, he'd seen a lot of nasty stuff. People did things in cheap motel rooms they'd never dream of doing in their own homes. He'd come across his fair share of dead junkies, hookers, and drunks. He'd even cleaned up after the results of do-it-yourself abortions. But nothing was as bad as this.

His first thought was that someone had put red sheets on the bed. Then he saw the flies rise in a cloud from the pillows. The smell of blood was so strong he was forced to breathe through his mouth to keep from gagging.

On closer inspection, he saw leather thongs tied to the bed's head and foot posts. The lamp next to the bed lay on its side, the shade gone and the remains of a shattered bulb still screwed into the socket. There was what looked like blood and shit smeared on the neck of the lamp.

Sykes shook his head, forcing down the bile rising in his throat, and turned away. "Sweet Jesus—"

There were words scrawled in blood on the wall facing the bed. They were stilted and uneven, looking like a deranged child's attempt at the alphabet. The words said:

HEALTER SCELTER

PIGGIES

and, most chilling of all,

HELP M—

Sykes staggered back, scanning the room for the woman he'd glimpsed with the punk the night before. There was blood—plenty of it—but no sign of a body. He checked the bathroom, expecting to see a mutilated corpse in the tub, but all he found were a handful of blood-caked towels.

As far as he could tell, there was no trace of her to be found. It was like she'd been swallowed whole—hair, guts, and all.

The cops were there in under ten minutes. Forensics made the scene in under a half hour. Sykes stood in the air-conditioned comfort of the front office and watched the police crawl in and around Room 410 like a battalion of army ants.

One of the homicide detectives came in and began questioning both him and Juanita.

"And you say you saw this guy?"

"Yeah. Looked to be about twenty-five. Had long white hair and a nose ring. Wore a black leather jacket with torn up sleeves. Oh, yeah! He had a tattoo—what looked like the head of a snake on his left hand, if that's any help."

"Can't hurt. Did this guy fill out a registration card?"

Sykes handed the detective the card. "Yeah, not that it'll do you any good. I didn't really look at it that hard last night. It was late—besides, he paid cash and cash customers here usually *don't* use their real names. . . . For what it's worth, he didn't officially check out."

The detective scanned the registration card and laughed humorlessly. " 'Roman Polanski.' Cute."

"Have you found anything?"

"You mean a body? No, but we *did* come up with something that pretty much cinches it that it's the woman's blood splashed all over hell's half acre up there."

"Like what?"

"Forensics found something behind the T.V. set. We're not sure how it got there—not that it matters, come to think of it. Forensic isn't a hundred percent certain, but they think it's a human clitoris. Or part of one, anyway."

That settled it. He was going to sell out to the Pakistanis and move the hell to Idaho.

Chapter Seven

Skinner was numb throughout the entire sentencing. Part of him knew that he was being brought before the judge on charges of drunk and disorderly, with vagrancy thrown in for good measure, since whoever it was who had kicked the shit out of him also lifted his wallet with all his I.D. and what little money he had left in it, but he couldn't bring himself to respond. He was still in a state of shock after learning of Luke's suicide.

Although he'd been thousands of miles away when it happened, Skinner felt responsible for his stepfather ending his life. He hadn't been there when the old farmer had needed him most. Instead of helping Luke through the grieving process, he'd run off on a half-baked search for his natural parents. He'd thought only of himself—of the promise held at the core of this most personal of mysteries.

He hadn't given his stepfather a single thought until he had landed in trouble and turned to him for help. But good-natured, big-hearted Luke had been unable to stand the strain of being alone in that empty house, widowed and lonelier than he'd ever been before.

Skinner barely registered the judge's verdict of ninety days. While he was innocent of the charges leveled against him, the decision somehow seemed appropriate. He deserved to be punished.

However, after he was returned to the holding tank, Skinner discovered disturbing news from his cell-mate, who had finally sobered up enough to sit upright and talk. It was enough to dispel the self-pity and angst that had clouded his senses earlier.

Los Lobos County was so tiny its own population didn't generate much in the way of trouble. However, it had a prison five times the size it needed because of an agreement with the nearby, and far more affluent, Pima County to handle their overflow. And Pima County was fond of sending the more troublesome prisoners to Los Lobos. And since Butter Junction didn't have a municipal jail, it shunted any prisoner with more than thirty days on his ticket to Los Lobos. Like Skinner, for example.

Two hours later, Skinner was manacled hand and foot and placed in the back of a police van and driven to his new home for the next three months.

After a half-hour drive, Skinner was unloaded just inside the gate of the Los Lobos County Correctional Facility. As correctional facilities go, it was hardly the Big House. But then, Skinner had never seen a *real* prison before, just ones on T.V.

Los Lobos was designed to house five hundred prisoners in three double-tiered cell block wings jutting from the central hub that housed a mess hall, sickbay, and administrative offices. It was

stuck out in the middle of serious nowhere, surrounded by fifteen-foot-high chain link fences
topped with spools of razor wire, guard towers
pinning down the corners.

There were men in the yard when Skinner arrived, dressed in identical blue workshirts and
denim pants. Some were doing laps on the track,
others pumping iron. Most of them, however, simply ambled about in clumps of two or three,
smoking hand-rolled cigarettes and talking
among themselves.

"C'mon! You'll have plenty of time to hang in
the yard once you're processed!" snapped the
deputy, prodding Skinner with the butt of his
baton.

They entered the central administration block
and were routed through Receiving and Release
by two men with the word "Trustee" stenciled
across the backs of their workshirts, who saw that
Skinner's manacles were removed.

First he was told to strip and then run through
a cold shower that made his nuts shrink to the size
of raisins, then squirted with delousing powder.

Naked and dripping, he was brought before an
inmate typist who recorded his name, Social Security number, physical description, next of kin, and
medical history. Once that was finished, he was
once again fingerprinted and photographed, then
hustled past the quartermaster's desk, where he
was issued a blue workshirt, denim pants, brogan
shoes, wool socks, two pairs of underwear, a
comb, and a toothbrush.

The deputy reappeared, this time armed with a
clipboard, and reconnected the leg chains, leading

Skinner deeper into the facility. The deputy checked the cell-assignment sheet and dropped Skinner off at Cell Block A.

The entrance to Cell Block A housed a couple of desks, a weapons closet, and a small card table with a Mr. Coffee and a box of stale donuts atop it. Two men, one middle-aged, the other somewhat younger, sat behind the desks.

"Got you a new fish, Stanton," yawned the deputy, handing over the cell-assignment sheet for the guard to okay.

Stanton—the older of the two—grunted and scribbled his initials on the form. "Tate'll see about getting him situated."

The younger guard stood up, fixing Skinner with a cold glare that was designed to make his guts knot. It did.

"C'mon, Cade. I'll show you your new home for the next ninety."

Cradling what few possessions he had against his chest, Skinner stepped through the heavy reinforced steel door that separated the foyer from Cell Block A, Tate literally breathing down his neck as he directed him down the corridor and into the cell block itself.

It was double-tiered, twenty-five cells on each level, each cell designed for two prisoners. Metal catwalks connected the tiers and levels. Since it was daytime, the doors to the cells were open and most of the inmates either assigned to chores or walking the yard. A few cells contained solitary occupants, most of which barely looked up from their magazines and letters home to note the new fish's arrival.

"Here you go, Cade. Lucky you! You get to bunk with Cheater!" Tate laughed.

Before Skinner had a chance to figure out whether the guard was being sarcastic, he found himself standing in one of the cramped cells, staring at a man old enough to be his father squatting on a stainless steel institutional toilet, perusing a less-than-current copy of *National Inquirer*.

The older man lowered his newspaper enough to fix Skinner with a mildly curious stare.

"Afternoon."

"Uh, I'm sorry—" Skinner looked at his shoes, the ceiling, and the wall in rapid succession. "I didn't mean to intrude—"

"If you ain't never seen anyone take a crap before," the older man sighed, "you better get used to it, kid." He folded his newspaper and stood to wipe and pull up his pants. He was big—well over six feet—and his graying hair was held in place with at least a tube of Brylcreem. His face was heavily seamed about the eyes and the corners of the mouth and his left eyelid drooped, but outside of that he seemed to be in good health. "My name's Croyden. But mostly I go by Cheater. What's your handle, kid?"

"Cade. Skinner Cade."

Cheater grunted again and lipped a cigarette, fixing his gaze on Skinner. "What you in for, kid?"

He tried to make his voice sound as tough and worldly as possible. "Drunk and disorderly. Ninety days."

Cheater snorted, sending a cloud of smoke from

his nostrils. "You've never been inside before, have you?"

Skinner fidgeted.

"You don't have t' say, kid. It might as well be tattooed on your forehead." Cheater settled onto the lower bunk, folding his arms behind his head, peering thoughtfully at the cracks in the cell wall.

"Ninety, huh? That ain't nothin'. I could do ninety standin' on my head blindfolded. But I remember what it was like being your age. Three months can feel like three years. Man can get himself in a lot of trouble in ninety days, if he don't know the ropes. Come in for vagrancy, find himself doing time for murder, if he ain't careful.

"Oh, by the way. You get the top bunk."

Skinner nodded and began putting away his few meager personal possessions. He was acutely aware of Cheater's eyes on him the whole time.

"You got family, kid? Anyone know you're here?"

Skinner felt his shoulders tighten without his willing it. "No. My mom died a couple weeks ago. My dad—my dad died when I was twelve. There's no one else."

Cheater nodded to himself, as if some unspoken question had been answered. "I like you, kid. I can tell you're a reg'lar joe; not like the trash that comes through here. Me? I been in an' outta the jug since I was twelve. I'm fifty-seven now. I figger I've spent over half the time in between coolin' my heels at the state's expense—whether that state be Alabama or Wyoming or Texas or wherever.

"Once you've got yourself situated, we can go for a stroll in the yard. I'll introduce you to some

of my homeys. They're okay joes—mostly bur-
glars and hold-up men, not trash like those fuckin'
crackheads or gangbangers.''

Later Cheater took Skinner on a tour of the
yard. It looked just like it had when he arrived,
only now he was one of the men dressed in the
identical workshirts and denims. It was late afternoon and the baked earth under their feet radiated
heat like a pancake griddle, but that didn't seem
to deter the men at the weight bench.

Skinner watched in awe as a tall, muscular
white man stripped off his shirt in preparation for
doing a set of military bench-presses. His skin was
coated with sweat, making the various jailhouse
tattoos that swarmed over his pecs, biceps, and
scapulars glisten and gleam. The con looked like
a one-man picture gallery, his body covered with
hard-case icons. There were skulls with daggers
through their eyes, skulls on fire, snarling pan-
thers, eight balls, crossed knives, spiders, coiled
snakes, grim reapers, and armlets of braided
thorn. And to top it all off, a solitary India ink
tear at the corner of his right eye.

Cheater followed Skinner's gaze and visibly
blanched. Without breaking stride, he grabbed the
youngster's arm and steered him away from the
weight area, doing his best to position himself between Skinner and the tattooed con. He spoke in
an even voice, although there was an undercur-
rent of urgency in his delivery.

''There's a few things you need to know so's
you can make it through your stay in this country
club in one piece. First thing is: don't go looking
a man in the eye while you're in here, less you're

looking for a fight or a fuck. I seen men get their guts handed to 'em on a sharpened spoon just cause some cracker didn't like the way he was being looked at."

Skinner glanced up at Cheater. He was suddenly aware how tall the old-timer really was. He rarely moved from his bunk while in his cell, but outside he straightened his spine and rolled his shoulders. Although now a bit stooped and flabby, Cheater had once been an impressive specimen.

"Don't screw around with the fags, as they'll get your ass every time. Just cause they're swish don't mean they ain't ready to lay you open like a butchered hog—or get one of their boyfriends to do it for 'em.

"And don't borrow shit, cause the first time you can't pay back a pack of smokes you'll find yourself some con's property, washin' his socks an' pullin' train to make up your debt.

"But the single most important thing you got t'remember, kid, is to do your own time and hold your mud. If it gets out that you've snitched—or it's suspected that you *might* have snitched— you're good as dead."

A slightly built con with a state-issue upper plate sidled up alongside Cheater. "See you're schoolin' yourself a fish, Cheat."

"Howdy, Top Gum. This here's Skinner, my new bunkie."

The old con nodded and smiled, careful not to send his ill-fitting dentures flying out into the yard. "How long?"

Cheater didn't even give Skinner a chance to

answer for himself. "Short-termer. Ninety. Green as goose-shit."

"You better make sure Mother and Rope don't get whiff of him, then." Top Gum's mouth was smiling, but there was no humor in his voice.

Cheater grunted but didn't say anything.

"Rope? Mother? Who are they?"

"You already saw Mother," Cheater muttered.

"You mean the guy with the muscles and the tattoos?"

"That's him."

"What's the deal with these guys? Why should I watch out for them?"

Top Gum shot Cheater a look out of the corner of his eye, waiting for the bigger man to take up the tale, but Cheater remained silent. He sighed and pressed his plate back into place with the ball of his thumb.

"Them's two bad-asses in this place you better steer clear of, if you got any sense. There ain't a nastier set of bookends to be found in Los Lobos.

"Mother—that's short for 'Motherfucker'—is trash that don't burn, as my mama used to say. He's got more jailhouse tattoos than Carter's got little liver pills. Tough *hombre* outta Texas, originally. Kilt himself a few, if the brag's true, but the Man's never been able to pin him for nothing worse than manslaughter.

"Mother's real specialty is rape, though. When he's on the Outside, he rapes women. When he's doin' time, he rapes boys. Don't seem to matter what kinda hole he sticks it in, long as the person attached don't have no say in the matter.

"He travels with his homey, a nigger called

Rope. Normally blacks and whites don't have much truck with one another in here, but Rope and Mother are tighter'n ticks at a nudist colony. I figger it's on account of nobody else bein' willin' to hang with 'em.

"Rope's as mean as Mother, but more *subtle* on account of him being mute."

"Mute? You mean he's deaf?"

"No, he can hear as good as you or me. Better, mebbe. He just can't talk on account of him gettin' hung."

"*What?*"

"Seems that when he was just a punk—no more'n thirteen or so—Rope got hisself accused of rapin' some white gal in Alabama. Mebbe he did, mebbe he didn't. Who knows? Anyway, he gets caught by some crackers and carried out to the piney woods, where they beat on him some, take a buck knife to his privates, then string him up. I reckon they'd thought they'd kilt him, so they drove off in their pickups and left him hangin' there. He weren't dead, though. Somehow he managed to get himself free, pretty much none the worse for wear, although it crushed his voicebox and left a mark on his neck he's gonna carry to his grave.

"Rope's been in and outta jail ever since— mostly on assault charges. And crime against nature. Just cause some Alabama crackers cut his pecker off fifteen years ago don't slow him down none. Seems he likes to use coke bottles, broomhandles, baseball bats, whatever's handy, when he's doing the dirty. Like I said; him and Mother is a mean machine you want to stay the hell clear of."

*   *   *

That evening Skinner had his first meal on the state of Arizona. It consisted of tomato soup, re-fried beans, corn bread, and something that claimed to be chicken-fried steak with gravy. He sat opposite Cheater, who devoured his meal with the indifference of a man who had known little else but institutional cooking.

"Lookee here. We got us a new fish in the tank."

Cheater froze, spoon halfway to his mouth, as Mother set his tray down beside Skinner with a loud clatter. A huge black man with a shaved head sat down beside Cheater. Although he did not speak, his eyes were focused directly on Skinner.

"I can smell fresh meat from a mile away." Mother grinned, displaying teeth the color of antique ivory. "There ain't a boy that comes into this place I don't know about. Ain't that right, Rope?"

The heavyset man grunted, narrowing his eyes into gun-slits. Skinner had a good view of the scar ringing the Negro's throat, and how it pulsed and twisted whenever Rope swallowed.

"You leave him be, Mother."

Mother pulled his lips back into something that might have passed for a smile if you weren't looking into his eyes. "Why? He your punk?"

Cheater shifted uneasily, dropping his eyes. He was too old to face down hardcases as young and mean as Mother anymore, and both men knew it. "I wasn't saying nothing, except that Skin here hasn't done you no disservice."

"He ain't provided no service, either. Ain't that right, fresh meat?"

Skinner's face was dead white except for hectic blotches of red marking each cheek. He stared down at the battered tin tray as if he could see the future in the gravy pooled atop his country-fried steak.

"I *said* ain't that right, meat? You deaf, or are you dissing me?"

Skinner turned to look Mother square in the eye, fighting to keep from spitting in his face. The rapist seemed momentarily taken aback by the color of his eyes, then broke into a slow, evil smile. "I'm gonna enjoy doin' you, meat. You need a few lessons on how a punk like you should act towards his betters, and I'm just the one to teach 'em to you."

He motioned to his companion, and the two picked up their trays and moved on to a different table.

Skinner leaned forward and whispered to Cheater, trying his best to keep the fear from making his voice waver.

"What am I gonna *do?*"

"Watch your back."

"That goes without saying! Can't I get the guards to do something? What if I tell 'em Mother threatened me? Can't they do anything to stop this?"

Cheater shook his head sadly. "You *might* be able to talk the warden into taking you out of General Population and putting you into Protective Custody. But that's not going to do you much good in the long run. Mostly Protective Custody's for snitches. If you get put in there for awhile, then released back into General Population, you'll be lucky to last a day."

Skinner was still mulling this information over later when the bell rang for lights out.

He lay there in the dark for a long time, arms folded behind his head, and stared at the cracks in the ceiling above his bunk. The sounds of the Mainline after hours echoed through the building; two hundred men whispering, snoring, praying, fucking in the dark. It sounded like a zoo full of animals on the verge of tearing at one another—and themselves.

He wasn't sure when he managed to finally drift off, or how long he'd been asleep. It could have been minutes or hours. He woke up suddenly, his muscles rigid and every hair on his body erect.

At first he wasn't sure what had woken him. Then he saw Cheater's silhouette looming in front of him, a blot of darkness set against the light drifting through the bars at the front of the cell.

He was certain the old con was going to rape him. Then he looked into Cheater's face and realized he was asleep.

"Cheater . . . ?"

"I—I had a dream . . . about you." Cheater's voice was thick, slurred. "You . . . were wearing . . . a crown . . . and a robe . . . and you were walkin' the yard . . ."

"Cheater? Wake up, man. You're givin' me the creeps!"

"I asked someone why . . . you were tricked out . . . and they said . . . you was really a prince . . . the Prince of the Foxes. . . . You walked right up to the fence . . . the guards was shootin' at you . . . but you didn't get hurt . . . and you parted the fence like it was a curtain . . . and walked on through. . . . You was so beautiful . . . so wild . . . so *free* . . . free'r than air . . . free'r than water. . . . I knew I had to follow you, then. . . ."

Cheater lifted a hand to his seamed face with its busted nose and droopy eyelid and began to cry. "So . . . free . . . so . . . beautiful . . ."

With that he lumbered over to the toilet in the corner of the cell and relieved himself noisily before returning to his bunk. Within seconds he was snoring.

Skinner did not sleep the rest of the night. Instead, he lay in his bunk, trying to deal with the dawning realization that his only ally in this hellhole was probably not entirely sane, at least by the standards held by the society that existed beyond prison walls.

Skinner's second day at Los Lobos started out calmly enough. He and the other one hundred and ninety-nine inmates of Cell Black A were awakened at six in the morning by the simultaneous sounds of the wake-up bell going off and the central mechanism that controlled their cells unlocking the doors.

Skinner showered in the company of one hundred and ninety-nine other men, returned to his cell and put on his clothes, and trooped off with fellow members of Cell Block A to the mess hall, where they were served cornbread, sausage patties, and powdered eggs.

After breakfast, Skinner reported to the duty officer, whose job it was to assess the new inmates' skills and assign them to whichever sector of the prison was short of manpower. Skinner was assigned grounds detail.

He and six other men were given the hellish task of resurfacing the basketball court. For the remainder of the day, while under the constant supervision of an armed guard, not to mention his fellow officers in the air-conditioned towers, they spread asphalt with shovels and rakes, coated it with an oily fixative, then pushed old-fashioned manual rollers over it in order to pack it down and smooth out the playing surface. All of this in ninety-degree heat, with a half-hour break for lunch and two fifteen-minute water breaks. Skinner had never worked so hard—and for no pay— in his entire life.

He stumbled back into his cell, back and shoulders aching, stinking of asphalt, to find Cheater reading a dog-eared porn mag. Unlike his previous roomie, if Cheater ever beat off, he kept it to himself.

"Phew! Don't you smell like a bed of petunias!"

"I hurt in places I never knew I had," Skinner groaned, crawling onto his bunk with the speed of a giant three-toed sloth.

"What are you complainin' about? You're a young feller! You'll get used to work details, soon enough. You gotta learn the government lick, or they'll work you right into the grave."

"It sounds obscene, whatever it is."

"It's simple, really. All you have to do is figure out how much work you can get away with *not* doing, then just do what it takes to get by without getting the bulls on your ass. You don't do a lick of work other'n what they tell you to do, how they tell you to do it. Don't go thinkin' for yourself, or tryin' to figure out a more efficient way of gettin' the job done. I call it the government lick on account of that's how civil servants do their jobs."

The dinner bell rang and Cheater quickly stowed his stroke mag under his mattress. "Time to eat! You coming or what?"

"I think I ought to clean up, first. I'll meet you in the mess hall in fifteen, twenty minutes. I can't stand to smell myself any longer."

"Gotcha. Don't take too long, though. You'll end up missing chow. A man can get awful hungry in the middle of the night."

Skinner grunted his understanding and, his towel draped over one shoulder, headed in the direction of the showers.

As Skinner peeled off his dirty clothes, he realized he had it all to himself. Cell Block A's showers resembled those found in any high school locker room, with a dozen individual fixtures and poured concrete floors. Normally you had to wait in line, with ablutions limited to three minutes per man. Those at the end of the line usually had to settle for lukewarm—if not outright cold—water. Skinner intended to take full advantage of the situation and enjoy a shower hot enough to get the oily residue of his labors out of his hair.

He was standing under the shower head, washing his hair, the thunder of falling water in his ears, his eyes shut to keep the soap out, when he was struck in the chest and knocked back against the shower's tiled wall. Skinner opened his eyes to see who'd punched him, swearing as the soap burned his tear ducts.

Mother flashed him a predator's grin, all teeth and menace.

"Bend over and crack yore Daddy some brown-eye, punk."

"Fuck you!" snapped Skinner, trying to keep the anger and fear from making his voice break.

"That's exactly what I intend to do."

Mother's fist crashed into the side of Skinner's head and for a brief second the world was without light, sound, or scent. When he regained his senses, he was lying on his side on the floor, the sound of running water filling his ears.

"Roll him over on his back," Mother ordered, nudging Skinner's flank with his boot as he opened his pants. "I want to look into his eyes while I'm doin' it to him."

He tried to say no, but Rope was already kneeling over him, shoving Skinner's own bunched-up underwear into his mouth.

Skinner had never seen an erect penis besides his own. The thing clutched in Mother's hand looked more like a blunt instrument than a piece of meat. Mother gave himself a few swift, angry yanks, as if his dick was made of leather instead of living flesh, until he was pumped full. There were red and black flames inked along its length, like the customizing on a hotrod engine cowling.

"Hold him still, damn it! How do you expect me to plug him if he's wiggling around like that?" Mother growled, spitting into his free hand.

Rope nodded and slapped Skinner hard enough to crack the back of his head against the floor. For a second everything went gray and seemed to go away for a few seconds—then the pain of Mother shoving between his buttocks brought him back to himself.

He screamed as the con slammed into him, but most of it was muffled by the gag blocking his mouth. It was like he was being torn in two, the pain increasing with each thrust of his attacker's hips. Tears of agony and shame filled his eyes, streaming from the corners into his ears.

This isn't happening.

"Look at me!" Suddenly Mother's face was looming over his, breathing hot, putrid air down on him. Skinner squeezed his eyes shut and turned his head away. "Look at me when I'm fucking you, punk!"

This isn't happening to me. I'm not really here. This can't be happening to me. When I wake up it'll have been nothing but a bad dream. A nightmare. Nothing more.

"I *told* you to look at me, punk!" Mother's fist smashed into Skinner's face, breaking his nose.

Blood flooded Skinner's sinuses and began backing up into his throat. He tried to spit it out, but the gag was in the way. The blood continued to back up and he began to strangle.

Die. I'm going to die. He's going to let me choke to death on my own blood and then let the other rape my body. I'm just meat to them. It doesn't matter if I'm alive or dead. I'm just something to use and throw away. Meat. Meat.

Mother grinned and grabbed Skinner's rapidly inflating penis in one blood-smeared hand. "Hey,

Rope! Lookit this! The guy's a faggot! He's gettin' off on it! Ain't that right, pretty boy?''

Skinner made a choking noise by way of a reply.

The convict's smile began to fade. Something resembling concern crossed his face, but it wasn't for his victim. ''Hey—something's wrong here. I-I think he's havin' some kinda fit—''

Skinner's limbs began to jerk and quiver, flailing about so violently Rope could no longer maintain his grip on the boy's upper torso. Mother swore and tried to disengage himself from his victim, but his penis was clamped tightly in place.

''Help me! Sweet Jesus, he's got my dick! I can't get out! I'm stuck!''

Skinner wondered what was going on. First there had been pain: unending, unendurable pain that had given way to a sensation so intense that it transcended agony and bordered on ecstasy. It was what he imagined junkies felt when they shot up.

Funny, he felt as if he was a thousand miles away, watching everything with the wrong end of a pair of binoculars. Everyone looked so little— so inconsequential. Why was the naked, bloodied young man sprawled on the floor? Before he could find out, his body kicked into overdrive and the Change was on him.

There was the sound of breaking bone and squelching cartilage. Mother screamed like a woman. Rope scrambled to his homey's aid, wrapping his arms under Mother's pits and yanking him free of the boy with a wet popping sound. Mother's face was gray with shock. He clutched at the front of his pants, now smeared with blood, anal mucus and feces, his lips pulled back in a rictus grin.

Mother said something under his breath— whether a curse or a call to God was moot—as the thing on the floor of the shower room got to its feet. It stood like an arthritic old man, its shoulders and legs twisted and bent, the elongated head cocked to one side as if listening to something only it could hear.

Its fur shone like moonlight on a still lake as it flexed its long-fingered, razor-taloned hands and rolled its stooped shoulders. It shook the beads of water from its silvery coat and grinned, licking its wrinkled snout with a long pink tongue.

When it saw Mother sprawled on the floor, whimpering and shivering like a newly whelped pup, it narrowed its golden eyes and growled.

Rope stepped forward, positioning himself between the beast and Mother. He pulled a homemade knife—a sharpened cafeteria spoon with a taped handle—from inside his shirt. Rope lunged at the creature, burying the makeshift weapon deep in its right breast.

The creature howled as bright red blood jetted from the wound, clawing at the protruding spoon handle. It swiped at Rope's head with one of its claws, slicing open his face.

The mute screamed.

Rope fell to his knees, trying to put his right eye back in its socket. Skinner stepped past him, reaching for Mother, who had recovered enough to prop himself against the wall, one hand still cupping his crushed genitals.

"No," the big man wept, his tears mingling with the tattooed teardrop at the corner of his eye. He tried to shield his face with his free arm. "No . . ."

Skinner reached down and grabbed a handful of Mother's hair, pulling him to his feet. He was amazed at how light the convict seemed. It was like he weighed nothing at all. The realization made Skinner smile, which made Mother start to cry even harder. Skinner found the sight of his enemy's tears exciting.

Mother looked into the creature's golden eyes. "Please don't kill me," he begged. "Please—"

Skinner's teeth snapped shut on Mother's throat before he had a chance to repeat himself. Blood, hot and fresh, spurted into his mouth. It tasted good. Better than anything he'd ever eaten before in his life. Suddenly he was so hungry—so very, very hungry.

A muscular, denim-clad arm as thick as a young girl's thigh wrapped itself around his throat, yanking Skinner free of his meal. It was Rope—one eye dangling by its optic nerve, the right half of his face displaying a skeleton's grin—coming to the aid of his homey.

The mute had Skinner in a choke-hold and was trying to crush his windpipe. And had he been battling Skinner Cade, gangly teenager from Seven Devils, Arkansas, he probably would have succeeded.

Skinner grabbed Rope's wrist and flipped the mute over his shoulder, twisting his arm a quarter turn as he struck the floor. There was a loud snapping sound, like a green tree branch being broken.

Rope opened his ruined mouth and issued a shriek only his killer could hear.

Jaws dripping long beads of saliva, Skinner gave the mute's arm a final wrench, grinning even wider when it came off in his claws.

The last thing Rope saw before he bled to death on the floor of the Los Lobos County Correctional Facility was the thing that had once been Skinner Cade hunkered down on its haunches, gnawing his still-twitching right arm like it was a leg of lamb.

Chapter Eight

Caged.

He was caged. Everywhere he looked, there were gray walls and no way out. Everything stank of human sweat and semen and other secretions. There was another smell, something far less tangible, yet equally real, that mingled with the other odors. It was a mixture of frustration, anger, hate, and desperation, impregnating the walls of the prison like a toxic perfume. It was the smell of rage, and it made Skinner's fur stand on end and his teeth ache.

As Skinner prowled the catwalks that connected the upper tiers, he heard the first of the humans return from dinner. He dropped to his belly, careful to avoid detection, and watched as a pair of humans—one elderly and missing his upper teeth—paused underneath his hiding place to chat and light their cigarettes.

Skinner watched the old human with hungry eyes. Although he'd fed less than fifteen minutes ago, his guts were already gnawing at themselves. He was so hungry. It was like he hadn't eaten in years. And what easier prey than an old and infirm human?

The human's companion waved farewell and walked away, leaving the old one behind. Now was his chance. Skinner gathered himself in preparation for the attack.

Top Gum yawned, scratched himself, and blew twin jets of smoke out his nose. Like his friend, Cheater, he'd spent most of his adult life in and out of jail. Since he'd always been on the puny side, he'd specialized in forgery and embezzling. Safe stuff. He left the risky business to the big guys. You lived longer that way.

Well, it was getting late. Time to return to his cell, read a couple chapters from that book his old lady sent him, maybe write a letter or two before lights out. He paused, suddenly overwhelmed by a memory of a dog he'd owned as a kid. A shaggy little mutt called Booker. Funny, he hadn't thought about that pooch in—well, dog's years. He wondered what might have sparked the memory.

His last coherent thought was: *That's odd. I could swear I smell a wet dog.*

Skinner jumped, landing in the middle of Top Gum's back. The old convict's spine snapped like a dry twig. He only had the time—and breath— to voice one hoarse cry of alarm before Skinner clamped his muzzle onto his throat.

The sound of boots hammering against the decks of the upper and lower tiers distracted Skinner from his feeding. Humans—dozens of them— were headed his way, alerted by their comrade's death shriek. He stood up, ready to abandon his prey, but it was too late.

The ones at the head of the mob came to a sudden halt the moment they saw Skinner hunched over Top Gum's corpse and began back-pedaling. The ones behind them, however, couldn't see what was going on and kept pushing forward, only to be met by those trying to escape. There were angry shouts and swearing and the air became electric with the smell of panic. Skinner grinned and dove forward, tearing at those closest to him with his claws and fangs, creating a stampede.

At least a half-dozen prisoners were trampled as their fellow inmates tried to flee the snapping, snarling, yellow-eyed beast. Cheater, who'd been toward the back, was knocked to the floor and narrowly avoided being crushed. He grabbed the railing and tried to pull himself upright, only to find himself staring into the grinning jaws of a nightmare.

The creature stared down at him, panting like a friendly dog. Its silvery pelt was marred by a wet crimson bib and its breath reeked of blood. The brows above the golden eyes momentarily bunched, then relaxed.

"Skinner?"

The creature lifted its snout and tested the air, made a high-pitched whining noise, and was gone.

Cheater watched the beast leave, waited a few seconds, then got to his feet and hobbled after his friend.

Stanton looked up from his girlie book and scowled at Tate. "You hear that?"

Tate, who'd been cleaning his nails with his Boy

Scout pocket knife, cocked his head to one side and frowned. "I don't hear—oh, shit!"

The sound of men screaming and yelling, distant at first, then growing louder, could be heard echoing up the corridor from the cell block.

Stanton pushed himself away from the desk, fumbling for the keys to the assault rifles and tear gas launcher locked in the closet next to his desk. "Sounds like we got ourselves a riot in Cell Block A!"

Tate stood at the security door that separated the corridor leading to Cell Block A from the guard's station, peering nervously through the bullet-proof window.

"Riot? Hell, it sounds like a fuckin' *massacre*! Where's Malone, Simpson, and Keller? They were in charge of patrolling the Mainline tonight. Why didn't they report trouble?"

"We'll worry about that later! Call the warden!" When his partner didn't make any move to respond, Stanton kicked the trash can next to his desk, denting in its side. "I *said* call the warden! *Now*!"

"Yes, sir!" Tate blurted, diving for the phone.

The noise coming from Cell Block A was growing louder. Stanton yanked open the closet door, his hands trembling as he reached for the riot gear.

He'd lived through a major riot at the state penitentiary six years back. There had been hostages and things had gone badly toward the end. The worst part had been the payback, though. The prisoners broke into the Protective Custody Wing, where they kept the snitches. One prisoner had been handcuffed to his bunk and dismembered with acetylene torches looted from the machine shop.

Stanton had hoped transferring to a smaller facility like Los Lobos would have kept him from having to deal with brutality on that scale again.

"We need backup right now—" Tate's other words were drowned out by the sound of a klaxon.

Stanton, armed with a tear gas launcher, the mask perched atop his balding brow, squinted through the observation port. "Shit! They've started a fire! The sprinkler system's cut on! Sweet bleedin' Jesus, where're Keller and the others?"

Los Lobos, like every other facility in the state, had suffered manpower cut-backs. If the riot succeeded in spreading to the other wings, there was no chance of them being able to put it down without the help of the National Guard. But he'd be damned if he was going to wade into a melee without at least ten other men tricked out in riot gear behind him.

"Anything coming up the corridor?" Tate asked, swinging the breach shut on his assault rifle.

Stanton squinted through the observation port again. "Hard to tell, what with the smoke and shit, but I don't think so. No! Wait a minute— I think I see something— It looks like it might be Malone!"

The two-inch thick reinforced steel door came off its hinges as if hit by a freight train, slamming into Stanton's face with such force it drove his nose up into his brain, killing him instantly.

Tate stared at the riot door lying on the floor and the blood seeping out from around its edges. Then he saw what was crouched atop it, its tongue lolling and eyes showing white. He aimed the assault rifle at the thing, but it was already moving, hitting him full in the chest with bared talons and fangs. His Kevlar jacket shredded under its claws like cheesecloth. The rifle went off as he fell, punching a hole the size of a man's fist in the ceiling. Tate's ears were ringing so badly from the blast he couldn't hear his own death scream.

Skinner cast back his head and howled as he entered the yard. The smell of the Wild was all around him. The acrid stink of smoke and spilled blood was still strong in his nostrils, clinging to his fur, but it could not hide the sweet, pure scent of the Wild.

He loped into the darkness of the yard, eager to put the huge concrete warren full of screaming, bellowing, dying humans behind him. All that mattered was the Wild on the other side of the metal fence.

A beam of light, hot and intense, suddenly shone down on him, swiveling to follow his attempts to avoid detection. A voice—angry and frightened—came from the nearest guard tower.

"Stop! Stop or I'll shoot!"

Skinner was moving before the guard had a chance to finish his sentence. He could hear the rifles crack, feel the bullets punch holes in the air around him, see the sprays of dirt kicked up as they impacted with the ground, but it made no difference. He had to be free of this place of men, with its cages within cages.

Something hit him in the right shoulder, then again at the back of his left leg. It felt like he'd stumbled into a nest of angry hornets. A third shot knocked him off his feet.

One of the guards was hurrying toward him, a pair of massive German shepherds snapping and snarling at the end of their leashes. They smelled like slaves. Skinner squatted on his hind legs and fixed the dogs with a defiant stare, his hackles raised and teeth bared.

The attack dogs dropped their ears and pulled their heads in, cringing and whimpering like un-weaned pups.

"God dammit, Satan! Stalin! What's gotten into you?" shouted the guard, tugging violently at their choke chains. The attack dogs pulled themselves free of their handler and ran, tails between their legs, back toward the kennels.

Skinner was on the guard in a flurry of fangs and fur before the man could draw his revolver. Someone in the tower fired a shot at Skinner, only to be yelled at by one of his superiors.

"Hold your fire! You might hit Jack!"

It was already too late for Jack. Skinner spat out the dying guard's larynx and loped toward the north fence.

He made a running jump at the fence, hitting it halfway up its fifteen foot height. He howled as electricity coursed through his body, contracting his muscles and igniting his fur, but he refused to let go. His body jerked and twitched painfully, his mouth filling with blood as he bit through his tongue, but he continued climbing.

There was a muffled explosion from the direction of the main building and the yard was plunged into darkness.

"Damn it! The generator's blown!"

Skinner could hear the shouts and screams and laughter of hundreds of men behind him as they poured into the yard. Then came the sound of automatic gunfire as the guards opened up on the rioters below. It meant nothing to him. It was human foolishness and had little to do with him.

He pulled himself over the top of the fence, his hide protecting him against the slicing edges of the razor wire, and dropped to the other side.

Free.

He was free.

Skinner tossed back his head and gave voice to a long, ululating howl, then loped off into the darkness, where he belonged. Into the Wild.

Chapter Nine

Skinner squatted atop an outcropping of rock atop a hill overlooking the highway, peacefully gnawing at the jack rabbit he'd just killed. The animal's blood was still hot, its meat stringy but palatable. It tasted gamier than human flesh, but lacked the acrid traces of preservatives and other manmade contaminants humans made a part of their diet.

Skinner's belly was stretched tight—he'd eaten more than his fill of meat that night—and the hunger that gnawed like a rat in his gut was finally beginning to fade. Still, he wasn't so full he couldn't savor cracking open the bones of his kill to get at the marrow.

He scanned the vast, star-strewn desert sky and yawned, curling his tongue inward. It felt good to be free. To run naked in the night air in pursuit of prey. To be surrounded by the Wild and not walls. Most of all, this shape—his *true* shape—felt good. It had been so long since he'd known this form. Much too long.

He could not remember the first time he changed, shifting from man to not-man, but he was certain this was not his first transformation.

Skinner yawned again. He was tired. His stomach was full. He was far removed from those who had tried to hurt and imprison him. It was time to rest. He took what little was left of the rabbit carcass and covered it with loose stones, saving it for later, then turned around three times before settling down, his muzzle resting atop his folded hindlegs.

Within three minutes he was sound asleep.

Within five he began to dream. And in his dreams, remembered the first time he Changed.

"Hurry up, Skin! You don't want to be late your first time out!" William Cade called to his son from the foot of the stairs.

It was an early morning in November—so early, in fact, the sun had yet to come up. William Cade was dressed in a flannel lumberjack shirt, a red plaid hunting jacket, khaki pants, leather boots that laced up to his knee, and a fluorescent orange cap with earflaps.

"I'm coming, Dad! Don't leave! Don't leave!" Skinner, all of twelve years old, hurried down the stairs, still struggling into his own jacket. From his hat down to his boots, he was dressed identically to his father.

Today was a very special day and he was very excited. He'd been looking forward to November 1 with the avid eagerness he usually reserved for Christmas and his birthday. Today was the first day of deer season, and he was now old enough to join his father in the woods.

He had undergone a rite of passage the night before—Halloween—when he'd put on his pirate's costume and gone trick-or-treating for the last time.

Today, he was putting aside childish costumes and candies in favor of hunter's garb and a gun.

No one in Choctaw County, outside of the handful of Catholics who attended St. Joseph of Copertino, knew that the day after Halloween was anything but the First Day of Deer Season.

All Souls Day, All Saints Day, Day of the Dead . . . these holidays meant nothing to the inhabitants of Seven Devils, Arkansas. Despite this ignorance, it was still a school holiday, the start of deer season being recognized and celebrated in rural Arkansas as a sacrament.

Edna Cade was in the kitchen, making sure her men didn't go out into the wilderness unprepared. She poured hot coffee into her husband's thermos and hot cocoa into her son's, and made sure each was equally provisioned with enough sandwiches to last the day. Satisfied they were warmly dressed, she kissed them on the cheeks and stood on the back porch and watched them walk across the field on the other side of the yard and enter the woods, their rifles slung across their backs. Before he disappeared into the forest, William Cade paused long enough to wave good-bye to his wife of forty years. And then he was gone.

Skinner's excitement doubled as they moved deeper and deeper into the woods behind his house. He was familiar with the forest from his years of playing underneath its trees and climbing its branches. But now it had been transformed into a different place. A place where wild things dwelled. A place where mystery lurked behind every bush.

"Do you think we'll see a bear or a bobcat, Daddy?"

His father laughed as he paused to light his pipe. "Son, we'll be lucky to see so much as a fox in these parts. Most of the bears and swamp cats were either scared off or shot long before you were even thought of."

"But Mama's always telling me to be careful when I play in the woods."

"That's because your mama's a woman. It's their job to worry about bears eatin' their young 'uns. And their menfolk."

William Cade spotted deer tracks and they moved even deeper into the woods, following its trail. Skinner's heart was hammering away in his chest like it wanted to get out. He'd never stalked anything before. Not with the intent of killing it, anyway. He'd become quite adept at tracking squirrels and rabbits and feral cats during his solitary trips to the woods, but he never did anything except watch them.

They caught up with the deer an hour later. It had paused to drink from a small creek in a part of the woods where the trees were so close the forest floor was cast in perpetual twilight. Skinner stood in awe of the creature as it drank. It was a large, healthy buck, boasting an eight-point rack and a pelt the color of caramel apples.

"Go ahead, Skin. Shoot," his father whispered, his lips pressed close to Skinner's ear. "Remember what I told you. Make sure you get it with the first shot. It's more humane. That way it won't run off into the woods and bleed to death."

As if in a trance, Skinner nodded and raised his rifle, sighting down the barrel at the deer standing fifty feet away. The buck lifted its head suddenly, water dripping from its wide black nose, and for a heartbeat he was afraid it had caught his scent and was ready to flee, its white tail lifted in warning to its brothers as it bounded into the surrounding forest. Instead it lowered its head and resumed drinking.

Two bullets punched into the buck's exposed throat. The deer screamed as it jerked backwards, away from the stream, its forelegs flailing about uselessly as its lifeblood pumped from the side of its neck. It fell among the dead leaves with a heavy thump, kicking and thrashing like a clockwork toy whose action has wound down.

Skinner's father clapped him on the shoulder. "That's my boy! You're a natural born hunter, there's no denying it! Now, let's finish the poor beast off. . . ."

The buck was still alive as they approached. It had stopped struggling, but was breathing, the massive rib cage rising and falling like a faulty bellows. The smell of blood and deer piss was so strong they had to breathe through their mouths.

His father handed him a Buck knife. "Here you go, Skin. Finish what you started."

The deer's eyes were already starting to glaze as Skinner squatted beside it, the oversized knife looking like a bayonet in his small hand. Without knowing why, he placed his free hand atop the dying animal's snout, stroking it gently. "Forgive me," he whispered as he slit the deer's throat.

The buck shuddered as its bowels emptied, then was still. Skinner stood up, dazed, and handed the knife back to his father.

William Cade squatted beside the deer and began sawing away at its underbelly. "Look at this booger! He must weigh a hundred twenty, hundred thirty! Once he's dressed out proper, we should be eatin' venison until Christmas! Check out those points! That's *gonna make one hell of a trophy, son!" He reached into the animal's steaming carcass and pulled out a length of intestine.*

He stood up, still holding the slippery length of gut, and motioned for Skinner to stand beside him. "That was a damn fine first kill. I've known men twice your age who couldn't shoot that good or clean. I'm proud of you, son."

With that, he wrapped the length of intestine around Skinner's neck and smeared his cheeks with blood.

And Skinner changed.

It was on him so suddenly there was no time to realize what was happening. There was only pain that went beyond the borders of human endurance, beyond the ability of expression. It was like being born and dying at the same time. The doors of perception were thrown wide, and for the first time in his life he knew what it was like to truly hear and taste and smell the world around him. And there was a hunger so overpowering it knotted his stomach like it was an empty bag.

There was blood and the tearing of flesh and screams and the memory of running low to the ground at speeds impossible for a boy crawling on his hands and knees. . . .

The next thing he remembered, he was lying naked on a pile of dead leaves, curled up with his knees pressed against his chest. He was covered with dried mud and feces, and he was gnawing what remained of a gray squirrel.

"Skinner . . . ? Skinner, baby, it's Mama. Can you hear me?"

His mother was there, kneeling in the dirt in front of him. There were tears in her eyes, and her face had suddenly become very old and colorless. She removed her coat and wrapped it around his shivering, naked form, wrenching the half-eaten squirrel from his gore-caked hands.

"We've got to get you back to the house before someone sees us."

He lay in bed for three days with a raging fever, recovering in time for his father's funeral. He had no memory of what had happened the day his father died. His mother insisted that he'd been ill the first day of deer season and been unable to accompany his father into the woods, as originally planned. Skinner always assumed she was telling him the truth.

Skinner woke up naked and shivering, curled into a fetal ball. Someone was shaking him. Asking him if he was all right. At first he thought it was his mother. Then he recognized the voice.

"Prince! Answer me, Prince! Are you okay?"

Cheater was kneeling over him, shaking him by the shoulders. Skinner slowly raised his head. It had all been a bad dream. A nightmare spawned by anxiety at being imprisoned and the guilt from Luke's death. He looked around, expecting to be greeted by Los Lobos' immutable gray walls, but saw open desert and sky instead.

"Man, I thought I'd *never* catch up with you!"

Real.

It was all real. The attack in the showers. The rape. The transformation. It actually happened.

And what I remembered. About what happened when I went hunting. It was real, too. Oh, God. God.

He wanted to scream, but all that came out was, "Ah. Ah. Ah."

"You alright, Prince? You don't look so good."

Skinner spewed forth a gut full of raw meat by way of a reply. Cheater nudged at the mess with his boot, then bent over to retrieve a human finger. He studied it for a moment before wiping it off and slipping it into his pocket.

"You feel better now?"

"*Better?* How the hell am I *ever* supposed to feel 'better'! I'm a murderer and a cannibal! I'm a fuckin' *monster*!"

"You're being too hard on yourself, Prince. Way I see it, you're a miracle."

"*Miracle?*" Skinner started to laugh uncontrollably.

"C'mon, Prince. We gotta get you some clothes before you catch your death. Then we gotta snag ourselves some wheels. They're gonna be lookin' for all the chickens that flew the coop last night."

"Let 'em find me, then."

"You don't want that, Prince."

"How do *you* know what the fuck I do and don't want? I—I—uhhh!" Another spasm of vomiting hit him, doubling him over with each racking heave.

Cheater shook his head sadly and picked up his friend as easily as a father might take a recalcitrant toddler to bed. "I don't pretend to know everything, Prince. But I think I have a better idea of what's good for you than you do right now."

Chapter Ten

Dawn had yet to break over the Potrillo Mountains of New Mexico, sixty miles northwest of El Paso, Texas, as the vans, one a Volkswagen minibus, the other a Dodge Caravan, drew to a halt in the foothills. Before the dust had a chance to settle, the doors flew open and six figures, five male and one female, piled out. The Caravan's sound-system was still on, shattering the early morning silence with the sound of Nirvana.

Ripper, relieved to be free of the confines of the minibus, danced about in a circle in time with the music, yipping at the retreating moon, kicking up clouds of dust with his scuffed combat boots, occasionally throwing himself onto the ground and rolling around in the dirt. Being the youngest, he tended to be the most enthusiastic of the pack.

Hew leaned against the side of the vehicle he'd been driving, sipping beer from a 30-ounce container, watching the drummer leap and jump like an Indian shaman, an indulgent smile on his face. Sunder prowled the perimeters, sniffing the wind, while Jag and Rend walked around to the back of the Caravan.

Jez stretched slowly, her arms lifted high over

her head, making sure all the males caught a glimpse of her exposed midriff, before hopping onto the hood of the van and curling her legs under her. "Any sign of intruders, Sunder?"

"I caught scent of a couple of coyotes and a puma, nothing more."

Jez frowned. "Coyotes? Are you sure . . . ?"

Sunder made a snuffling noise and spat in disgust. "I know true coyote when I smell it!"

"I'm not saying you don't, Sunder-my-pet," she purred. "It's just that—well, we *are* in the very heart of enemy territory. We can't be *too* careful . . . not after what happened to poor Bender back in L.A."

Sunder grunted and rolled his shoulders in a surly shrug, but he did not meet Jez' gaze.

"Stop squabbling and get ready!" barked Jag, tossing his hair out of his face with an angry shake of his head. "We don't have much time, and we've still got to make that sound check in Albuquerque!"

Jez rolled her eyes as she slid from her perch. "*Yes*, brother-dear."

Jag fished the keys to the back of the minibus from his hip pocket and unlocked the double doors, swinging them open so hard they banged against the sides of the van. Rend crawled in and a few seconds later two bodies, hands cuffed behind their backs, were dumped onto the hard dirt. The female cried out as she struck the ground.

Jag squatted on his haunches and smirked as the prey struggled to roll over. "What's the matter, my friends? Are my little 'restraining devices' a bit too . . . realistic . . . for your tastes?"

The male, dressed in tattered jeans and what was left of a Temple of Psychick Youth t-shirt, tried to roll onto his back, but Sunder put his booted foot between his shoulder blades, forcing his face into the dust.

"Screw you, Jag! What's this mind-fuck control shit you're trying to pull, huh? You trying to freak us out, or what? You said you and your weirdo sister wanted to play doubles. You didn't say nothing about bondage and gang-bangin', man!"

"I don't know what your problem is, friend. You were the one who came to me after the show in El Paso and told me you were into rough trade. Well, they don't get any rougher'n me!"

"Perry, don't say any more. He's crazy. They're *all* crazy," pleaded the female. She was a bottle blond, evident now that her black party dress was up over her hips, exposing the lace tops of her silk stockings and the dark patch of hair between her legs. She was barefoot and her stockings were spiderwebbed with runs. There was also a nasty welt under her right eye from where Jag had popped her one for struggling.

"Shut up, Sheri!" Perry hissed, somehow managing to make it seem like it was all her fault.

Jag leaned over, thrusting his face into the terrified woman's. "*Crazy?* Sweetheart, we're a *lot* more than crazy!"

Jag stood up and snapped his fingers. Rend produced a pair of keys and tossed them to him. Jag caught them in midair without even looking. "Despite what you might think, we're not crazed drug-addicted psycho-killers. No, we're sporting types. And there's no sport in shooting fish in a barrel. So we're going to give you a fighting chance. It's more fun that way. We're going to unlock the handcuffs and give you a five-minute start.'' Jag quickly removed the cuffs and stepped away.

Perry and Sheri sat up, exchanging uncertain looks as they massaged the circulation back into their wrists.

"The clock is running, friends.'' Jag grinned, exposing far too many teeth for a human mouth.

Rend made a noise somewhere between agony and orgasm and dropped onto his knees, his spine twisting and bunching underneath his leathers.

Sheri scuttled backward on her heels and hands, her eyes suddenly huge. "P-Perry?''

Perry lurched to his feet. "Run! Run, Sheri!''

Sheri staggered after her boyfriend, wincing as the rocks and loose gravel cut her feet.

Ripper barked and growled in anticipation of the hunt, hopping about on first one foot, then the other, as he took off his boots. Sunder unbuckled the bondage straps that held his jeans together and joined Ripper in his dance, his flaccid penis growing abruptly rigid as he shifted.

Hew tossed back his head as the Change came over him and gave voice to a strong, lusty howl of exultant pain. Jez cried out, whipping her head back and forth as her bones restructured themselves, her shrieks turning into a yowl of release.

Jag shook out his white mane and leapt atop a nearby rock. He was happy with the way the pack was working out. They might have their differences in human form, but once they shifted into their true selves—their *vargr* selves—these petty annoyances disappeared. They were a tightly knit, fiercely loyal, self-reliant team. And he was the leader of the pack.

His was a wonderful life.

"Come on, damn it! They'll be after us in no time!" snapped Perry.

They were halfway up the side of a low hill, its face studded with scrub and small boulders. Sheri was leaning against one of the boulders, sobbing in pain from the damage done to her feet. She wiped at her tears, smearing mascara across her cheeks.

"What *are* they, Perry?"

"They're not a speed-metal band, that's for fuckin' certain! Now, hurry up!"

"I *can't*! Look at my feet!"

He didn't need to look. He'd seen the bloody footprints a half-mile back, and he was sure whatever was chasing them had noticed them as well. Even if they somehow managed to survive their ordeal, Sheri would be crippled for life.

"So what do you expect me to do? *Carry* you?" he snapped.

Sheri stared up at him with those big, stupid Bambi-eyes that she saved for those occasions where she refused to admit that she loved him more than he loved her. Fine. He never asked her to fall in love with him in the first place.

"Perry, I *love* you!"

"Forget it, shitball! I'm not gonna get my ass killed lugging you through the fuckin' wilderness!" He resumed his climb, scrabbling over loose rock and brush.

Sheri stared after him, open-mouthed, for a couple of seconds before finding her voice. "Perry! That's not funny! Come back!"

Perry paused long enough to shoot her a venomous glance over his shoulder. "I mean it, bitch! You're on your own! I told you when I picked you up at that party last year I wasn't into commitment! You were the one who wanted to be my girlfriend! Nice knowin' you, kid!"

"Perry!" She tried to follow him but slipped in her own blood and fell. She lay there, sprawled in the dirt, and wept his name like a mantra.

Fuck her. Everyone else had. As far as he was concerned, Sheri was nothing more than a screwed-up little tramp who was either stupid enough or desperate enough to do whatever he told her to do, whether it was pay his rent or blow his friends. He didn't owe her a Goddamned thing. Let those . . . those . . . *creatures* do whatever they wanted with her. It had nothing to do with him.

"Females can be a real ball and chain, eh, Perry?"

There was something squatting atop the rise of the hill, grinning down at him. It had eyes the color of freshly minted gold coins and was covered in white fur. It looked something like a wolf, except that it was jointed wrong and was wearing a black leather jacket with torn sleeves and had a stainless steel ring piercing one nostril.

Behind him, Sheri began to scream. There was the sound of tearing fabric and what was either barking or laughter. Perry refused to look.

"You don't want me—you want the girl! Go

ahead and take her! I don't care! Just let me go, okay? I won't tell anyone what happened out here. Who'd believe me, anyway? Right? Right?"

Jag's grin grew even wider and sharper than before. "Thank you for reaffirming my faith in human nature, Perry. Your offer is most generous, but I'm afraid I can't take you up on it. You're right. I *do* want the girl. And I'll have her, as will the others. But I have my sister's desires to consider, as well . . . Isn't that right, Jez?"

Perry gave an involuntary yell as a taloned hand clamped onto his shoulder, the nails sinking into the flesh beneath his shirt. Jez' breath was hot and redolent of decay.

"What's the matter, Perry? Afraid I'd forgotten you?"

Jag waved farewell as his sister dragged her prey, kicking and screaming, behind the bushes. "Good-bye, Perry! Nice meeting you! And thanks for coming out to the show!"

Chapter Eleven

"Try these on, Prince. They look like they might fit you," Cheater said, tossing a bundle of loose clothes at Skinner's bare feet.

Skinner quickly pulled on a pair of blue jeans and shrugged into a plaid long-sleeved shirt. Both were far from new and somewhat loose on his wiry frame, but the pants held themselves up without the aid of a belt.

"You'll have to wait awhile before getting some boots, I'm afraid."

"Where'd you get these clothes, Cheater?"

"They were hanging in someone's backyard. Where th' hell you *think* I got 'em? Now we've got to locate ourselves some transportation. . . ."

"How are we gonna manage that?"

Cheater's laugh was slow and easy, the laugh of a free man. "That part's easy, Prince. These fuckin' redneck farmers never learn. They live out in the middle of nowhere, so they get in the habit of leavin' their front doors unlocked and the keys in the car. A man can get himself some free pussy and a ride that way, if he has a mind to take it."

An hour later, they came across a squatter's shack. The truck was sitting there like it had been waiting for them.

It was a battered late fifties Ford pickup with a paint job comprised of equal parts primer and rust, but it had four good tires and the keys hanging from the ignition.

"See? What'd I tell you?" Cheater grinned as he slid behind the wheel.

"I don't know about this, Cheater . . . It's not like the guy who owns this truck is rich or nothing."

"He's richer'n us, ain't he? He's got a truck and a house, don't he?"

"Well . . . yeah."

"And it ain't like we're taking his *house*, right?"

"I guess so."

"See? You just got to look at things the *right* way, Prince. There's a *right* way and a *wrong* way to look at things. If you insist on lookin' at life the *wrong* way, you'll end up never getting anywhere, except screwed!" Cheater turned the key in the ignition and threw the truck into gear.

As they were backing down the drive, the front door of the shanty flew open and a middle-aged man, dressed in long johns and a pair of cowboy boots, charged into the front yard.

"Come back with my truck, you goddamned sonofabitch!"

"Shit, Cheater! He's got a—"

The shotgun thundered, peppering the passenger side with a spray of rock salt.

"You'll have to do better'n that, shit-kicker!" Cheater crowed, spewing gravel and dirt in the face of the truck's owner.

"Did you see the look that guy gave you?" Despite his misgivings, Skinner found himself giggling so hard he nearly slid onto the floor of the wildly bouncing cab.

"Yeah, like he just found a turd in the punch bowl!"

That one was good for a solid five minutes of guffaws. Finally, Cheater wiped at the tears at the corners of his eyes and gestured at the glove compartment.

"Check that out, why don't you? Maybe there's a map or something. . . . Find anything?"

"Uh . . . a flashlight . . . what looks like half a bologna sandwich . . . a Texaco map . . . and this." Skinner pulled a .38 handgun from the tangle and showed it to Cheater.

"Alright! Now we're shittin' in high cotton and wipin' with the top leaf! Any spare ammo with that?"

"Doesn't seem to be. But it's loaded."

"Could be better. But I'm not about to cuss my luck so far. Now we've got to find me some new duds, too. We sure as hell won't get far with me wearin' state issues."

A few miles farther down the road, Cheater caught sight of laundry flapping in the dry desert breeze behind a dilapidated shack. Skinner hopped out of the truck and hurried across the dry, rocky ground, snatched an armload of clothes from the line, and returned to the waiting truck.

Cheater gave him a strange look out of the corner of his eye. "You made that dash like you were walking on a shag rug! Don't your feet hurt?"

Skinner blinked and looked down at his naked feet. He'd actually forgotten that he wasn't wearing boots. "I guess they don't." He reached down and touched the soles of his feet. They felt rough and calloused, as if he'd lived his entire life without the benefit of shoes.

Cheater laughed and shook his head in admiration. "I've gotta hand it to you, Prince. You're really something!"

"Yeah, but what?"

Cheater's original plan was to stay on back roads and old highways and head for Texas, where he knew an old cellmate who owned a ranch in the Panhandle. They could lay low out there for a few weeks then hit the road again once the heat died down. Skinner didn't really care where they went. He no longer had a home to return to, or family to worry about. What difference did it make where he ended up?

They'd kept to the smaller state roads and highways, and were headed south on U.S. Highway 666, near the border, when Cheater noticed the needle on the fuel gauge was heading toward "E." While both men were wearing borrowed pants, neither had come equipped with a wallet.

"We're ridin' on fumes, Prince. Keep an eye out for a gas station."

"You mean like that one?" Skinner pointed at a faded wooden sign nailed to a telephone pole that read BUNNY'S: LAST CHANCE FOR GAS BEFORE MEXICO: FIVE MILES.

"Looks like we're shittin' in tall cotton again, Prince!" Cheater grinned. "Hand me the gun, would you?"

Skinner's smile faltered. "You—you're not plannin' on holding up a gas station, are you?"

"You think Standard Oil's gonna *give* us gas for this clunker out of the goodness of their heart?"

"Well . . . no. . . ."

"I ain't gonna shoot no one, if that's what you're scared of. Now, hand me the gun."

Bunny's was a tiny clapboard shack with a couple of antique gas pumps—the kind with round glass heads—stationed out front. A weather-beaten metal sign hanging from a curved pole advertised cold drinks, maps, and restrooms. A slat-ribbed yellow dog sat in the shade of the overhang, scratching itself wearily.

Cheater coasted up to the pumps and cut the engine. The yellow dog stopped in mid-scratch and lowered its ears and whimpered. An old man, almost as skinny as the dog, tottered out of the shack, wiping his gnarled hands with an oily bandanna. Dressed in stained overalls and long-sleeved undershirt, a battered baseball cap pulled low over his brow, he looked like the epitome of a geezer.

Skinner, acting on Cheater's orders, hopped out of the truck and moved to one of the gas pumps. The yellow dog got to its feet and stood stiff-legged, growling deep in its throat.

"Hush, Sheba! What's wrong with you, dog? Don't bother with that pump, son. I'll get it for you," the geezer said, pushing his bandanna into his hip pocket.

"That's what you think, pops." Cheater was suddenly towering over the old man, the muzzle of the .38 pressed against the baseball cap. "Take it easy, and no one will get hurt."

The yellow dog sank its teeth into Cheater's

shin, tearing at his pants cuff. He kicked the animal free and shot it, point-blank, blowing off one of its hind legs. The dog yelped and jumped straight up in the air, collapsing against the nearest gas pump, blood gushing from its wound.

"Sheba! You shot my Sheba!" the gas station owner wailed.

"Come on, Grandpa," Cheater snarled, shoving the old man ahead of him. "Let's go see what you got in the till, huh? Prince! Gas up the truck!"

Skinner stared at the dying dog. The animal turned its head toward him. Its eyes were already beginning to glaze. It gave a pained, low whine, which Skinner recognized as its death-song. He squatted alongside the beast and touched its head, whimpering in sympathy. The yellow dog, now completely blind, licked his hand, shuddered, and died.

"Stop messin' with that damned critter and put some gas in the tank!" Cheater was striding back from the office. The geezer was nowhere in sight.

"Where's the old man?"

"I tied him up with a length of clothesline. Don't know why he put up such a fuss. All the old coot had in the till was a couple of tens, anyway...."

Skinner cast a nervous glance back at the office. "You didn't hurt him, did you? I mean ..."

"He didn't take kindly to me shootin' his dog, so I had to pacify him with the gun butt. He'll have one hell of a headache when he comes to, that's for damn sure! Now let's put some gas in this jalopy and blow this popsicle stand before one of the locals shows up!"

Skinner filled the truck's tank and hopped back into the cab. He watched the gas station dwindle in the rearview mirror, until it was nothing but a dot on the landscape. When he looked down at his hands, he noticed they were smeared with dog's blood.

Once they made Douglas, Cheater switched to State Highway 80 Northeast, which would take them safely into New Mexico. Once out of Arizona, they were free to travel the interstates as they saw fit.

"We'll be home free, Prince! Once we get to Texas, all our worries will be behind us!"

"I'm not so sure about that. This guy you know from jail—what's his name again?"

"You mean Chic?"

"Yeah, him. How come you're so sure he'll be willing to let us hide out at his place?"

"Chic an' me, we go back years! We've known each other since before Korea! We used to hop freights together, after the Big One. We pulled a few jobs, here and there. We held up this mom 'n pop joint in some pissant town in South Dakota and all we got to show for it was fifty stinkin' bucks. Chic was so mad he raped the cashier, just for spite! When I asked him why he'd gone and done something like that, he tells me, 'Mebbe *that* will teach 'em to leave something in the register!' That Chic! He's really something, I tell ya. . . ."

Skinner chewed his thumbnail as he stared out the window of the car. He was trying hard not to look at the .38 resting on the seat between him and Cheater, but it was no use. It was as if the gun was a malign magnet, drawing his eyes to its blued steel barrel.

It was hard to believe that less than a month ago he'd been a college student, studying hard to make the dean's list. Now he was on the run with a convicted felon. Within the contained society of Los Lobos, Cheater had seemed harmless, almost quaint. Compared to jailhouse badasses like Mother and Rope, he was the salt of the earth. But now Skinner was seeing his companion for what he truly was: dangerous. But who was he to condemn Cheater for his lack of morals? At least Cheater wasn't a cannibal and a patricide.

He squeezed his eyes shut in an attempt to blot out the images rising, unbidden, inside his skull.

He was a monster. There were no two ways around it. He would have preferred to believe himself mad, but there was no use in deluding himself. He was a werewolf. Or at least what *seemed* to be a werewolf. But how could that be? In all the movies he'd seen, the doomed heroes fell victim due to the bite of another werewolf. But he was certain he'd never been bitten by anything larger than a squirrel. Unless . . . unless this had something to do with the mysterious circumstances surrounding his birth.

When he first set off on his journey of self-discovery, he'd possessed so many hopes and dreams. Now it had turned into one long, endless nightmare. Luke had been right. There *were* things better left unknown.

When Skinner woke up, it was dark and the truck was no longer moving. He sat up, rubbing the sleep from his eyes. As far as he could tell, they were parked at a rest area, somewhere along Interstate 10 in New Mexico. Cheater was nowhere to be seen.

Skinner climbed out of the cab, stretching stiff muscles in his arms and legs. He scanned the parking lot, which was empty save for a large, dark-colored sedan three spaces down.

"Cheater?"

No response.

Skinner frowned and scratched his head. Where the hell could he be? The pressure tugging on his bladder drew his mind away from the whereabouts of his traveling companion. He had to take a wicked piss. He headed toward the squat adobe-and-brick comfort station, fumbling with the zipper on his fly.

The interior of the men's restroom smelled strongly of industrial disinfectant and stale urine. Skinner stood at the urinal, sighing in relief as his bladder let go. Riding in that rusty bucket of bolts had really done a number on his kidneys. He moved to wash his hands at the sink, only to have his attention captured by his reflection in the mirror.

His dark hair had gone almost completely silver. What had once been touches of gray at his temples were now shocks so wide he resembled a skunk in reverse. Stunned, he reached up and plucked one of the strands free. It was real, all right.

His reverie was suddenly broken by a noise from one of the stalls behind him. It was the sound of men fucking.

Skinner froze, uncertain as to whether to leave or not. Before he could decide, there was a muffled cry and the sound of something hard hitting something soft. A few seconds later, Cheater stepped out of one of the stalls, zipping up his pants. When he saw Skinner, he smiled and held up a set of car keys and jingled them.

"Looks like we got ourselves a new set of wheels, Prince!"

Skinner didn't say anything, walking around Cheater to peer into the stall he'd just vacated. A middle-aged man dressed in a rumpled business suit, the pants of which were still around his ankles, lay unconscious on the stained concrete floor, his hands bound with what looked to be his own tie. There was a large bump visible on his bald spot from where Cheater had pistol-whipped him.

"He'll be okay, kid. The cleaning staff will find him in a couple of hours. By that time we'll be long done."

"You could have *killed* him, hitting him like that!"

Cheater shrugged. "So? He's just a fag."

"Oh, yeah? And what does that make *you*?"

Cheater looked genuinely insulted. "Hey, I only pump butt when I'm doin' time, or I need something. Like right now. When I'm on the outside, I'm a straight pussy-man! And no one can say otherwise! Guys who do it because they *want* to— now *that's* perverted. C'mon, let's get goin'!"

Minutes later, they were heading down Interstate 10 toward Las Cruces in a 1989 Olds, Cheater behind the wheel.

"Lookit this baby! It's even got cruise control! This sure beats ridin' in that junk heap, don't it, Prince?"

Skinner grunted and turned to look out the window. It was a moonless night and it should have been too dark to see anything, but for some reason his vision was perfectly clear. He thought he saw something just beyond the shoulder of the road. Something light-colored, moving at the same rate of speed as the car.

It was a dog made out of blue light.

No. Not a dog. Something *like* a dog, but bigger and wilder. It ran alongside the car, pacing it effortlessly, its tongue hanging from the side of its open mouth. It was both beautiful and fearsome in its freedom, and Skinner felt a kinship with the beast that went beyond human words and emotions. And for the first time since he'd lost his illusion of humanity, Skinner wondered if his journey might end in something besides a brick wall.

"Are you sure about this, Cheater?"

"Sure as shit! Believe me, Prince, nothing is gonna go wrong. All we gotta do is walk into the store, I point the gun at the clerk, you clean out the till, and then we hightail it outta there 'fore the cops arrive. It's foolproof!"

"Have you ever held up a store before?"

"Sure, plenty of times! There was that package store in Arkansas—did three years for that—then there was that gas station in Oklahoma—did five for that 'un—"

"Forget I asked."

"You worry too much, Prince. That's the problem with straights and suits, see? They spend so much of their time worrying they never do nothin' cause it might not work. Me, I never let that bother me. If I wanna do something, I do it. If I want something, I take it. Or try to, anyways. It's instinct, man. You gotta learn to go with it."

Skinner shuddered. "That's what I'm afraid of."

They waited until after midnight to pull the job. Cheater had picked the convenience store earlier that day, loitering by its magazine rack, thumbing through magazines with pictures of tattooed women in halter tops and cutoffs straddling Harley-Davidsons while he kept one eye on the register.

"We should be able to get outta there with a couple hunnert bucks. They're one of them small independent stores, not like Circle K or 7-11. They don't have one of them damn time-lock safes where you can only get thirty, forty bucks out every ten minutes. Hate those fuckers."

Skinner went in first and pretended to browse the front of the store. The cashier was a young, slightly overweight woman with two-tone hair, blond at the ends, dark at the roots, and too much eye makeup. She wore a badly fitting synthetic blouse emblazoned with the store's logo on the breast pocket. She barely glanced up from the true crime magazine she was paging through when Skinner entered the store.

A couple of minutes later, Cheater walked in, hands in the pockets of his jacket, and headed for the beer case in the back. He selected the most expensive import available and strode purposefully to the checkout counter.

Skinner moved to join him, doing his best to

look casual. His heart was beating so hard it felt like it was trying to jam itself between his ribs.

The cashier rang up Cheater's purchase and he handed her a ten-dollar bill. The till drawer opened.

"Anything else?" asked the cashier, her breath made sickly sweet by the cud of gum parked in her cheek. Funny he should be able to smell that, since she was still a good ten feet away....

Cheater pulled the .38 from his pocket and pointed it at her. "Yeah, baby. Give it up."

The cashier stopped chewing her gum and stared at Cheater as if she'd been suddenly turned to stone. Cheater swore and motioned for Skinner to empty the till.

He tried to keep his hands from trembling as he raked out the money. He showed Cheater the fistful of dollar bills and the two crumpled fives and cringed when he saw his partner's face darken.

"Is that *all*?"

The woman's fear came off her in waves, breaking through her initial barrier of shock, the scent hot and rank. There was something erotic in its smell and Skinner felt himself become aroused. The trembling grew worse, only now it wasn't just nerves that made his hands shake.

"I *said*, is that *all*, bitch?" Cheater prodded the terrified cashier's shoulder with the barrel of the .38.

She nodded dumbly, her eyes never leaving the gun.

"You're lying! I know you got more'n this!"

"C'mon, man. We got the money, let's *go* before

the cops get here!" whispered Skinner. The look of rage on Cheater's face was enough to shake him from his pheromonal trance.

"No way! This bitch is fuckin' with us, man!"

The cashier shook her head, tears forming in her eyes. "That's all there is. I just came on shift an hour ago. The boss takes all the money out of the store just before midnight and makes a deposit. That's all the cash, I swear!"

Cheater's anger was replaced by a stoic calm that Skinner found almost as unnerving as his rage. He nodded a couple of times and muttered something to himself under his breath and stepped back, letting the barrel of the gun drop.

"Figures. Fuckin' figures."

Before Skinner could react, Cheater lifted the .38 and fired two rounds into the cashier's forehead, knocking free the wad of bubblegum parked inside her right cheek.

The cashier went down in a spray of brains, toppling the cigarette display rack behind her. She lay sprawled amid scattered packets of Winston 100s, Camels, and Pall Malls, a halo of blood radiating from her ruined skull. Gray matter dripped from the Slushpuppy machine.

Cheater blinked rapidly and stared at the dead girl as if he was seeing her for the first time. "Shit, Chic! Why'd you go and have t'do *that*?" he mumbled.

Blood. So much blood. The smell of it was sharp and bright and coppery. Skinner realized his dick was hard and his mouth was watering. And then the change was on him, turning him inside out, pushing his muscles and bones into a new geometry. He gave a brief cry of ecstatic pain that became a howl as he vaulted over the counter that separated him from the fresh kill.

Cheater's previous psychopathic cool had completely evaporated. His face was pale and he was shaking and sweating like a junky. "Shit, man! We got no time for that! The cops are gonna be here any second!"

Skinner didn't hear him. He was too busy savoring the taste of still-warm flesh and the sweet smell of freshly spilt blood. He emitted a whine of delight as he ripped free the dead woman's liver. Tasty. So very tasty. It felt like he hadn't eaten for days.

"Leave it, man! We gotta get outta here!" Cheater leaned across the counter and tried to grab his friend's shoulder, but Skinner growled and flashed crimson-stained fangs in warning. He was not going to leave such an easy meal before having had his fill.

The sound of sirens approaching from the distance made Cheater jump. The bitch had managed to trigger a silent alarm before he iced her. He glanced back in the direction of Skinner, still squatting over the body of the slaughtered cashier, feasting like a starved pitbull.

He was fucked. Fucked big time. He was sure to get the chair or the gas chamber or whatever the hell they used to put born losers like himself out of society's misery in this godforsaken state.

Lord only knew what they'd make of his beloved prince of foxes. Probably stick wires in his head and run tests on him before they put him away somewhere where no one would ever find out the truth. Psychopathic cannibal killers are one thing, werewolves something else entirely.

The thought of Skinner locked up in a cage for the rest of his life made Cheater sick. He knew what it was like not to be free. For Skinner it would be a hundred times worse than his hardest stretch had ever been.

It was cruel to keep a wild thing locked up.

The patrol cars fishtailed to a stop in the convenience store's parking lot just as Cheater stepped outside the door, gun in hand. The headlights turned the front of the store into a hideously overlit stage, with Cheater the star.

"Toss down your gun and keep your hands where we can see them!" shouted a voice from behind the blinding glare.

Cheater replied by shooting out the lights on one of the two patrol cars.

Four service revolvers returned his fire. Cheater felt the hollow-point bullets enter his body and mushroom, sending shrapnel throughout his vital organs. There was a moment where he could feel his insides rearrange themselves, and he wondered if this was how Skinner felt when he underwent his transformations. Then he died.

Skinner looked up from his meal at the sound of tires squealing against pavement, a length of entrail still gripped between his teeth.

Cheater?

He abandoned the kill, leaping over the counter in one smooth jump. He growled at the harsh glare filling the store, lifting a taloned hand to shade his eyes. There was one shot, then another, and the light was reduced by half. The answering volley of gunfire nearly deafened him and he howled his pain.

Through the plate glass windows of the storefront he could see his friend dancing in the parking lot. Cheater jerked and spun like a badly handled marionette, his arms flailing and head lolling. Skinner wondered why his friend had chosen such a time to dance. Then he saw the blood.

The police moved cautiously toward Cheater's body, guns held at ready just in case he decided to take one of them with him at the last second. One of the officers knelt to retrieve Cheater's dropped weapon. As he did so, he glanced in the direction of the store and saw something silvery, its eyes glowing like molten gold, launch itself through the front window.

It landed on all fours beside the dead holdup man, slivers of glass shining in its heavy pelt, and snarled, displaying a muzzle full of razor-sharp teeth.

"It's a fuckin' dog!" marveled one of the cops. "One of those wolfhounds or something. . . ."

The beast growled and stood up on its hind legs, crooking its fingers into claws.

The cop closest to Skinner swore and fired, hitting him in the rib cage. The gunshot stung like a bad cigarette burn. Skinner grabbed the hapless officer by the front of his uniform and ripped him open from nipples to belly button with one swipe, spilling his guts onto his shoes. The human's screams hurt his ears, so Skinner snapped his jaws shut on his larynx.

"Don't shoot! You'll hit Malloy!" yelled one of the cops, not realizing that Malloy was past worrying about being the victim of friendly fire.

Skinner hurled the dead patrolman's body at the others and turned to flee. Cheater was dead. There was nothing he could do to help his friend. He'd spilled blood in his name, which was tribute enough. There was no time for mourning—he had to get away before more humans arrived.

He could hear the angry, frightened shouts of the police as he loped into the darkness, then the sounds of gunfire, and he felt vicious burning stings stitch their way across his unprotected back. The pain was enormous, but he did not stumble or fall. He could feel the blood pumping from the holes in his body, darkening his coat with russet streaks.

The agony was intense, worse than anything he'd ever known before, but he kept running. If he stopped for even a moment he was doomed— the humans would catch him and put him back in the cage. And that must never happen again. Never.

He ran through the darkened streets, keeping to the deepest shadows, cutting through alleys, crawling through drainage pipes and scaling fences until the pursuing sirens began to fade.

Satisfied that he'd finally succeeded in eluding his enemies, he slumped against an alley doorway and began licking his wounds.

Although his silvery pelt was stiff with blood, not all of it his, he was no longer bleeding. His chest felt like someone had used a sledgehammer to crack his rib cage open. His back and shoulders throbbed as if he'd run naked through a swarm of killer bees. From the way his left side ached, it was likely he'd taken a bullet in the hip.

His vision was starting to fade in and out, like the reception on an old television set, going from black-and-white to full-color to black-and-white again. Just before he passed out, he noticed for the first time the van and the minibus parked in the alley.

Chapter Twelve

Skinner woke up with angry hornets in his head, ground glass in his bladder, and loose feathers in his lungs. He coughed violently, bringing up clotted blood and discolored mucus.

"Cheater?"

He struggled to open his eyes and bring his blurred vision into focus. The first thing he saw was a young man with long dark hair and a high, wide forehead, his eyes obscured by tinted mirrorshades, leaning over him.

"Wh-where am I?" he rasped, trying to sit up.

The stranger gently pressed against his shoulder, pushing him back down. "It's okay, cousin. You're safe now. The pigs won't be looking for you in this van."

"Van?" Skinner tried to sit up again, but the hornets buzzing in his head stopped him. "The—the last thing I remember, I was in an alley somewhere. . . ."

"Yeah, I found you passed out behind the garbage cans next to the stage door. You looked like you needed some help, so I brought you here."

"Where's Cheater?"

"Cheater?"

"My friend. He and I were ... Oh." The memory of Cheater dancing in the spotlight, his body riddled with bullets, suddenly reemerged. "Oh, God. He's dead. Cheater's dead. They shot him." He covered his eyes with a trembling hand.

"Look, friend, you're safe here, understand? You don't have to worry about the pigs finding you. ..."

"I appreciate your kindness. I really do. But you don't understand. I'm *dangerous*. More dangerous than you could ever possibly think. If you could loan me some clothes, I'll be on my way. I'm alright, honestly I am. You needn't worry about me."

"You're in no shape to travel right now, cousin."

"I can't stay here! You're in serious danger! You don't know what I am ... what I'm capable of doing! And I'd rather you didn't find out. ..."

Skinner's benefactor leaned forward, bringing his face close to his. There was a squelching sound as his features rearranged themselves, growing hairier and more lupine. His mirrorshades slid down his snout, revealing eyes the color of gold.

"But I *do* know, cousin."

The transformation was so sudden, so *natural*, it frightened Skinner. He involuntarily scrabbled backward on his elbows, his heart banging against his ribs like it wanted out.

"You're new to all this, aren't ya?" The werewolf grinned, his face resuming its human appearance.

Skinner nodded, too dumbstruck to speak.

"My name's Rend. What's yours, cousin?"

"Skinner. Skinner Cade."

Just then the doors to the back of the van banged open. Rend seemed to cringe at the sight of the man with long white hair.

"What th' fuck's going on here? Who's this lame-o?"

"His name's Skinner, Jag. I found him in the alley. He was hurt pretty bad. . . ."

Jag crawled into the van, closing the doors behind him. He fixed Rend with a withering stare. Skinner noticed that his eyes were gold as well. "That's just fuckin' *great*! Did anyone see you?"

Rend shook his head, insulted. "You know I'm too smart to slip up that way! I'm not Ripper or Hew, damn it!"

"I'm not doubting your abilities, Rend. I'm not so sure about our 'friend' here, though. He's probably left a trail so obvious even a *human* could follow it." Jag leaned forward, sniffing at Skinner like a wary dog. "What's your story, Rover?"

"Skinner. My name's Skinner."

"Whatever." Jag shrugged and settled back onto his haunches. Skinner found his eyes drawn to the snake's head tattoo on the back of his hand.

"I—I was arrested and put in jail. While I was there I—I changed. I killed some men. There was a riot. I escaped with a friend. We got as far as Albuquerque, then we held up a convenience store. The cashier was killed and I changed again . . . and . . . and the next thing I know, my friend's dead and I'm being shot at by the cops. I managed to get away, but not before I caught a few slugs. . . ."

"You were damn lucky, too," Rend explained.

"*Vargr* are close to indestructible—but if you catch a bullet in the head or have your spinal column shattered, you're dead. Or as good as. From what I could tell, some of those shots came awful close."

"*Vargr*. What the hell does it mean?"

Jag rolled his eyes in disdain. "Great. Just what we need. A fuckin' *mutt*!"

Rend shot Jag a disapproving scowl. "Cut him some slack, why don't you? Most *vargr* know nothing about themselves. Not all of us were privileged enough to be raised within the pack. Me included. It wasn't that long ago that I was as green and ignorant as he is."

"Good. You can fuckin' school him, then! Because *I'm* sure as hell not going to waste my time!" Jag opened the back doors of the van and hopped outside, turning to point an angry finger at his companion. "Remember! He's *your* mutt, Rend! And as far as I'm concerned, he's on probation until after the Howl!" With that, he slammed the doors shut.

Rend smiled apologetically at Skinner. "Don't mind Jag. He's pack leader; it's his job to run roughshod over the rest of us. He can be something of a snob sometimes, though. He likes rubbing it in our faces that he's purebred, not mongrel."

"What do you mean?"

"Jag's full-blooded. So's his sister, Jez, since they're twins, natch. Their parents were both *vargr*. They were raised in the pack instead of human society, like most of us. I guess it makes them special—but I sure get tired of them bragging about their damned pedigrees!" Rend laughed and Skinner was surprised to find himself joining in, although weakly.

"I'm afraid there's still so much I don't understand . . . so much to take in. First I thought I was crazy . . . then I thought I might be the only one like—like I am."

Rend nodded his understanding. "I know where you're coming from, cousin. We all do— except for Jag and Jez."

"You keep saying 'we.' How many of you are there?"

"You mean in this particular pack? Six, counting myself. We're a speed-metal band, actually. We call ourselves *Vargr*. It was Jag's idea, really. Kind of a joke. I wanted to call us the Thrill-Killers, but someone was already using the name. Uh, look. I'm going to have to leave you alone for awhile, okay? I've got to help tear down the equipment."

Fifteen minutes later, the side door on the van rolled back, waking Skinner from a light doze. He could tell someone had entered the van and was looking down at him from the back seat.

"Rend?"

"No. Not Rend." The woman's voice was like honey poured over ice. She leaned over the backseat, her chin resting atop her folded arms. Her hair was a shock of stark-white, short-cropped cotton candy. Her red lacquered fingernails ticked against the upholstery. "He asked me to look in on you, however. He said your name is Skinner. He didn't tell me you were handsome, though."

Skinner, acutely aware he was completely naked, turned the color of a freshly boiled lobster.

"You're blushing! How quaint! My name's Jez."

"Uh. Hello."

"Looks like you've been in some trouble." She pointed to the bruises and scars that were all that remained of the bullets that had entered his body only hours ago.

"I guess you could call it that."

Jez smiled, exposing strong white teeth. "Were you *brave*? Were you *very* brave? I *like* brave dogs."

"I don't know if you'd call it *brave.* . . ."

"*Jez!*"

Jez jumped, emitting a small yelp of surprise. She quickly composed herself, exchanging her startlement for a belligerent pout. Jag reached in the van and grabbed her by the arm, pulling her outside.

"What do you think you're doing out here?"

"Checking on the new member, that's all, brother-dear."

"No doubt!"

Jez's look of indifference suddenly faltered. She bit her lower lip and tried to pull away from her twin. "Stop squeezing my arm, Jag! You're *hurting* me!"

"I *don't* want you near that mutt, understand?"

"You can't tell *me* what to do!"

Jag's scowl deepened and he increased the pressure on his sister's arm.

"Ow! Ow! Ow! Okay! Okay! I understand!"

Jag glowered at Jez as she petulantly massaged her bruised upper arm. "Damn straight you understand! Now go back in there and help Rend." Satisfied that Jez was gone, Jag thrust his head back inside the van. His face was livid with anger, his eyes glowing with a lambent energy. Although he retained his human features, the image of the beast was lurking just below the skin.

"As for *you*, mutt! Stay away from my sister, is that clear? *Stay away!*"

Without waiting for a reply, Jag slammed the van door shut and stormed off, leaving Skinner to lie naked in the dark, wondering just what the hell he'd managed to get himself into *this* time.

Chapter Thirteen

Ten minutes passed after Jag's abrupt leave-taking, then there was a knock on the side of the van. It was Rend. He handed Skinner a bundle of mismatched clothes and a pair of patent-leather wing tip shoes.

"Here, I found you something to wear. At least for the time being. Hope they fit."

"Thanks," Skinner muttered as he pulled on the proffered garments. There was a badly wrinkled gray silk jacket with padded shoulders and narrow lapels, a pair of charcoal stovepipe jeans, and a tattered Temple of Psychick Youth t-shirt. Skinner wasn't thrilled with the sartorial selection, but at least he wouldn't be bare-assed naked.

Just as he finished tying his shoes, the rest of the group showed up, lugging instruments and sound equipment. Skinner got out of the Dodge and stood beside Rend, watching the newcomers cautiously as they loaded the Volkswagen.

"Who's the dweeb?" asked Ripper as he muscled his drum kit into the rear of the mini-bus.

"He's not a dweeb. He's one of us. He's *vargr*," Rend announced.

"Not fuckin' likely," grunted Hew, carefully

lowering Jag's Marshal amp onto the minibus' bed. "What's your opinion, Sunder?"

Sunder gave his fellow roadie a slow, nasty smile and tossed the Fender Bassmaster amplifier he was carrying at Skinner as if it was a beach ball. "Think fast, low dog!"

Skinner instinctively moved to catch the heavy piece of sound equipment before it hit the ground and, to his surprise, caught it. The fifty-pound amp seemed to weigh as if it was made out of papier-mâché.

"Smooth move, low dog!" Sunder laughed, clapping Skinner on the shoulder.

Jag stormed out of the stage door, a Fender hardcase in one hand and a wad of money in the other. "What the hell do you think you're doin', assin' around like that?" he snapped. "What if somebody had seen you pull that stunt, numb-nuts? We can't fuckin' eat *every* witness!"

"Yeah, but we could *try*." Ripper giggled.

Jag smacked the drummer on the side of his shaved head with a clenched fist. "Shut up, you! This isn't fuckin' *funny*! It's not a *joke*, Ripper! Get it through your thick head, why don't you?"

Ripper cringed, rubbing his skull and watching Jag with the eyes of a chronically abused child. "I got it, Jag. You didn't have t' hit me."

"Yeah, right." Jag swung back to face the others. "It's your job to ride herd on these bozos while I'm dealing with the bar, Rend! You know better than this!"

"Sorry, Jag. You're right . . ."

"You better fuckin' *believe* I'm right! Now, let's

blow this stinkin' burg before your new little buddy here brings the heat down on us, okay?"

Skinner moved toward the van, only to have Jag block his way with his guitar case.

"And where do *you* think *you're* goin', low dog?"

Skinner looked in the direction of the Dodge. Jez was lounging on the front passenger seat, idly filing her nails. She looked up from her task and flashed him a smile that made him break out in a cold sweat. "I was, uh, just going to get back in the van, that's all. . . ."

Rend grabbed Skinner's upper arm, leading him toward the minibus. "You're ridin' in the *equipment* van, Skinner. Not with the *band*. I'll keep you company, okay?"

"Uh, yeah. Sure. That's cool."

Skinner didn't look back, but he could feel the twins' eyes boring into his back. He wasn't sure which one worried him more.

"Awright! Munchies!" Sunder crowed as Rend climbed into the cab of the minibus with a sack of junk food and a six-pack of beer from the convenience store.

"Slim Jim?"

"Thanks," Skinner mumbled, accepting the stick of jerked beef. He was sandwiched between the band's equipment and the front seat, squatting atop a couple of unzipped sleeping bags and several scattered back issues of *Flipside* and *Reflex* magazine. Although his butt was insulated from the hard, grimy bed of the Volkswagen, his muscles were already starting to cramp from the close quarters.

Sunder popped open a beer as he threw the minibus into gear, Motorhead's "Eat the Rich" thundering from the sound system. "Next stop— the Howl!"

"Is that a bar?"

Sunder laughed and shot Rend a "get *him*" glance. Rend smiled wanly and handed Skinner a beer. "No. It's not a bar. It's an event. I guess you could call it a gathering."

"You mean for werewolves?"

Rend grimaced. "We prefer to call ourselves *vargr*. 'Werewolf' is *their* name for us."

Skinner sipped his beer in silence for a few minutes. There was so much he wanted to know— *needed* to know—about himself and those like him, only now he was fearful of asking stupid questions and looking like an idiot. To his surprise, Rend was the one that broke the silence.

"So. How long have you known you were different?"

"All my life, I guess."

"Hmph. I bet you were real unpopular with the other kids. Always ended up getting the stuffing kicked out of you by the jocks, right?"

"Yeah. Right. How did you know?"

"It's the same with all of us. Leastwise the ones raised in human society. Humans can tell we're not like them. That's why they hate us."

"Not all humans. I've met a few who were nice."

Rend shrugged and produced a joint from the breast pocket of his leather jacket. His eyes were unreadable as he lit up. "They're in the minority, believe me. Most humans either hate us or fear us. I think they can sense what we're after, kinda. The same way cattle get antsy when they catch a wolf's scent. Occasionally, you get the self-destructive groupies who want to fuck you; they can tell you're dangerous, but don't know how much. Until it's too late. When was the first time you shifted?"

"When I was twelve, I guess. I didn't do it again until a week ago."

"Kill anyone?"

Skinner shifted around uncomfortably. "Yeah. My father."

Rend lifted an eyebrow. "You too, huh?" Skinner blinked and fought to keep his jaw from dropping. "Don't look so surprised, cousin. Patricide isn't exactly rare in *vargr* society." Rend laughed. "But he wasn't your *real* father, was he?"

"If you mean was he my biological father: no, he wasn't. I don't know who my *real* father is."

Rend nodded his understanding. "Most of us don't know who sired us, except for the full-bloods. There aren't many *vargr* bitches, for some reason. The majority of male *vargr* wander loose, mating with whatever they can hunt down, human or wolf, and they usually don't hang around after the deed. Hell, I've *never* had consensual sex with a human woman.

"So—you killed your old man. What happened? Was he beating you? Trying to ram it up the old poop-chute?"

"*No!*"

The vehemence of his denial caused Sunder and Rend to exchange glances.

Sunder looked into the rearview mirror, meeting and holding Skinner's gaze. "Hey, you know what they say about d'Nile not just being a river...."

"You don't understand ... my father *loved* me, and I loved *him*! He never did anything to hurt me in his life! It was all a horrible accident. We were out hunting and I killed a deer and ... and when I smelled its blood, I *changed*. It was so sudden, so unexpected ... I didn't know what was happening to me and I—I killed him."

Sunder shook his head in open astonishment. "Wow. You actually sound *sorry*!"

"My adopted parents loved me. Both of them. I didn't even know I wasn't, you know, their own flesh and blood until my mother died last month."

Rend was looking at him with a strangely wistful expression on his face. "What was it like?"

"What?"

"Having parents that loved you," Rend said softly.

"C'mon, don't give me that! You know what it's like." Skinner laughed.

"No, I don't. It was different for me. I didn't get lucky, like you apparently did. You ended up with people who actually *wanted* you. Far back as I can remember, my parents hated me. I don't mean they gave me a hard time about my clothes or my hair or my attitude. I mean, what kind of *attitude* can a baby have, right?

"My first memory—I couldn't have been more'n—what? Fourteen? Sixteen months old? I was still wearin' a diaper, whatever the case. I don't recall what it was I was doin'—or if I was doin' *anything*—to piss off my dad. Maybe I dropped my cup or spilled my cereal. Something. Next thing I know, my old man's bellowin' like a fuckin' bull and throws me up against the wall. I cry real hard and run to my mom—thinkin' she'll kiss it and make it better, right? But she gives me the back of her hand, instead. That's my first real memory. It was just a taste of what was to come.

"I'd catch my mom and dad lookin' at me like I was some kind of *disease.* Like being around me made 'em sick. They never loved me. They never cared.

"My big brother Raymond used to climb on top of me in bed and choke me and stick his dick in my mouth when I opened it to try and breathe. I was seven and he was twelve. I was eight when he started putting it in my ass. Everyone knew he was doin' it to me, but they wouldn't make him stop. Then my dad found out Raymond was making my little brother, Timmy, put it in *his* mouth. He went nuts, punching Raymond in the gut and slamming his head against the wall, screamin' until he was red in the face.

"I watched Dad beat Raymond with his belt until blood ran down his back—and I knew I ought to be *happy* that Raymond was finally getting some of his own back. But you know what I felt *instead*? I was jealous! I was jealous Dad would *care* enough about Timmy that he would beat Raymond to a pulp for doing to him *once* what everyone knew he'd been doing to me three or four times a *week* for over a *year*!

"When I was ten, my mom ran away with a woman from her prayer circle. That's when everything went to hell and didn't come back. Dad had been a boozer since before I was born—but after that he hit rock bottom and didn't care anymore. Raymond moved away and began selling his ass to strange men in cars, which kept him away from me, at least. That left my older sister, Melissa, who was thirteen, Timmy who was eight, and Erin, who was six, still in the house.

"Dad encouraged the others to beat on me. I got slapped, punched, pinched, pushed down stairs, burned with cigarettes, hit with baseball bats—you name it, they did it to me. It was like I was a pillow they could throw around and do things to without anyone telling them to stop.

"And since Raymond was no longer putting his thing in me, Dad took up the slack. One time he got his whole fist up there. It really hurt and there was a lot of blood. Dad beat me afterward for ruining the sheets.

"Melissa used to practice her judo flings on me and toss me down the basement stairs. Another favorite pastime was tying me up and tossing me into a tub full of scalding hot water. Sometimes Dad would make me walk around the house nude with a coke bottle up my ass.

"Often they'd lock me up in the basement for days on end. They wouldn't allow me water, then force me to drink and beat me for it. I'd be tied up for days and get beat for soiling myself. They made me eat shit and drink piss—both mine and theirs.

"You'd think the neighbors would have noticed,

huh? Well, if they did, they didn't let my screamin' bloody murder worry 'em. Sure, some kid was
gettin' whipped pretty good next door. But, hell,
it's the parents' right to beat their kids. Besides, I
probably deserved it, right?

"I was twelve when Dad came home one night
drunker'n usual—which is sayin' something, believe me. He came stumbling into my bedroom—
I thought he was going to try and stick his thing
up me again—then I see the knife. He's slurring
something about making sure I never do anything
like the bastard who did it to my mother. He starts
trying to pull off my underpants while waving the
knife in my face. And I *changed.*

"I realized this pathetic, drunken excuse for a
man wasn't my *real* father, and these sadistic, perverted creeps had never been my real family. It
was like all the fear in me melted away and all
that was left was anger and hate. For the first time
in my life I was free. It was *beautiful.*

"Next thing I remember, I'm naked on the
couch. I'm covered in blood. So's the couch. And
the walls. The first thing that crosses my mind is
that Dad succeeded in cutting my thing off. Then
I see Timmy's head is sitting on top of the T.V.
set, the rabbit ears punched through the top of
his skull.

"I found Erin stuffed inside the toilet. Melissa
was still alive—crawling around in circles on her
hands and knees, dragging a lap of gut behind
her. Dad—Dad was in my bedroom, the knife he'd
tried to castrate me with rammed between his
eyes. His dick and balls had been chewed off.

"I packed my *Star Wars* lunch box with a couple

of Oscar Meyer bologna sandwiches and a thermos of chocolate milk and ran out the kitchen door. I never went back."

"How did you manage to live on your own?"

Rend shrugged and took another hit off his joint. "I managed. There was this one guy who took me home who wore a diaper and paid me to poop on his nice white rug. Then there was the old fucker who liked to have boys pee up his ass—I think he was a judge or something.

"I didn't kill them all, though, if that's what you're thinking. At first I was like you—I didn't have control over my shifts. Usually I had to be threatened with serious bodily harm in order for it to be triggered. But other times all I had to do was, you know, get *excited*.

"By the time I was fifteen, I'd learned how to shift at will. I was in New York City at the time. That's when I ran into Raymond, hustling the meat packing district. He had a serious drug problem and, at twenty, he could no longer pass for chicken. The last five years hadn't exactly been good to him. He'd been living hard and fast, and it'd taken its toll on his looks. He was barely a step above a coke whore.

"He didn't recognize me at first. When I told him who I was, he seemed genuinely *glad* to see me. We went to this sleazy little coffee shop over on the Bowery to 'catch up.' Talking to him, I realized he didn't know that the rest of the family was dead. I didn't see any reason to clue him in.

"I asked him if it was true about Mom being raped and he tells me yes. She'd been working as a waitress to make some extra money for Christmas. One night, as she was walking to the car, someone jumped her. The guy knocked her unconscious and fucked her in the parking lot. They never found out who did it.

"Not long after that, she discovered she was pregnant. Dad wanted her to have an abortion, but she wouldn't do it. She was convinced it was his baby, not the rapist's. Then I was born. When the blood tests proved I wasn't her husband's child, Mom's attitude toward me changed completely. She hated the very sight of me. She even refused to nurse me. But she wouldn't put me up for adoption. She thought she could teach herself to love me, but it was impossible.

"Looking at me every day and being reminded of what had been done to her ended up poisoning her relationship with Dad. Even though she had two more children by him, their marriage was pretty much ruined once I was on the scene. Raymond told me that's why he'd done those things to me as a kid. He knew I wasn't his *real* brother, so it hadn't been incest, therefore no sin was involved.

"After about a half-hour, he reaches under the table and squeezes my thigh and asks if I want to go back to his place 'for old times sake.' I say okay.

"He was living in this shit-hole of a welfare hotel over on Avenue C. It was nasty: full of rats and junkies and drag queens. When we got there, I overpowered him and tied him to the bed. I told him I wasn't the puny little eight-year-old he used to butt-fuck anymore. He whined and complained about the ropes being too tight, but he didn't get genuinely scared until I brought out the lighter and the pack of cigarettes.

"I burned the words 'I am a whore and proud of it' into his bare chest and belly. He screamed the whole time, but if anybody heard, they didn't bother to stop what was going on. He was still alive when I shifted into my *vargr* form. While I was fucking him, I got carried away and ripped his head off his shoulders.

"The way his sphincter reacted right before he died was really something. Same with women's vaginas, too. You ought to try it sometime, Skinner. Nothing quite like it."

"Uh, I think I'll pass."

"Don't knock it till you've tried it, cousin."

Chapter Fourteen

Skinner started awake, his inner eye full of fading dreams. He lay curled atop the sleeping bags on the floor of the minibus and wondered what it was that had wakened him. Then he realized they were no longer moving.

Yawning, he sat up and looked around, scratching his head. It was not yet dawn, but he could tell they must be somewhere in the national forests north of Santa Fe.

"Rend? Sunder?"

Skinner crawled out of the minibus, sniffing the air cautiously. It smelled of high country pine and wild things. It made the hair along his arms prickle.

The Dodge Caravan was parked a few yards away. It, too, was empty. He could make out the telltale burble of rushing water and, beneath its camouflage, the sound of laughter. Following the sound, he discovered a small footpath that led to a rocky creek bed. There he found the others, splashing in the cold mountain spring water, in various stages of undress.

Rend was squatting at the edge of the creek, bare-chested, vigorously scrubbing his face with a piece of soap. Jag emerged, nude, from the water, shaking out his white mane like a dog after a bath. Hew and Ripper were amusing themselves by hopping from rock to rock across the creek, skipping stones across its surface and whooping like children at play. Sunder lay flat on his belly, lapping at the briskly running water like a beast of the field.

"Look who's here. It's the low dog."

Skinner turned in the direction of Jez's voice in time to see her emerge from the surrounding foliage. She was stark naked, allowing him a good view of the small surgical-steel rings piercing her nipples and outer labia. He also noticed that her pubic thatch matched the color of her hair exactly. She stood there, idly toying with a fern frond like an ancient woodland nymph, and watched him look at her.

"Jez!"

The sound of her brother's voice spurring her to action, Jez moved past Skinner—lingering long enough to give him a sultry smile and a wink. She presented herself to Jag, who was standing with his hands on his hips, scowling in Skinner's direction. Jag grabbed his twin's hair and pulled her face close to his. She made a small whimpering sound and quivered in anticipation. His eyes still locked on Skinner, Jag thrust his tongue into his sister's mouth and his hand between her legs, working his fingers past the gaping lips of her vulva.

Skinner looked away and tried not to pay attention to the sudden heaviness between his legs. He walked toward Rend, who had halted his ablutions and was watching him out of the corner of his eye. Skinner hunkered down beside him and tugged off his t-shirt.

"What's with those two?" he whispered.

"Jag is Jez's consort. Without her, he's no longer the Alpha. He's somewhat—shall we say—jealous of her attentions."

"Huh? You mean *she's* calling the shots?"

"*Vargr* males outnumber bitches ten to one. The bitch is the linchpin that holds a pack together. Ours is a matriarchal society."

"You're shitting me."

"Couldn't be more serious. If you think Jez is a piece of work, wait until you meet her dame, Lady Erzule. Same goes for Jag and his sire, Lord Feral."

"One big happy family, huh?"

"You could say that."

Skinner splashed a handful of water in his face. It was cold and unbelievably clean, waking him to the core of his soul. Shivering, he splashed another handful onto his bare chest, cleaning away the residue of blood—both his and his victims'—that still clung to his naked skin.

"Where the hell are we?"

"We're in the Santa Fe National Forest, somewhere near the Abiquiu Reservoir, off U.S. Highway 84 North," Rend explained, talking around his toothbrush. "We still have a way to go before we reach the Howl."

"You mentioned that before. What is it, exactly?"

"It's the most sacred of *vargr* observances. It is the gathering where full-bloods and halflings alike come together to do battle for the right to mate with females in season. It is the time of the rut melee."

"Oh."

"It's great fun! You'll see! It's held at this secret mountain lodge bordering the Sun Juan Primitive Area in Mineral County, Colorado—" Rend suddenly lapsed into silence, staring at something Skinner couldn't see.

"Rend? Rend—?"

Skinner turned and followed his companion's gaze. As he did, he realized that every member of the pack had fallen equally silent. Then he saw the deer.

It stood on the opposite bank of the creek, about a quarter-mile upstream. It was either accustomed to humans larking about the creek bed or they were far enough up-wind of the creature for it not to realize they were there. Skinner was reminded of the deer he'd shot the day of his first transformation, years ago, and he felt his blood start to bubble and boil inside his veins.

Jag and Jez's full attention was now riveted on the stag, their lust abruptly forgotten. They dropped to their haunches, their noses lifted to the winds, their eyes fixed on the deer as if it was the focus of their entire universe.

Slowly, as if in a trance, Skinner began to remove his clothes, making sure his eyes never once left the deer.

Ripper was standing on a slippery rock in the middle of the creek, balanced perilously on his right foot as he tried to remove his left combat boot. Tugging it free, he overbalanced and fell into the stream.

The deer jerked its head up, its nostrils flared wide and its eyes rolling with fear. It smelled them now. And the stink of fear that radiated from its hide as it bolted into the woods told them that what it scented was not humans—but an enemy far more ancient. Far more dangerous.

Jag was the first to move, splashing across the shallow creek in a crouch, the call to the hunt rising from his throat. The others were quick on his heels, each lifting his or her voice in accompaniment as the Wild filled their bodies and fueled their flesh, shifting naked skin in favor of thick, luxurious pelts, blunted nails for fearsome talons, and pathetic pieces of ivory for a mouthful of knives. And to Skinner's amazement, his howl joined in with those of the others. And it felt *good*.

As Skinner ran, he was aware that the overhanging branches and tangled undergrowth no longer slapped and stung his exposed skin. His senses were so acute he could smell their prey's fear, hear its ragged breath, hear its heart thundering as it fled for its life.

Ripper leapt forward and bit the fleeing beast's hindquarters. Hew then attacked in a similar fashion, slashing the stag's other flank. Sunder immediately moved to grab the deer's snout, causing it to bellow sharply and toss its head in an attempt to free itself, sending him sprawling. Rend leapt to take Sunder's place, latching onto the stag, somehow avoiding its sharp rack of antlers.

While their prey was held fast in front, Jag and Jez leapt forward, tearing large lumps of flesh from its struggling hindquarters. Jag bit a large piece from the anus and swallowed it immediately. Skinner tore at its intestines with his teeth and talons, savoring the taste of the dying beast's fresh blood and quivering, still-living tissue. The hapless deer was yet standing, its eyes bugging out of its skull, uttering a low, moaning cry. It suddenly gave out a shrill scream and collapsed first to its knees, then to its side.

The pack descended on the slaughtered animal, gorging themselves on its still-warm meat. After they were finished, Jag and Jez each pissed near the kill. One by one, the others sniffed at the puddles of urine, then peed as well. Skinner was the last to add his own fluid to the collection. It seemed the natural thing to do.

"Hey! Lookit me!" Ripper pulled the stag's head free of its body, superimposing it over his own. The stag's eyes were already glazed and its blackened tongue hung limply from the side of a mouth still dripping blood and froth. "I'm Bambi!" he laughed, skipping around in a circle.

For some reason, this struck Skinner as the funniest thing he'd ever seen in his life. He began laughing and was quickly joined by the others. He was overcome by a strong surge of camaraderie. For once in his life, he'd found others who understood him—who knew what it was like to be painfully different, and to be punished by society for that difference. He felt a powerful bond between him and these six strange and awesome creatures that only a full belly after a successful hunt could forge.

Skinner licked his lips and patted his rounded stomach. "What next?"

Rend stretched and yawned, scratching himself behind the ear with his hind leg. "Next we crash. We've still got a long drive ahead of us. G'night, Skin." With that, he got up and moved into the surrounding brush.

Jag reached over and fondled Jez' middle pair of tits, smearing them with blood. He nuzzled at her throat, nipping playfully at her exposed jugular. In return, Jez openly fondled her brother's genitals. Skinner watched in voyeuristic fascination as Jag's erect penis emerged from its furred pouch. It looked like a big, wet pink crayon, already dripping pre-cum.

The twins retired to the privacy of the nearby woods to complete their mating ritual. Apparently inspired by their leader's display, Ripper and Hew were licking their privates vigorously.

Sunder made a disgusted wuffling noise through his snout and yawned, then tore a final morsel from the deer's carcass for a bedtime snack and headed back in the direction they had first come.

"If anyone wants me, I'll be guarding the vans."

Skinner nodded and waved goodnight, then went off to find his own place to sleep. He found a natural shelter formed by a couple of small bushes and crawled underneath their protective canopy. Unless they were specifically looking for him, the casual nature lover out on a hike would never know he was there.

Well-fed and weary, he lapsed directly into a sleep without dreams.

He did not know if he'd only been asleep for a few minutes or several hours when she came to him.

He woke up the moment he heard the twig break. His eyes were wide open and his ears pricked before he was fully conscious. A warning growl vibrated deep in his throat.

"Don't be afraid, Skinner. It's only me."

Jez wriggled forward on her belly, pressing herself tightly against him. All six of her nipples were erect. Her snow-white pelt was streaked with mud and the dried blood of their kill, mixed with leaves and forest litter.

"Where's Jag?"

"Don't worry about him," she sneered, twirling a lock of his fur around her over-long ring finger. "He sleeps like the dead. Did anyone ever tell you what beautiful fur you have? It's such a pretty silver—"

"Jez—why are you here?"

"Why do you think?"

She smelled of female. Not the way human women reek of powders and deodorants and all the other toiletries that try to mask the primal essence that marks one sex from the other. She smelled of sweat and vaginal secretions that signaled a need so vast, so urgent, it triggered his own sexual appetite, like the growling of an empty belly fueling another's hunger. Still, his erection hadn't completely cut off the flow of blood to his brain.

"What—what about Jag?"

"What about him? He doesn't own me. In fact, he's *nothing* without me!" She giggled, sounding like a mischievous schoolgirl. "He's a washout in the sack, if you want to know the truth. He's won the rut twice, and each time I didn't get pregnant. Winning the melee is a hollow victory if no cubs are produced. At least that's what our dame says. And she should know."

"But—"

Jez wrapped her hand around his snout, clamping his muzzle shut. "Are you going to talk or fuck, low dog?"

Skinner jerked his muzzle free, snapping at her in display.

Jez' voice was low and husky with excitement. "Now *that's* what I like . . . a *brave* dog. Are you a brave doggie, Skinner? Hmmm?"

Her smell was all over him, clinging to his fur like an exotic perfume. It made it so difficult to think straight . . . to think at all, except for how everything wrong with the world would right itself if only he could stick his dick in her.

He took her from behind, her middle pair of tits clutched in his trembling claws. She made noises like his puppy used to make when it slept and dreamt of chasing rabbits. When he came, he sank his fangs into the thick fur protecting her shoulders and the back of her neck. Then he rolled off her and they lay together, drowsing, for several mintues, and she licked his face.

When he woke up again, she was gone. The only evidence that she'd been there at all was the mixture of jism and vaginal lubricant crusted on his crotch and the lingering smell of female.

Chapter Fifteen

It was close to twilight when Skinner returned to the creek to wash the blood, mud, and cum from his body. Rend was there, waist deep in the icy waters, vigorously shampooing his pelt. The moment Skinner set foot in the water, the shock shifted him back into his human form.

"Damn! That's *cold!*"

Rend barked a laugh. "That's why I elected to keep my coat on." He sniffed Skinner and wrinkled his muzzle, his ears swiveling atop his head like radar dishes. "So, you fucked Jez, huh?"

Skinner cringed. "It's that noticeable?"

Rend shrugged. "There are no secrets in the pack. Besides, it was only a matter of time before she added you to her collection. Hope you enjoyed it, cousin. She doesn't do repeat performances."

"She slept with you, too?"

"I don't know if 'slept with' is the right word. I've fucked her, yeah. We all have—even the losers like Hew and Ripper. But just once. It's part of the bonding ritual that makes the pack work as a team." Rend clambered out of the creek and shook himself dry. Seconds later, he shifted back into his human form and began putting on his clothes.

"What you need, Skinner, is a crash course in the birds and the bees—*vargr* style—before you wander into more trouble than you can handle.

"Full-blooded *vargr*—those raised within the pack—are comparatively rare. Bitches remain with the pack and don't travel alone, unlike the males. And while a bitch may copulate whenever and with whomever she likes—she can only conceive while in season. And that only occurs every few years.

"This is where the Howl comes in. To insure that the genetic structure of the pack is kept from stagnating, there's a rut melee—"

"Rut melee?"

"That's where all the assembled males, pedigree or mongrel, battle for the right to mate with the bitch in heat. It doesn't have to be a fight to the death, but it often ends up that way. Whoever wins the right to mate with the bitch becomes her consort, thereby making him the Alpha of the pack."

"Jez said something about Jag winning the rut melee twice."

"That's a sore spot for Jag. He won the melee fairly each time . . . but he has yet to sire any cubs. It's uncertain which one of them is sterile. Jez has only experienced two heat cycles and Jag . . . well, he has a tendency to devour his human sexual partners. Seems he has this thing against siring mongrels. He wants his issue to be full-blooded. Like I said: there are no secrets in the pack."

Skinner hurriedly left the water and joined

Rend on the bank, pulling on his clothes while his teeth chattered. "All this talk about rape ... I mean ... is it really necessary?"

"Did you have a girlfriend when you were growing up?"

"Well ... no. I—I wasn't very popular. I never dated."

"How about college, then?"

"I—I didn't get much of a chance. . . ."

"Ever beat off?"

Skinner could feel the blood rushing to his face. "I—well, sure—doesn't everybody?"

"What do you think about when you're pulling it, cuz?"

"I don't see where that's any business of yours—"

"Did you fantasize about how sweet her lips would taste? Or how tight her box would be?" Rend's lips pulled into a nasty leer. "Or did you fantasize about hurting her—making her scream and cry and bleed? Is that what got you hard? Did thinking about *taking* what you wanted make you pop your cork?"

"I—I—" There was a knot of anger and shame blocking his throat. Skinner's face burned as if it was on fire.

Rend's features abruptly softened. "I'm sorry, cuz. I didn't mean to get you upset like that."

"How—" Skinner swallowed, fighting to keep his voice from wavering. "How did you know?"

"Because I've been there, cousin. You see, even if you *had* a girlfriend, it still wouldn't have been any good. *Vargr* males are only capable of the act while in their *true* form. Their Wild form. As long as we wear our human skins, we're impotent. Because of this, consensual sex is alien to our kind. We are creatures born of rape and violence, and it is our destiny to repeat the circumstances of our creation. And once every few years we are given the chance to lay with one of our own kind and know something like love. *That* is what attracts us to the Howl like moths to the flame. *That* is why, within the span of the next few days, dozens of us will die at the hands of our brothers."

"Aw, you're over-romanticizing again!" Rend and Skinner looked up, startled by Sunder's unheralded approach. "We go to the Howl because it's a bang-up party and we can hang out without worrying about shifting back and forth. Me, I could care less about fucking something that actually *wanted* it. I participate in the melee because—well, when I get a whiff of bitch in heat, the little head takes over from the big head, know what I mean?"

"Always the philosopher, Sunder."

"Hey, don't I know it? Anyway, Jag sent me to tell you two to get a move on. It's time to go."

Rend grunted and began hiking back to the vans, Skinner in tow. The others were waiting for them in the clearing. Jez was sitting cross-legged on the grass next to the Dodge Caravan, retouching her nails with Fire Engine Red #1. She didn't look up as Skinner approached.

"Okay, let's get this show on the road!" Jag barked. "We've still got a long drive ahead of us before we make the lodge." The others made various groaning noises and began piling back into the vehicles.

Before Skinner had a chance to return to the minibus, Jag grabbed him by the upper arm, pinning him against the side of the Volkswagen. His face was millimeters from Skinner's and he gave off the hot, animal smell of raw aggression.

"What'd she tell you? What did she say about me?"

Rend coughed nervously and tried to draw his friend's attention away from Skinner. "Jag, cut the poor bastard some slack—"

"Stay out of this, Rend! This is between me and low dog!" Jag flashed bared fangs at his subordinate and Rend automatically stepped back, ritually exposing his throat in deference.

To his own surprise, Skinner jerked his arm free of the other's grip and stood, stiff-legged, his shoulders tensed and hair bristling, fixing Jag with a tense, angry stare. "I've had enough of you, buster! I've put up with bastards bullying me around all my life—but I'll be damned if I'll take it from you!"

Jag seemed genuinely surprised by Skinner's challenge. He took an involuntary step backward, his eyes searching for a way to extract himself from the confrontation. "I don't have the time to settle this properly, mutt. But once we get to the lodge, your ass is *mine*, understand?"

"I'll be waiting, Jag."

Chapter Sixteen

After leaving the Santa Fe National Forest, they followed U.S. 64 West, crossing the Continental Divide beyond Brazos Peak. Then they turned back onto U.S. 84 and followed it north into Colorado through the town of Chromo and then into the San Juan National Forest. There they switched over to U.S. Highway 160, heading east into the Rio Grande National Forest, passing tiny mountain towns such as Pagosa Springs along the way.

During the winter, when Eagle Mountain and Del Norte Peak were under a thick blanket of snow, the area was supported by thriving ski resorts. However, during the off-season, it was all but deserted, except for those hearty souls brave enough to endure the rigors of the San Juan Primitive Area. All things considered, it was a perfect place for a band of marauding, murdering nonhuman beast-men to hold a jamboree.

The vans turned onto a tiny dirt road just off Wolf Creek Pass that looked more like a dry riverbed than an actual byway. After twenty minutes of teeth-rattling, kidney-punching pothole dodging, Skinner caught a glimpse of a huge building made from native lumber and natural stone looming ahead. An old-fashioned wooden entry gate blocked the road.

The vans came to a halt and three hulking figures emerged from the surrounding shadows; one carried an automatic weapon, and although all three were wearing human skins, they were clearly *vargr*. Sunder rolled down the window and gave the armed *vargr* a quick hand signal.

"Snuff! Long time no see, cousin!"

The *vargr* guard sniffed at Sunder, then Rend. "Greetings, Sunder, Rend ... yeah, it *has* been awhile." Snuff fixed Skinner with a curious, somewhat suspicious eye. "Who's the new dog?"

"Name's Skinner. We picked him up in Albuquerque a couple of days ago. He's cool."

Snuff grunted and snapped his fingers. One of the others handed him a clipboard. He scribbled something down and handed it back to his subordinate. "You'll have go get clearance from Lady Erzule on that one."

"Don't worry, Snuff—I'll vouch for him."

Snuff shrugged and waved the vehicle into the compound. "Whatever. Okay, you're free to enter. Welcome home, cousins."

"Why all the security? I thought the only people who knew this place existed were *vargr* themselves."

"As you might have guessed, there's more than one kind of *vargr*. The most common is the mongrel, or mutt. They're the product of a *vargr*-human mating. I'm one, you're probably one as well. Most of us were born outside the pack and raised as humans. Those of us who learn of our blood heritage—who are capable of shapeshifting—are recognized as true *vargr*.

"Those who are incapable of shifting are shunned as *esau*. They are the crazed cannibal wild-men of legend—the ones who fell into the hands of the Inquisition and, in later centuries, the police.

"Then there are the half-wolves, known as the *ulfr*. They are the product of true *vargr* and wolf matings. These are quite scarce nowadays, since there are so few wolves left roaming the Wild. They are almost indistinguishable from true-wolves, except for their intelligence and their unusual size. The guards are here to make sure no *esau*, *ulfr*, or true-wolf makes it onto the lodge's grounds."

"Why? I thought this Howl thing was supposed to bring *vargr* of all kinds together."

"Unlike humans, not all *vargr* are created equal. There are probably more *esau* than there are pedigreed and mongrel *vargr* combined. They are pathetic creatures, trapped in the flesh and form of man, but possessing the nature and appetites of *vargr*. Gilles de Rais, Albert Fish, Jeffrey Dahmer, Jack the Ripper were all *esau* . . .

"While we, their blood kin, sympathize with their plight, we keep ourselves distanced from them. *Esau* are consumed by their needs, and that makes them dangerous running companions. They are careless and leave . . . trails. Even the most cunning, like Bundy and Lucas, eventually end up betraying themselves. The last thing we need is to have the spotlight of human attention trained on us.

"We have dwelt in the shadows for centuries—preying on mankind at our leisure. It suits our needs that they continue to dismiss our kind as myth—a quaint superstition to frighten their children into good behavior, or to be turned into grist for their entertainment mill."

"And the *ulfr*? Why are they excluded from the rut?"

Rend blinked, apparently genuinely surprised that Skinner would even bother to ask. "Why—that would be bestiality."

Before Skinner could say anything else, the Volkswagen came to a halt. "All out for Wolfcane Lodge!" Sunder crowed, hopping out from behind the steering wheel.

Skinner crawled out of the back of the minibus, surprised by the wide selection of automobiles parked on the gravel apron. There were late-model Detroit rustbuckets, fuel-efficient Japanese imports, expensive European sports cars, a couple of limousines and a '59 Cadillac that could have passed for the Batmobile.

Rend clapped him on the back and nodded toward the lodge. "Looks like we're the last to arrive—as usual! C'mon—let's go ahead and get you cleared!"

The front entrance to the lodge was imposing—the doorway flanked by huge statues of rampant, snarling wolves carved from black walnut. It made Skinner nervous to walk between them.

The central lobby resembled a rustic cathedral, with a huge domed ceiling that seemed to disappear into the dim smoke from the vast natural-stone fireplace that ran the length of the back wall.

Rough-hewn staircases connected the hub to the east and west wings. In many ways, it was no different from dozens of ski resorts in the state. Except instead of elk or mountain lions, there were stuffed humans on display.

One of the stuffed humans was an older man dressed in the long black robes of a judge, a gavel fitted into one hand, a volume of New York State Municipal Code, circa 1930, clutched in the other. A fine layer of dust clung to his robes and the surface of his skin. Skinner squatted on his haunches and squinted at the brass plate affixed to the base of the tableaux. It read "Judge Crater."

There was no need for him to read the plaque at the base of the tableaux featuring the squat, jowly, middle-aged man dressed in an early seventies polyester-blend business suit. He'd seen pictures of Jimmy Hoffa before.

"Rend! I was just wondering when you'd finally make it."

Skinner looked in the direction of the voice bellowing his friend's name, and was stunned to see a man tricked out in Nazi regalia striding across the lobby. As he came closer, Skinner realized he was wearing an authentic Gestapo S.S. uniform and not an elaborate costume.

Rend clasped the Gestapo officer's hand warmly. "Fenris! It's good to see you, cousin!"

"Same here, my young friend!" The Nazi turned his toothy smile in Skinner's direction. "And who's this? A new pack mate?"

"Skinner, I'd like you to meet Colonel Fenris."

Fenris clicked his highly polished jackboot heels

and delivered a full-fledged Nazi salute. *"Heil Hitler!"*

Skinner felt his mouth drop open, but there was nothing he could do about it. "I—I—uh—"

Fenris grinned and began to laugh. "You should have seen the look on your face, my dear boy! I swear, even after fifty years, it still gets them every time!"

"Some jokes never lose their punch."

"Rend! You handsome dog! There you are!" This came from a man dressed in the flowing red robes of a Roman Catholic cardinal, who approached them with the determination of an ice cutter plowing its way through the Arctic Ocean.

"Amadeo!" Rend took the older man's hand and kissed his ring. "And how have you been keeping yourself, Excellency?"

The cardinal pushed back his broad-brimmed hat, revealing a tangle of dark curls and a carefully maintained goatee that made him look like a picture-book devil. "Well enough, my pet. And you?" He spoke with an identifiably Italian accent.

"I can't complain."

"Are you still traveling with those wretched brats?"

"Yes, I'm still running with Jag and Jez."

Amadeo rolled his eyes and grimaced. "Honestly, my boy! I don't see what you find so attractive in those hellions!"

"Jag's my friend."

Amadeo chuckled and winked at Fenris. "My, isn't *he* the loyal little doggie? And who is this fine figure of a youth? Another member of your ragtag band, no doubt, judging from his abysmal taste in clothes."

"Skinner, this is Cardinal Amadeo."

"Uh, hi."

"Charmed, I'm sure."

"Who else is here? I haven't had a chance to look around yet. . . ."

Fenris took off his hat and ran leather-gloved fingers through his salt-and-pepper hair. "I saw the Hound an hour ago in the bar . . . he was drunk, as usual. He had Shaggybreeks with him and they were starting to reminisce about the Viking invasions by the time I left. There's nothing more tiresome than listening to them rehash the 'good old days' while they're in their cups!"

"It's good seeing you both, and I'd really love to hang and chat, but I've got to see to it that Skinner is cleared before I get settled in. I'll catch both of you later in the bar. Does that sound good to you?"

"Sounds perfect, my pet! And bring your delightful little friend with you, why don't you?"

"We'll catch you later, okay? C'mon, Skin, let's get you situated!" Rend waved a casual farewell to the older *vargr* and guided Skinner away, steering him by the elbow.

"Is that guy *really* a Nazi?" Skinner whispered as soon as they were out of earshot.

"*Was* not 'is,' if you please. Yes, Fenris was a high-ranking member of the Gestapo during World War II."

"But that was over fifty years ago! He can't be any older than forty-five!"

"He's closer to two hundred and forty-five,

Skinner. I know you just fell off the turnip truck, but do you have to be so damned obvious about it? *Vargr* aren't like humans in a lot of ways—one of which is aging. Mixed-bloods can live up to four hundred years—full-bloods even longer. Hell, Amadeo was born the year Christopher Columbus sailed for America!"

"Christopher Colum— You mean to tell me he's *five hundred years old*?!"

"Yep."

"Get outta here! You're shitting me, right?"

"It's a fact! Amadeo's sire was none other than Rodrigo Borgia, better known as Alexander VI."

"Wow! You mean he's one of *the* Borgias? I've heard of Cesare and Lucrezia, but not this guy. . . ."

"Amadeo is a full-blood. Yeah, there was a *vargr* pope. He had a different dame than his half-siblings. They were *esau*. That's why Cesare and Lucrezia are dead today and Amadeo is still farting around."

Rend led Skinner into the east wing's ground floor and up a narrow flight of steps that twisted back on themselves like the chambers of a nautilus.

"Where are we going?"

"To see the bitch queen."

"Huh?"

"Lady Erzule. The big mama who runs Wolfcane Lodge."

"Jag and Jez's mother?"

"Dame. The full-bloods prefer the word *dame*."

The narrow staircase ended at a doorway big enough for a twelve-year-old child to walk through, but which required an adult to bend over double. Then again, a *vargr* in its wild form would have no trouble entering or leaving. Rend rapped on the low-hanging frame. A panel slid open in the doorface and a *vargr* male poked its snout out, sniffed inquiringly, then withdrew. A second later came the sound of locks being turned and the door opened.

The *vargr* guard glowered first at Rend, then Skinner. Like the ones posted at the entrance to the lodge, he was outfitted with an automatic rifle. The Uzi slung over his twisted, hairy shoulder seemed highly superfluous, like a shark carrying a switchblade.

"We're here to see Lady Erzule."

"Is she expecting you?"

"Of *course* she's expecting them, you moronic lickspittle!" This came from a tall man dressed in a black frock coat and dark trousers, his neck held rigid by a stiff Gladstone collar. His long, luxuriant white hair was pulled away from his face and fastened in a loose ponytail that hung well below his shoulders. His accent hinted of the finer British public schools.

The guard cringed in deference to the other's superiority. "Yes, Lord Feral."

Feral nodded curtly to Rend. "Her Ladyship was alerted by the perimeter guards that you had a new pack mate. She is looking forward to making his acquaintance." Feral fixed a disdainful eye on Skinner, making it clear that this eagerness was not shared.

Lord Feral led them down a richly appointed hallway, the walls crammed with expensive objets d'art. Skinner watched the older *vargr* with keen interest. He walked with a military carriage, his spine ramrod straight, his hands clasped together in the small of his back. Put a ferule and a Bible in his hands, and he could pass for a Dickensian headmaster. So, this was Jag's father. Despite the extreme difference in their dress and personal mannerisms, Skinner could see familial similarities between the two. The most obvious physical trait was their cornstarch white hair, yet they also shared an aggressive hauteur that made them bristle with hostile energy.

They were ushered into a sumptuously appointed bedroom, hung with rich tapestries and appointed with gold fixtures. The canopied bed and huge vanity table littered with various jars of ointments, unguents, and perfumes made it clear that they were in a lady's boudoir. And if there was any further doubt, the lady herself stood in front of the mirror, propped up by a metal support that allowed her to remain perfectly still as servants applied the last of her toilet.

Lady Erzule glanced up as they entered and waved aside her retinue with an impatient flutter of a lace-trimmed handkerchief. "That will do for now, *mes enfants*!" She descended from her dressing post, flashing a brilliant smile with freshly carmined lips. "Rend! How marvelous to see you again, *cher*! And you've brought a new little friend, *mais non*?"

Skinner was having a hard time keeping his jaw from dropping open. Of all the bizarre fancy dress costumes he'd seen so far, Lady Erzule's certainly took the prize. She wore a pale lavender taffeta dress, the long V-pointed bodice laced up the front over a stomacher, the wide neckline edged with ruffled antique lace, as were the elbow-length puffed sleeves. The long flounced skirt opened in the front and was gathered full at the hip, shored up by stiff petticoats, a bustle, and strange basket-like projections worn under each side of the skirt, accompanied by a series of hoops of graduating size. She looked more like a cake decoration than an actual woman.

Her face was painted dead white, a small beauty mark pasted to the corner of her left eye, her lips and cheeks so brightly rouged she looked like a porcelain doll. She wore a powdered wig, dressed high and shaped with pads of cotton and wool to resemble a stylized atomic mushroom cloud. In one hand she held a shepherdess' crook, decorated with colorful satin ribbons, while in the other she clutched a lace trimmed handkerchief.

She smiled at Skinner and motioned for him to approach with her shepherdess' crook. "Come closer, *chien.* I will not harm you. I just want to look at you."

"Yes, ma'am."

"How polite you are for a whelp of this century," purred Lady Erzule, fixing him with a lidded gaze Skinner recognized all too well. "I like that. Are you a good doggie?"

"Yes, ma'am."

"What is you name, *jeune chien*?"

"Skinner Cade."

A look of distaste flickered across Lady Erzule's enameled face. "You won't be using your last name after this weekend," she sniffed. "We surrender our previous human identities once we embrace the pack. Still, Skinner is an appropriate name for one of the *vargr*. You may keep that."

Skinner glanced at Rend, who silently mouthed the words *say thank you.* "Uh, thank you, ma'am."

Lady Erzule smiled coquettishly and rapped Skinner playfully with her crook. "You *are* a delicious pup! And such lovely markings!" She gently stroked Skinner's hair. "It really is quite striking. You know, you look like you could be one of Feral's by-blows. Don't you think there's a resemblance, my dear?"

Lord Feral's shoulders stiffened and the muscles in his jaw knotted themselves tighter. "That is unlikely, my lady."

"Perhaps so. Perhaps not," Erzule mused. "You are given to rambling, are you not, my dear? Where did Jag find him, Rend?"

"Actually, I was the one who located him, milady."

Erzule raised a delicately tweezed eyebrow in his direction. "You brought an initiate into the pack instead of Jag?"

"There was little choice—he was badly wounded. If I hadn't acted when I did, he would have fallen into the hands of the police. Besides, we lost Bender only a few weeks before. . . ."

"Bender's dead?" Erzule had lost all trace of her previous gaiety.

Rend coughed and looked somewhat uncomfortable. "Yes, milady. He was killed by *coyotero* in East L.A. I thought Jag—I thought you knew."

"No. I— That is enough for now." Lady Erzule turned her back on them, the audience over.

"Who's this 'Bender'?" Skinner asked as they headed back down the stairway.

"He was a member of our pack, and one of Erzule's favorite whelps."

"He was her son? Jag and Jez' brother?"

"*Demi*-brother. His father was Lord Mammon, Feral's immediate predecessor. Erzule was genuinely in love with Mammon, and she made no secret of preferring Bender to the others."

"What happened to this Mammon?"

"Feral killed him in the rut melee, twenty-five years ago. That's how he became consort."

"You mentioned something about coyotes. . . ."

"The *coyotero*. You'll find out about them in time."

"But—"

"Man, you're full of questions!" Rend groaned. "All you have to do is keep your eyes open the next day or two and you'll learn *everything* you need to know about *vargr* society. C'mon, let's go check out the bar and see who's here!"

Chapter Seventeen

If anyone had ever told Skinner that he would one day be drinking beer in the company of werewolves, listening to them reminisce about the Dark Ages, the Reign of Terror, and Nazi death camps, he would have laughed. And if they'd told him he'd be bored stiff on top of it, he would have thought they were nuts as well. Funny how life is.

"And then I shook off their guards and grabbed a knife from the village chieftain and asked them 'Who dies first?' Well, that gave 'em pause, don't you know!" Shaggybreeks belched to punctuate his story, wiping the beer foam from his thick mustache. "Then, to make it look good, I went ahead and jumped into the pit full of half-starved wolves *anyway*! The humans assumed I was dead—torn to bloody ribbons—but I knew I had nothing to fear, what with my great-dame being a true-wolf, eh! They were family, don't you know?"

"Really?" Skinner said, trying not to yawn.

"I'm quarter true-wolf, and I'm proud of it!" Shaggybreeks brought his tankard down hard on the top of the table, sloshing its contents. "Not like some blue-nosed pantywaists I could mention! Way they run things nowadays, I wouldn't even be born!

"My dame—bless her sweet hide—was *ulfr*. Not many female *ulfr*, even back then. My sire was a *vargr* by the name of Tarquin. He was a Roman general stationed on the Rhine when he wore his human skin. After she whelped me, he brought us both back to the outpost. He claimed I was his bastard by a Teuton woman he'd raped, while keeping my dame as a 'pet.'

"We were a happy secret family for several years—until my parents were caught fucking. They were condemned as necromancers and drawn and quartered. I managed to escape into the Black Forest." Shaggybreeks fixed Skinner with a drunken stare, made all the more penetrating by his single eyebrow. "What about you, pup? What's your pedigree?"

"I don't know. I was raised human."

"You look like one of Feral's by-blows, if you ask me. Your dame—she wouldn't have happened to have been raped while out taking a stroll one fine evening?"

"I was adopted by humans as a baby. I never knew my birth-mother."

Shaggybreeks grunted and got to his feet. He was big and burly and excessively hirsute, tufts of thick body hair peeking out of the neck of his tunic. He also wore a wolfskin cape, fastened about his throat by a bronze fibula, woolen hose, and cross-gartered sandals. It wasn't hard to believe that this hard-drinking, foul-smelling drunkard had once been one of the most feared Viking warriors to terrorize the coasts of Western Europe.

"That's the trouble with *vargr* today. No sense of roots. I need to make room for more ale."

"Don't let us stop you, cousin," sneered Fenris. After the Viking lumbered off in the direction of the bathroom, the Gestapo officer leaned forward and spoke to Skinner, sotto voce; "We no longer encourage the participation of those with such—bestial—pedigrees at the Howl. Shaggybreeks is—well, he's a *character*. He's one of the last of the old breed, really, so he's been granted special dispensation. The same holds true for the Hound—the red-headed *vargr* over there in the kilt and woad. Genetically, they're dinosaurs. Remnants of the time when man still dwelt in the land of myth and dream."

Skinner pushed aside his drink and got to his feet. Suddenly, the interior of the lounge had become uncomfortably close.

"Excuse me ... I think I need ... some air...."

He staggered through the lobby and out the front door. The smell of aspen leaves and high-altitude pine from the surrounding mountains was bracing, clearing his head.

It was close to dusk, the setting sun throwing lengthy shadows across the lodge's carefully manicured lawn. He decided to take a walk and scout out the surrounding area. Anything was preferable to spending the rest of the evening listening to the others drone on and on about their murderous exploits.

Although it was almost summer, there were still patches of snow and crusted ice underneath the trees and shrubbery. The wind coming down off the nearby mountains was sharp, threatening to become frigid after sunset. Still, Skinner found being close to such raw nature invigorating, regardless of the cold.

Following an instinct he did not fully comprehend, he dropped to his haunches and rolled vigorously in the litter of aspen leaves and pine needles. It felt good. Without realizing it, he shifted into his Wild skin.

The sound of high-powered rifle fire in the near distance made him sit up, sniffing the air cautiously. He smelled blood. He loped off in the direction of the gunshot.

He found the *vargr* called Snuff standing over a badly wounded human male, speaking into a hand-held radio.

"... Sector Nine ... intruder located and immobilized...."

Skinner moved closer for a better look at the man bleeding to death at Snuff's feet. He was a white male, apparently in his mid-thirties, with long, matted hair and an equally unkept beard. There was blood on his lips and blood flowing from his nostrils, as well as what was leaking from his side where the bullet had passed through, doing irreparable damage to his spleen and liver. He wore dirty, ragged clothes and a tattered cloth coat that was unsuited for the harsh climate of the Continental Divide.

"Please ..." the dying man gasped, a bubble of bloody froth forming at the corner of his mouth. "Let me see her ... I just want to see her ..."

"Damn fool *esau*...." muttered Snuff. "This is the third one we've shot in the last year. If this keeps up, we'll have to relocate the lodge."

The *esau* clutched a canvas rucksack to his blood-smeared chest, fumbling at the straps with numb fingers. "I want to be like you . . . please, tell her . . . tell her . . . I brought gifts . . ."

Skinner plucked the rucksack from the dying *esau*'s grasp and looked inside. It was full of human scalps. Some were dried and leathery, others still quite fresh.

"See . . . ?" The *esau* smiled, blood drooling into his beard. "I'm one of you . . . one of . . . you. . . ."

Snuff set aside his rifle and pulled a 9mm semiautomatic handgun out of his belt, working the action to chamber a round. He noticed Skinner watching him. "Silver-jacketed bullets. We save these for the kill," he said, holding the gun up by way of explanation. He pointed the muzzle at the *esau*'s temple. "Sorry, Charlie." He sighed and pulled the trigger. The *esau* jerked once and then lay still.

Snuff holstered the gun and thumbed the walkietalkie back on. "Snuff to Thrasher. Intruder eliminated. Proceeding with perimeter check, over." He hesitated before leaving, eyeing the sack full of scalps. "You want that?" he asked.

Skinner shoved the grisly "gift" at Snuff. "No. You want it? Here, take it!"

Snuff grinned. "Thanks! Don't mind if I do, cousin. Oh, and watch out for the traps we've got set for the true-wolves and *ulfr*. They really can't do much permanent damage to *vargr*, but they hurt like hell and it'll take you a couple of days to regenerate your foot." With that final word of warning, the *vargr* guard shouldered the rucksack and strolled off into the gathering dark, leaving Skinner with the body of the dead *esau*.

Skinner stared at the rapidly cooling corpse. He wasn't exactly sure what to do about the *esau*'s body. He certainly wasn't hungry enough to eat it. Besides, there was something cannibalistic about the thought of chowing down on the hapless bastard, kind of like a human devouring a chimpanzee. After a couple of minutes, he lost interest in standing vigil and decided to continue investigating the grounds.

He found the wolf caught in a trap about a mile into the treeline behind the lodge. It was big and gray, its shoulders easily twice the width of a rottweiler's. When it saw him, it lay its ears against the side of its head and bared its fangs.

"I'm not going to hurt you, big fella," Skinner said, trying to make his voice as nonthreatening as possible. He eased forward, trying to figure out how to pry the trap open without getting too close to the biting end of its catch.

It was obvious the beast was in pain, although far from incapacitated. As he drew closer, he got a better view of the wolf's wounded foreleg—and saw what looked like a human thumb in place of its dewclaw. Skinner jerked back, staring hard into the eyes of the trapped wolf. They were blue and possessed of an intelligence he found both disturbing and compelling.

"Do you understand me?"

The *ulfr* made a short bark Skinner assumed was an affirmative.

"I'm going to try and help you." He grabbed

the jaws of the trap and pulled them apart. Even with his *vargr*-born strength, it wasn't easy.

The *ulfr* yanked its foreleg free, whimpering and licking the mangled paw. It raised its head and fixed Skinner with a quizzical stare, then turned and fled, limping, into the forest.

As he turned to leave, a shadow separated itself from the dark and moved to intercept him. It was a heavily built *vargr* male with dense black fur. Even before he spoke, Skinner recognized Shaggybreeks by his scent.

"I saw what you did."

"So?" Skinner replied, his withers beginning to prickle.

"No need to get your back up!" Shaggybreeks laughed, clapping the younger werewolf on the shoulder. "I approve wholeheartedly! I'm just surprised a *vargr* your age would help an *ulfr*."

"Why shouldn't I? We share Wild blood, don't we?"

Shaggybreeks gave Skinner a long, hard look, as if trying to decide whether he was serious. "You're new to *vargr* ways. In time you'll see that those of us who boast true-wolf blood are considered less than full *vargr*. The rules for the rut melee insure that the thoroughbreds continue to reproduce. There's too much human blood diluting the breed, if you ask me."

"I may not know much about *vargr* ways, but I know setting traps is wrong."

Shaggybreeks grunted and pulled on his beard. "You're better off keeping such opinions to yourself, pup. Even if there are those who are sympathetic to your views."

"You're not going to tell are you?"

"If you hadn't freed the *ulfr*, I surely would have done it myself. Come along, cousin. It's almost time for the Grand Bal Masque. You don't want to miss out on the party, eh?"

Chapter Eighteen

The ballroom was all polished crystal and refracted light. The hardwood floors were buffed until they gleamed like the hide of a well-fed animal. A large stage, draped in black bunting, dominated the far end of the room. There was a deranged version of a prom queen's throne on a raised dais in the middle of the platform flanked on the right by a smaller, more austere chair. Heavy black velvet curtains hung behind the throne, obscuring any view of who or what might be waiting backstage.

There were at least thirty *vargr* in various historical costumes circulating on the dance floor, talking among themselves and sampling the buffet table and its array of specially prepared meats, when Skinner and Shaggybreeks entered.

"Make yourself comfortable, pup. And don't worry; no one will learn of our little secret," Shaggybreeks said, giving him a wink. "Enjoy the feed—Erzule really knows how to provide a spread, that much I'll grant her!"

"*There* you are! I was wondering where you'd gotten off to!" Rend had a highball glass in one hand and looked more than a little drunk. "I thought you'd run out on us. . . ."

"I was taking a walk, that's all. Anything wrong with that?"

"My, aren't *we* being oversensitive! Here, try some of this—it's human veal." He thrust a plate heaped with paper-thin slices of pale white meat in Skinner's face. "It melts in your mouth! Truly exquisite!"

Saliva pooled in Skinner's mouth, but he pushed the offered delicacy aside. "No, thanks."

"You've got to get over thinking of humans as anything but what they are: meat. You'll starve otherwise."

"I'll deal with it in my own way, in my own time. What's the rush?"

"Just tryin' to help, that's all," Rend replied sullenly. "It's not like you've never eaten human flesh before."

"I appreciate the concern, but I've got to work this out myself. Besides, it's different when you kill to defend yourself. Eating something that's been specially butchered and prepared . . . It just seems, I don't know, *wrong*."

Rend rolled his eyes in disgust. "Save me from fuckin' dilettantes! I used to think if I only preyed on junkies, muggers, pimps, and other sleaze and left 'good people' alone, it would make a difference. Now I can't tell if they're serial killers or Sunday school teachers. Meat's meat."

Skinner grunted and shrugged. There was no point talking to Rend while he was drunk. He glanced around the room, studying the different costumes and the *vargr* wearing them. He spotted Shaggybreeks talking to a *vargr* in the uniform of a Napoleonic general, while Fenris held forth with a dark, wild-haired *vargr* in a cassock who looked suspiciously like Rasputin.

As he scanned the ballroom, Skinner noticed all the attendees were white males who, at least physically, seemed between the ages of thirty-five and sixty.

Skinner nudged Rend and whispered in his friend's ear. "You call this a party? Where are the women?"

"There are only two *vargr* females here: Erzule and Jez. Jez is about to go into estrus. She doesn't dare show herself until the rut melee. Just one whiff would start a riot. The *only* bitches I've ever seen have been Erzule and Jez. And in a few years, there'll just be Jez."

"Why? I thought you said the full-blooded *vargr* are nearly immortal."

"Technically, yeah. But the bitch queen's eggs are growin' old, if you get my drift. The last time she went into heat was twenty-five years ago— that's when Jag and Jez were conceived. And it was ten years between that heat and the one which produced Bender. Once Erzule hits menopause, she's dead meat. It's Jez' turn, then. Assuming she isn't sterile."

Fenris stepped forward, the steel death's head adorning his Gestapo colonel's hat gleaming in the light from the crystal chandelier. "I hope you two don't mind my attaching myself to your conversation, but I couldn't help but overhear. . . . Actually, this is a unique situation. Normally, Howls are held once every five or six years, coinciding with the mating cycles of the dominant bitch. The older the bitches get, the longer the spaces in between mating cycles, of course.

"But this is the third Howl in as many years. All because the lovely Jez has yet to pop a pup. Personally, I don't think it's her fault, poor child. I believe her brother is the one to blame—faulty genetics, don't you know. Speak of the devil, there he is now."

Jag strode into the ballroom, flanked by Ripper and Hew, Sunder trailing behind him. He still wore his motorcycle boots and black denim jeans with the knees slashed out, only now he was bare-chested underneath his black leather jacket. When he caught sight of Rend and Skinner, he motioned for the others to stay put.

"Looks like I'm needed elsewhere," Fenris muttered under his breath, leaving before Jag could arrive.

"Where the hell have you two been?" he snapped, his complexion ruddy with anger.

"I—I had to get Skinner's clearance approved."

Jag's face reddened even further. "You introduced him to Lady Erzule? Without my say-so?"

"I—I'm sorry, Jag. I thought it would be okay."

"*I'm* the alpha, Rend! *I'm* the one that makes decisions and tells the others what to do and what *not* to do—not you! Is that understood? It was bad enough you brought this mutt in without asking me! Now you go and introduce him to Lady Erzule—are you *challenging* me, Rend?"

Rend cast his eyes down, all but tucking his tail between his legs in submission. "No, Jag. You know I'd never do that."

"How about your little butt-buddy, here?" Jag

thrust his face into Skinner's. "Does *he* understand?"

"Look, Jag, why don't you just get off my back, okay?" Skinner growled, bringing his hackles up and his lips back. "You've done nothing but chew my tail since I first showed up, and I've taken all I'm going to from you!"

"As long as you run with my pack, mutt, I'm the one who calls the shots." Jag's face began to twist and sprout hair, his teeth suddenly becoming very big and sharp. "And right now I'm gonna rip you a new asshole, low dog!"

"Children! Children! Save it for the melee!" Amadeo was suddenly between the two young *vargr*, waving his hands and clucking his tongue like a teacher riding herd on schoolyard ruffians.

Skinner shrugged and lifted his hands, palms outward. "Okay. I'll wait."

Jag however, surged forward, only to have the collar of his jacket grabbed by Amadeo. "I *said*, save it for the melee. Perhaps you did not hear me, brother-dear? I would hate to think you were willing to disgrace our dame with such— bestial—behavior."

Jag glowered at Amadeo for a long moment then spun on his heel and rejoined his pack mates. Rend moved to follow him, but Skinner caught his forearm.

"Where are you going?"

"With him."

"You don't have to go running after him!"

Rend opened his mouth to say something, but pulled his arm free instead, hurrying after Jag's retreating back.

"You're not one of Jag's admirers, I take it," Amadeo observed dryly.

"You could say that." Skinner turned to look the clergyman directly in the eye. "Did I hear you correctly? Is Jag your brother?"

"*Demi*-brother. I stress the word '*demi*.' We share maternity, not paternity." Amadeo sniffed. "I was one of Erzule's earliest whelps. All I can say is that as she's grown older, she's become lax concerning the raising of her cubs. I would *never* have pulled such a stunt when I was Jag's age! Ask Fenris, if you don't believe me."

"Did you two grow up together?"

"Hardly. He's my son. By Lady Erzule."

Not knowing what to say to that particular revelation, Skinner excused himself and headed for the open bar. Before he had a chance to pour himself a beer, a large, calloused hand clapped him on the shoulder. Skinner turned around and found himself staring up into the broad, grinning face of a *vargr* with a bristling red beard and braided hair that hung almost to his waist. The strapping giant was completely naked except for a kilt and bluish-purple bodypaint.

"Well-met, pup! I am called the Hound. My good friend Shaggybreeks told me of your deed earlier this night!"

"Oh, great!" Skinner muttered under his breath.

"Fear not, young cousin. The tale will go no farther than I. You see, like Shaggybreeks, I too am of *ulfr* heritage. I boast the blood of dire wolves in my veins, and none can ever make me ashamed of it!" He cast an angry eye about the room. "There was a time, my friend, when humans worshipped our kind as demi-gods and heroes!

"Why, in *my* day, the humans made me their official champion! I was so fierce in my battle-rage and moved so swiftly that I was said to have faces on every side of my head and six arms—each clutching an instrument of destruction!" The grinning, redheaded giant's smile faltered and he absently pulled on his chin whiskers, now liberally shot with threads of gray. "But that was a *long* time ago. . . ."

Before the Celtic warrior could continue, the lights dimmed and a recorded fanfare blared from hidden speakers.

Everyone in the room turned to face the stage. The black velvet curtains parted and Lord Feral strode forward, his demeanor as rigid as ever. He moved to the rococo throne, picked up a handheld radio microphone, and addressed the crowd.

"Greetings, cousins, and welcome to the Howl."

"Greetings, cousin," the *vargr* responded with one voice.

"Before the festivities get underway, let us first consecrate ourselves to that which makes us different! That which makes us *vargr*!"

Feral clapped his hands and a servant dressed in livery walked onto the stage, carrying a long black leather box that looked like a cross between a guitar case and a pool cue sheath.

At the sight of the box, the assembled werewolves dropped to their knees, throats exposed in symbolic surrender. Not sure what was happening, Skinner followed the others' lead.

The servant knelt before Lord Feral, holding the

leather case up to him. Feral snapped open the catches that held it shut and opened the lid with the caution and reverence of a priest attending the ark of the covenant.

He lifted from the crushed velvet interior of the case a strangely fashioned staff roughly five feet in length. The body of the staff was made of a single piece of ebony, polished to a high sheen. The head of the staff was the size of two doubled fists and was a facsimile of a snarling wolf cast in silver. The wolf's head boasted fangs of antique ivory and eyes fashioned from rubies that sparkled and flashed. Feral held the cane aloft by the haft, careful not to touch the decorative silver head.

"Behold the Wolfcane! Emblem of our power! Symbol of our superiority over the herds of mankind! Heed the Wolfcane's credo: 'Those who are weak are destined to be food for the strong'!"

The assembled *vargr* whimpered like frightened cubs and averted their eyes from the Wolfcane's baleful gaze. But not Skinner. As he stared at the silver head, his eyes began to burn and swim with tears. Through the tears he saw what looked to be an aura of bluish-white light radiating from the Wolfcane. He wanted to see more, but the pain became too much and he finally had to look away.

Having satisfied the needs of ritual, Feral returned the staff to its protective case, dismissing the attendant.

"Now, without further ado, let me introduce your hostess—Lady Erzule!"

As the audience got back onto its feet, the curtains parted once again and Lady Erzule, resplendent in her Louis XV finery, glided out onto the stage. A chorus of barks, howls, and applause rose from the audience, which she acknowledged by blowing kisses and waving her beribboned shepherdess' crook.

Smiling like a cross between Little Bo Peep and an airline stewardess, she took the microphone from Feral and addressed her subjects.

"I welcome you, one and all, to Wolfcane Lodge. I trust my servants have seen to your needs, *mes cousins*? *Bon!* Let it never be said that Lady Erzule is inhospitable!"

There was a roar of agreement, which she accepted with mock humility. Skinner shook his head as if trying to dislodge an earmite. Whatever he had envisioned when Rend and the others first mentioned the Howl, he hadn't expected to find himself in a ballroom full of werewolves tricked out in masquerade costumes, paying court to an aging she-wolf dressed like Marie Antoinette on Quaaludes. All they needed was to have Bert Parks step on stage and sing "There She Is: Miss Lycanthrope" while Erzule twirled along the runway like an escapee from a Ken Russell movie.

Erzule held up a delicate hand for silence. "But lest we forget, I would like to announce to those assembled tonight the names of our brethren who have perished since the last time we met." She removed a piece of folded parchment from the bodice of her costume, clearing her throat into the microphone.

"Gone from the pack is Lykos: eldest of the *vargr*, who once marched alongside Alexander into Persia. He died of that rarest of *vargr* ailments—old age.

"Also gone is Womanslayer, who the human press so crudely dubbed 'The Northside Slasher.' He was killed while evading arrest in Billings, Montana. Operatives loyal to me in the coroner's office made sure Womanslayer's body was promptly cremated before further investigations could be brought to bear."

Erzule waited out the smattering of applause, biting her lower lip in preparation of making her third, and final, announcement. When she spoke, there was a noticeable waver in her voice.

"And, lastly, it pains me to announce the death of Bender, who was cruelly taken from us by our enemies, the accursed *coyotero*, while in eastern Los Angeles."

There was an audible gasp as the *vargr* exchanged shocked looks among themselves.

"While we shall each mourn Bender in our different ways, my cousins, at least the vengeance that is our due will begin this very evening. I'd been planning on keeping the little surprise I had in store for you secret until after the melee, but in light of the news concerning Bender, I see no reason to wait, *mais non*?"

Erzule clapped her hands and two young *vargr* males dressed as footmen emerged from backstage, wheeling a circus animal cage covered by a sheet in front of them.

"As you are all well aware, we of the *vargr* have waged war with the *coyotero* since we first set foot in the New World, five hundred years ago. Many of our cousins have fallen to their ambushes over the years—yet we prevail! Their spies and assassins are everywhere!

"Just two days ago one of my loyal guards captured one such spy. And tonight, *mes cousins*, I give you the chance to see one of the *coyotero* up close!" With that, Erzule snatched away the sheet.

The assembled *vargr* moved forward, pressing themselves against the lip of the stage in hopes of getting a good look at the captured enemy. Skinner stood on tiptoe, trying to get a clear view of the figure huddled inside the cage. The *coyotero*—whatever it might be—seemed human in appearance and refused to look in the direction of the audience.

"Show them your face, *espionne!*" Erzule snarled, viciously poking the captive with the butt of her crook.

The *coyotero* jerked in response to the prodding, and the entire room gasped when they realized the captive was female. Skinner gasped as well, but not because of the captured enemy's sex. He *recognized* her.

He knuckled his eyes in disbelief and looked again. The *coyotero* spy that sat huddled on display in the cage, her clothes torn and her face bruised, was none other than Root Woman's granddaughter, Rosie.

Chapter Nineteen

Skinner lay sprawled across his bed, staring up at the raw pine rafters, a joint drooping from the corner of his mouth. Rend's portable tape player was busy booming out Sonic Youth's song "Schizophrenia."

"What are they going to do to her?"

Rend stepped out of the bathroom, fresh from his shower. Instead of using a towel, he shook himself dry, sending spray in every direction. Skinner noticed his friend had shaved his forehead again. "Her who?" Rend yawned, taking the joint from Skinner.

"Ro— The woman they captured."

Rend shrugged. "Probably use her in the Hunt."

"The Hunt?"

"Yeah, it's an official part of every Howl. Normally they use a human or an *esau*, but this is a special occasion. The Master of the Hunt—in this case, Feral—sticks the prey in a big burlap bag and drags it through the woods, so it'll leave a scent trail. Then he hangs the bag from the limb of a really high tree. The first *vargr* to the scene gets to keep the ears. It's not much different than a foxhunt. Except that we don't use horses."

"Doesn't sound very sporting."

"Did I say it was supposed to?" Rend flopped down on his own bed, folding his arms behind his head while he toked on the joint. "What's it matter to you? She's *coyotero*. It's not like she's *vargr*."

"What's this shit about *coyotero* and *vargr* all about? They're werewolves too, aren't they?"

Rend shook his head, grinning ruefully. "You better not let Jag or any of the other purebreeds hear you say that."

"But they *are* shapeshifters, right? Shaggybreeks said they are. . . ."

"Yeah, but they're not were-*wolves*, they're were-*coyotes*!"

"So?"

Rend pulled a moronic Goofy-face, crossing his eyes and sticking his tongue out of the side of his mouth. "Duh, *so*? What do you mean, '*so*'? They're not *vargr*!"

"I still don't get what's the big difference."

"*Vargr* and *coyotero* have been warring with one another for five hundred years—ever since Columbus first set foot in the New World. The *coyotero* are native to North America."

"You mean they're Indians?"

"I guess so. They didn't take to the idea of sharing their territory with their European cousins, so they declared war against the *vargr*. We've been actively fighting one another—mostly through guerilla actions—for five centuries now. Our side started getting the upper hand, thanks to Manifest Destiny, about a century and a half ago. The *coyotero* won't admit it, but their days are numbered.

It's only a matter of time before the *vargr* reign supreme."

"And the *coyotero* murdered Bender?"

Rend turned his face to the wall and murmured something.

"What? I didn't hear what you said."

"I said 'maybe.'"

"Maybe? aren't you *sure*? I thought you told Lady Erzule he was killed by *coyotero*. . . ."

"That's what Jag says."

"But you're not sure?"

"I wasn't there when it happened. But why should he lie?"

"I dunno. You tell me."

Rend fidgeted, swore under his breath, and got up. Skinner remained on his bed, legs crossed in the lotus position, and watched his friend pace back and forth.

"You think Jag killed him, don't you?"

"Maybe."

"But they were brothers!"

"*Demi*-brothers. Erzule favored Bender over Jag. Everyone knew it. He was her favorite. There was a lot of bad blood between the two—especially after Erzule insisted that Bender run with our pack. It didn't help that Bender was trying to beat Jag's time with Jez, either. Supposedly, he and Bender were waylaid by *coyotero* while in East L.A. I saw Bender's body—he'd been shot through the head with a silver bullet."

"If you think Jag's responsible for Bender's death, why didn't you say so to Lady Erzule?"

"Will you lay off Jag, okay?" Rend snapped. "Interfamilial intrigue and murder is hardly unheard of among the *vargr*! For the purebred, it's a fuckin' way of life!"

"I don't get it—why do you insist on protecting him?"

Rend sighed and ran his hand over his high, gleaming forehead. "Five years ago, I was a know-nothing mutt like yourself. Sure, I'd been on my own for nearly a decade—I'd even run across a couple of others like me, but they were as confused and clueless as I was.

"Then I met Jag. He was the one who taught me what my heritage really meant. He offered me a place in his pack and schooled me in the ways of the *vargr*. Before then, I had been a loner—without friends or family, preying on those society shunned: junkies, hookers, hustlers, queers, runaways, pimps, and johns.

"I was nothing more than a murdering cannibal, incapable of sharing my thoughts with anyone for fear of exposing myself. My loneliness was driving me mad. Jag gave me the chance to be part of something bigger—for the first time in my life, I knew what it was like to feel secure.

"Jag gave me all this, Skinner. I can't rat on him because of what happened with Bender. While I don't always approve of the things Jag does, or how he does them, he's still my friend. I'll never turn against him, no matter *what* happens.

"Now get to bed. Tomorrow is the rut melee. You're going to need all your strength if you want to survive."

Just before dawn, there was a light rapping on the door. Someone was going up and down the hall, knocking on each of the doors. Rend tossed back the covers on his bed and leaned over and shook Skinner.

"Wake up! It's time for the melee!" His voice held the excitement and anticipation of a child announcing Christmas morning had arrived.

Skinner reached for his clothes, but Rend stayed his hand.

"There's no need for that. Come, follow me."

Skinner followed Rend out into the hall. There were several other *vargr* there as well, all of them naked. Silently, they padded along the carpet toward the central lobby. Close to four dozen nude men of various ages and physical builds moved down the stairs and headed out the front door. Skinner had to force himself not to giggle at the sight of some of the older *vargr*, who were far from imposing when seen butt-naked, trying to maintain their dignity.

The brisk morning air hit Skinner's bare flesh the moment he stepped outside, tightening his scrotum and raising goose pimples on every available surface. His first instinct was to drop his human skin, but Rend caught his eye and shook his head.

They continued walking across the neatly manicured lawn, heading in the direction of the treeline. Skinner felt something pass through him like a jolt of low-voltage electricity. It made his scalp prickle and the tips of his fingers and the bottom of his feet pulse. With every step he took, the throbbing in his extremities grew more intense, until it felt like his body was keeping time to an unheard drumbeat. He glanced down and saw that his penis was completely engorged, pointing the way for him like a divining rod.

After a few minutes, he came upon a natural clearing in the woods half the size of a football field. In the middle of the clearing was a huge boulder that jutted out of the ground like the fossilized shoulder blade of some long-extinct beast. Perched atop the boulder was Jez, naked except for body paint and a necklace fashioned from rawhide and dead men's teeth. Jag hunkered at the base of the rut-altar, the ruling consort protecting his office.

Jez got to her feet and surveyed the congregation. She was now obviously the most important member of the pack, deciding the pace and direction in which the rut would go. Smiling to herself, she squatted on her haunches and let loose with a stream of hot, pungent urine that steamed in the cold morning air.

Her heat wafted down to her waiting suitors, filling the clearing with the scent of the most primal of needs. The assembled males moaned and growled, sprouting fur and fang in response to her fragrance.

As he shed his human skin, Skinner felt the last traces of reason slip away. There was only a hot coal between his legs and the knowledge that the only way it was going to stop burning was if he plunged it into Jez.

The assembled males moved into the clearing, converging on the rut-altar. Jag shifted, revealing bared fangs and ears flattened against his skull, and prepared to stand his ground. Then all hell broke loose.

The first males to accidentally brush up against one another went berserk, lashing out with their claws and teeth, biting and slashing indiscriminately. It looked and sounded like the world's biggest dog fight.

Skinner found himself under attack from a heavyset *vargr* with a dark, thick pelt whose eyes rolled in their sockets like a drunken lunatic's. The *vargr* directed powerful snapping movements at his throat. Skinner averted his head, growling loudly. The *vargr* tried to go for his throat again, only this time Skinner was ready for him, sinking his teeth deep into the fur at the back of his opponent's neck and shaking him vigorously. The bigger werewolf began to yelp and scream, but Skinner refused to let go. Finally, his opponent tore himself free, yowling in pain, and abandoned the field. Skinner spat out the mouthful of fur and flesh and continued trying to fight his way to the front.

Fur, blood, and feces flew in every possible direction as the *vargr* males set among themselves, tearing at one another with their talons and teeth. The weaker, more submissive males were quickly chased off or exited the fray, shitting themselves in fear.

Those who had received serious wounds or were hurt badly enough that self-preservation overrode the desire to reproduce, did their best to crawl from the surging mass of snarling, snapping beast-men. Even these crippled noncombatants were still subject to being savaged by their fellow *vargr*. Hew leapt atop the Hound, whose left leg had been all but severed at the hip, as he was dragging himself across the blood-soaked battle-field with his bare hands. Hew snatched up a nearby rock and began pounding it against the old Celt's skull until blood and brains flew.

In the midst of the rut melee, there was no recognition of friend, brother, or lover. Fenris bit off Amadeo's first and second fingers on his left hand, swallowing them ring and all. Ripper leapt onto Hew's broad back, slashing at his neck with razor-sharp talons. Rend sank his fangs into Skinner's shoulder, worrying him like a terrier would a rat. Skinner howled and broke Rend's right arm like a dry stick.

And during all the blood and pain, Jez sat atop the altar stone and looked down at the frenzy she had created and giggled like a demented school-girl, clapping her hands and rocking back and forth.

Suddenly, Skinner found himself confronting Jag. The reigning consort's spoiled cream pelt was stained with gore, his muzzle darkened with the blood of his sister's would-be suitors. When Jag saw who was challenging him, his brows tight-ened and his hackles rose even higher than before. The two surged toward one another, teeth bared and fur bristling.

Jag's teeth sank into the shoulder Rend had wounded earlier, causing Skinner to shriek in pain. Skinner tried to free himself, but Jag would not let go. Blood pumped from Skinner's shoulder, staining his silvery pelt. He knew the moment he fell, Jag would be at his throat. Howling his anger, pain, and defiance, Skinner clawed desperately at his attacker's face, plunging a talon into Jag's eye.

Jag let go of Skinner's shoulder, staggering backward with one hand clamped over his wounded socket. Blood and a clear, viscous jelly oozed from between his fingers and down his cheek. He screamed something unintelligible and abruptly left the battleground.

Skinner scaled the altar stone, leaving the confusion and bloodletting of the melee behind him. His nostrils flared, drawing in the smell of Jez' heat. The burning in his loins was so strong now it erased all thought. All that mattered was the bitch awaiting him.

Jez presented herself to Skinner in the manner of a she-wolf, approaching him sideways and then in front, her rump turned to one side. With a growl of agonized anticipation, Skinner mounted her from behind, pushing his rigid member deep into her bleeding vagina. Jez yowled and shivered as he penetrated her. After a few vigorous thrusts, the two locked as Skinner's penis swelled within her vagina.

Jez began to panic, squealing loudly and trying to bite Skinner. Firmly seated, Skinner cuffed her ears and dug his teeth into the nape of her neck, pinning her to the rut-altar's stained surface as he continued humping her from behind. He was vaguely aware that the others had ceased their fighting below and were now watching them.

One of the males still left standing made a tentative approach toward the altar, only to have Skinner halt in mid-thrust and display his teeth and growl. The other quickly backed off. Besides, while Skinner and Jez remained locked at the groin, none of the others stood a chance. After a few minutes, the failed suitors began to leave the clearing, indifferent to the companions they'd wounded earlier, left dead or dying on the battlefield.

As far as Skinner was concerned, nothing existed beyond the thrusting of his penis. His full attention was fixed on relieving the ache in his balls as he pounded relentlessly against Jez.

They still lay locked, belly to back, as the sun came up, drying the blood that covered the surrounding grass like morning dew. Every movement Jez made further excited Skinner's engorged organ, setting off round after round of frenzied rutting. Skinner had already climaxed at least three times, but his penis remained trapped within Jez's swollen vagina. Exhausted, he fell asleep, firmly entrenched, only to wake an hour later to find Jez squirming against his crotch, begging him to quench the fire gnawing at her womb.

They copulated furiously until Skinner was shooting air and Jez jerked and flailed like a monkey on a stick. Fatigued and dehydrated, the lovers collapsed into a deep sleep. When Skinner woke again, it was to find himself alone and the sun dipping behind the trees. His pelt was stiff from sweat, blood, and vaginal secretions, and his penis felt like he'd spent the last twelve hours masturbating with sandpaper.

His joints creaked and his muscles ached as he climbed down and surveyed the carnage that radiated from the rut-altar like spokes from the hub of a wagon wheel. He spotted the Hound's carcass almost immediately, the back of its skull staved in so fiercely what was left of the face was buried in the blood-caked soil. A few yards away from the fallen Celtic warrior, Amadeo lay surrounded by his own buzzard-gnawed viscera. As he walked from the clearing, Skinner came across more *vargr* corpses. The sight of their savaged bodies, looking like broken toys mired in the churned mud and gore of the battlefield, made his gut tighten.

He'd been weak. He'd allowed himself to be overwhelmed by a bloodlust that made him fight friend and foe alike. And what had he won? The privilege to empty his seed into a woman he didn't even like, much less love.

As his memories of the rut melee began to resurface, Skinner groaned and clutched his stomach. Unable to fight his revulsion any longer, he fell to his knees and vomited until his ribs ached.

God.

What am I turning into?

Chapter Twenty

"I guess this changes everything, huh?" Rend said, standing in the open bathroom doorway, watching Skinner through the frosted glass pane of the shower.

"I don't see why it should," Skinner replied, soaping the matted blood, sweat and jism out of his pubic hair.

"You don't see ...?" Rend sounded genuinely incredulous. "Skinner! You won the rut melee! You're Jez's consort! That means you're the Alpha of our pack!"

"I thought that was up to her to decide—you know, assuming I pleased her. What if she still prefers Jag?"

"She's not going to want him hanging around her, now that he's missing an eye."

"Yeah, but that'll regenerate, won't it?"

"Eyes, brain tissue, and the spinal column are the only things on a *vargr* that once damaged stay damaged. You marked him for life, Skin. And for *vargr* that can be a damn long time—especially for someone as vain as Jag. You're in like Flynn, cuz!"

"So?"

"You don't sound very excited."

"That's because I'm not. None of this means anything to me, Rend."

"If it doesn't mean anything to you, why did you fight your way to the rut-altar?"

"Instinct, I guess. It had nothing to do with *me*, though. It was something I did, that's all. I'm neither proud nor ashamed of it."

Rend shook his head in wonder. "I don't understand you at all, cuz." There was a light touch on his shoulder. Jez was standing behind him, dressed in nothing but a towel. She jerked her thumb in the direction of the door. Rend nodded his understanding and slipped away silently.

Jez let her towel fall to the tiled floor and stepped into the shower with Skinner, who was standing under the running water with his eyes shut, rinsing the shampoo from his hair.

"I just don't see what's so important about—" He gasped as Jez reached out and grabbed his freshly washed cock. Skinner nearly jumped through the frosted glass door.

"Rend?" Skinner opened his eyes, blinking rapidly in order to keep the soap from running into them.

Jez smiled up into his face, pressing herself against his slick, naked body. "Hi there, lover," she purred. "Miss me?"

"Jez! What are you doing here?"

"What's it look like, brave dog?" She dropped to her knees, running her lips over his belly, her tongue flicking against the head of his penis. He was sorely tempted to simply close his eyes and surrender to the sensation, but he pushed her away.

"Stop it, Jez! Who said you could come in here? What about Jag?"

Jez laughed huskily, tossing her wet hair out of her face. "You don't have to worry about him, my brave little doggie. *You're* my consort now. I can fuck you whenever and wherever I like. . . ." She reached out and cupped his testicles in her warm, soapy hand. "Doesn't that sound just *yummy*?"

Skinner ground his teeth together and tried to maneuver himself so that their bodies weren't touching in the close confines of the shower. "Look, Jez . . . I don't think you really understand how I feel. . . ."

Jez smirked and caressed his rapidly swelling penis. "Oh, I know how you *feel* alright, lover. You feel *damn* good!"

Skinner's muscles began to bunch and shift under his skin. He was on the verge of an involuntary shift. He knew if he succumbed to Jez, he'd end up screwing her again. And again. And again. His hand closed on the water faucet and, with a sudden, violent motion, twisted it to the left.

Jez screamed and jumped out of the shower as the ice-cold water sluiced over her flesh. Skinner's skin puckered into goose pimples and his penis shrank, short-circuiting his shift from man to *vargr*.

"What's *wrong* with you?" Jez hissed, wrapping her shivering body in a towel.

Skinner stepped out of the shower, brushing past her into his room, where he quickly pulled on his pants. "You said you're free to fuck me whenever *you* want. You didn't bother asking *me* whether I was interested in participating or not."

"What are you saying?"

"I'm saying go away. I don't want you."

Jez stood there, clutching her towel to her bosom and gaping at him as if he'd just told her the sky was falling.

"That's impossible! I've chosen you as my consort! You *have* to want me!"

"Oh, yeah?" Skinner grabbed her by the elbow and all but dragged her to the door. "Just *watch* me!" With that, he propelled her into the hallway.

Skinner slammed the door in Jez' shocked face, sagging against it in relief. That was close. He had never dreamed he'd see the day when he would deliberately throw a beautiful naked woman who wanted his body out of his bedroom. But then, he'd never dreamed of being a murderer, either.

"He did *what*?" Lady Erzule looked up from her tea, the porcelain cup frozen halfway from the saucer.

"He threw me out of the room!" Jez sobbed.

Erzule blinked in confusion, then looked at her consort. "I've never heard of a *vargr* male doing such a thing—he's not homosexual, is he? There have been incidents where homosexual *vargr* have won the rut melee. If my memory serves me, I had a cub by Lord Reynard under similar circumstances. . . ."

"He's not gay, Mother!" Jez sniffed. "He said he didn't want me!"

"You don't *have* to take him as your consort, *ma petite*. There is no rule that states the winner of the rut melee *must* be your consort. It just usually works out that way."

"But I want *him*!"

"Let me kill him."

Jez and Erzule turned to look at the figure standing in the doorway. Jaz stepped forward, one hand straying to the black satin patch that covered his ruined left eye. "He has disgraced my sister. Let me kill him."

Erzule flared her nostrils in contempt. "You will do no such thing! You no longer have any say in your sister's affairs!"

Jag glowered at his mother reclining on her chaise lounge, wrapped in yards of diaphanous negligee. Lord Feral sat in a nearby straight-backed chair, hands clamped atop his knees, watching his son with quiet intent.

"I want to hear Jez tell me that, not *you*," he snarled. "*She's* my queen, not *you*, old bitch."

Erzule's spine stiffened and Feral's shoulders tightened. Jez blushed and cast her eyes downward.

"How dare you speak to me in such a fashion!"

"Because it's *true*," Jag retorted, deliberately showing his teeth in a humorless grin. "Your time is almost up as bitch queen. You know it. I know it. The whole fuckin' *pack* knows it, Mother dearest! Your only hope of remaining in power is by manipulating Jez—keeping her dependent on you. Otherwise, she'll have you ostracized—just like you had your demi-sister chased from the pack when she became sterile, six hundred years ago." Jag knelt beside his sister, folding her hand in his, and looked up into her face. "Please, Jez . . . let me kill him."

Jez stared into her twin brother's remaining eye, then glanced nervously at her mother. "I—I—"

"Please, Jez . . ."

She bit her lower lip and shook her head. "No. I don't want him dead."

Jag snarled and jerked his hand away from hers, storming out of the room.

"Jag! No! You don't understand—" Jez cried out, hurrying after her brother.

Erzule shook her head in disgust and resumed sipping her tea. "Jag has far too much influence over her. It's unbecoming."

"Such is the nature of twins," Feral observed.

"I suppose so. I had hoped she would end up mated with Bender this time out, though. . . ." She fell silent at the mention of her favorite's name, her eyes glazing.

Feral fidgeted uncomfortably. He had spent twenty-five years living in the shadow of Mammon, his immediate predecessor, and loathed it whenever Erzule became nostalgic for her former consort. Despite her claims to the contrary, Feral knew Erzule would never truly forgive him for killing her lover.

Feral cleared his throat, hopefully derailing Erzule's train of thought. "Still, we must address the problem concerning Skinner, my lady."

"Indeed." Erzule shook her head. "What kind of *vargr* is this young Skinner, anyway? If he's uninterested in Jez, then what exactly is it that he wants?"

They were keeping her locked in the basement. This much Skinner was able to find out without drawing attention to himself. He knew he didn't have much time to act, whatever the case. Soon Feral would have Rosie removed and dragged through the surrounding woods as prelude to the Hunt. If he was going to do anything, it would have to be now.

He had noticed several of the attendant *vargr*, the ones who seemed to be permanent members of the lodge's staff, coming and going via the service elevators. After scouting around, he found a disused stairwell that led to the lower depths of the lodge.

He found himself in what looked to be the boiler room, over half of which was dominated by a coal-fed monstrosity that looked like a postmodern Hindu god, its myriad pipe arms branching out and upward. Luckily, no one was tending the furnace when he made his appearance.

He scouted the corridor before stepping into it, and heaved a sigh of relief. He hadn't exactly figured out how he was going to find Rosie in the first place, much less rescue her, but he couldn't stand by and let Feral and the others use her as blood sport.

The one thing he was certain of, however, was that he was completely on his own. He could not rely on anyone but himself. While he considered Rend and Shaggybreeks to be sympathetic, they saw themselves as *vargr* first and foremost, and neither was willing to risk their standing in the pack for the sake of a *coyotero*.

Skinner crept along the hallway, trying to keep to the shadows, casting about for a trace scent that might give him a clue to Rosie's whereabouts. There were several rooms along the corridor, left-over from the days when the lodge had actually been a resort. A few of the doors had what looked like peepholes drilled into them at eye-level. Curious, Skinner peeked into the first room.

He saw two young human males, naked except for the manacles that tethered them to the canvas cots, which were the only furniture in the tiny cubicle. Both men were unnaturally pale and swaddled in roll upon roll of fat. The stink of human feces and urine was so potent he could smell it through the door.

Skinner moved to the next room, which hosted a couple of unwashed young women, each obviously pregnant. Like the males, they too were naked and handcuffed to their beds. Their eyes were glazed, their faces slack. It was hard to tell whether they were drugged or simply driven mad by their ordeal.

The third, fourth, and fifth rooms contained women fattened to enormous proportions. Their eyes flickered about nervously at the sound of the peephole's covering being slid back and shifted their bulks uneasily. They reminded Skinner of livestock about to enter the slaughtering pen. And as far as Erzule, Feral, and the other *vargr* were concerned, that's exactly what they were.

He was beginning to despair of ever finding Rosie when he looked into the sixth cubicle. What he saw shocked and angered him so greatly, he shifted into his Wild skin without being aware of doing so.

Rosie, naked except for a studded leather dog

collar big enough for a rottweiller, was chained to a ring set in the wall. Her long black hair had come unbraided and hung loose, shrouding her shoulders and face. She was on her hands and knees, and a *vargr* male with a pelt the color of tobacco juice was mounting her from behind. The automatic weapon slung over his crooked, hairy shoulder marked him as one of the guards.

Skinner snarled and kicked open the door, knocking it off its hinges. The surprised *vargr* yanked himself free, standing there with his glistening erect penis jutting out of its furry sheath, just as Skinner's jaws clamped onto his throat. The guard's neck snapped between his teeth like a chicken leg. He didn't even have time to whimper.

Skinner knelt beside Rosie, brushing her hair out of her eyes. There were bruises dappling her velvety skin and several fresh scratches and bite marks across her back and on the insides of her thighs. The sight made him so angry he growled.

She looked up at him, struggling to understand what was going on through her drug-induced haze. He could tell it was all she could do to lift her head and squint in the direction of his voice. At first she cringed at the sight of the *vargr* male with the silvery pelt reaching out for her, issuing something between a whimper of fear and a snarl of defiance.

"Don't be afraid. Please . . . don't be afraid. I'm here to help you, Rosie."

She frowned, her brow creasing. "You—know my name. . . ." she said, the words coming out as a dry, cracked whisper.

"My name's Skinner. You met me at Root Woman's house, back in Arizona."

Rosie's lids fluttered and her eyes rolled in confused circles, flashing alternating glimpses of gold and white.

"Grandmother . . ." she croaked. Her body suddenly went limp in his arms.

Skinner removed the dog collar from her throat, wincing when he saw the blisters on her neck and collarbone. He had to get her as far away from this place as fast as possible. There was no telling what kind of tortures she'd been put through in the last few days. Skinner was uncertain exactly how *coyotero* differed from *vargr* physically, but it was a sure bet they were mortal.

He turned his attention back to the slain guard. It wasn't a pretty sight. During his last few seconds of life, the *vargr* had attempted to shift back into his human skin and was now permanently frozen between the two states. Still, there was enough there for Skinner to recognize him as Snuff, the guard who had executed the *esau* the night of the Bal Masque.

Skinner stripped the corpse of its Uzi, checking the clip to make sure it was loaded. A magazine of silver-jacketed hollow-point bullets gleamed reassuringly in the dim light. He also took the dead guard's discarded corduroy shirt and dressed Rosie in it. Slinging the automatic weapon over one shoulder, he gathered Rosie's unconscious body into his arms and hurried back the way he'd come.

As he climbed up the stairwell, Skinner wondered what the hell he thought he was doing. He

had no earthly idea how he was going to smuggle
Rosie out of the lodge without anyone spotting
them. And even if he succeeded in getting outside,
there was still the problem of getting off the
grounds themselves. Snuff might be dead, but
there were certainly other guards patrolling the
area. And since Rosie was currently incapable of
aiding in her own escape, he was uncertain just
how far he'd be able to get on foot saddled with
dead weight. And it certainly didn't help that the
only thing going through his mind at the moment
was a little rhyme his mother had been fond of
reciting when he was a child:

When in trouble,
or in doubt,
run in circles,
scream and shout.

Skinner stepped out of the stairwell and into the
ground floor hallway just in time to hear someone
approaching. Testing a nearby door and finding it
unlocked, he quickly ducked inside.

The room was illuminated by subdued colored
track-mounted spotlights, the walls hung with me-
dieval tapestries depicting the glories of the hunt.
Rosie moaned slightly, forcing Skinner to clamp
his hand over her mouth for fear the *vargr* passing
outside would hear her.

". . . wanted it that way." He recognized the
basso profundo rumble as belonging to
Shaggybreeks.

"I suppose it's the thought that counts," responded his companion, one of the younger *vargr*. "By the way ... was he Viking?"

"Celt."

"Oh."

As they continued to discuss the Hound's funeral arrangements, Skinner lowered Rosie to the floor and turned to study the room further. It was then he noticed the altar.

It was roughly the size and shape of an old-fashioned hope chest, fashioned from rosewood and draped in the skins of true-wolves. The Wolfcane was fixed into a special notched holder that kept the staff held upright, flanked by two huge black smoldering tapers as thick as a man's arm.

Skinner stared up into the Wolfcane's frozen snarl, marveling at the rich detail of the ornamentation. He could almost count the hairs on its head. In the light from the spots, it seemed as if the Wolfcane's ruby eyes were alive and aware, bidding him to draw closer.

Feeling as if pulled along by a string, his eyes still fixed on the staff's gleaming silver head, Skinner took a step forward. The Wolfcane was suddenly enveloped by a radiant halo of blue witchfire. Instinctively lifting a hand to shield his eyes, Skinner noticed that his fur was standing on end, the tips crackling with static electricity.

Before he could react, a tongue of bluish-white light leapt from the head of the Wolfcane and struck him between the eyes, knocking him to the floor.

Skinner saw a great wolf made of blue fire running toward him. As the creature came closer, it grew bigger and bigger, until it was the size of a grizzly bear. The beast loomed over Skinner, straddling his body with its forepaws. When it breathed, it sounded like a steam engine idling at the station. Somehow Skinner knew this was the spirit of the great dire wolf, the prehistoric monster made extinct during the Pleistocene, ten thousand years ago.

The dire wolf thrust its massive head forward until its huge muzzle nearly touched his own, forcing him to look into its eyes. Skinner saw twin orbs of bubbling liquid fire, as if the beast leaning over him was filled with boiling lava.

Skinner looked again, and he saw a world of endless forest and far-reaching grasslands, filled with wooly mammoths, shaggy rhinoceroses, sabertoothed tigers, giant ground sloths, four-pronged antelope, and fierce cave bears. And he saw man. Or what was to soon call itself man.

The world within the dire wolf's eyes changed. Ice and snow claimed the forests and plains. The mammoths and sloths and antelopes grew thin and collapsed, the bones of the predators soon mingling with those of their erstwhile prey.

The dire wolf spoke, its words rumbling deep inside Skinner's head. It was the voice of the god of all wolves.

Beware the return of the Great Extinction.

Skinner saw the world inside the dire wolf's eyes suddenly wither. He saw the ancient forests disappear amid a haze of smoke and the scream of chainsaws. He saw the rivers and lakes choked by agricultural runoff. He saw ice caps melt and farmlands turn to desert. He saw both man and animal burn like insects trapped under a child's magnifying glass. Only this time there would be no new beginnings. Only starvation, disease, and strife, leading to the ending from which there is no return.

The dire wolf growled, its chest rumbling like a volcano about to explode, and its huge fangs flashed downward, closing on Skinner's throat. He tried to scream, but all that came out of his mouth was the crackle of electricity.

The dire wolf was gone as if it had never existed, although the room stank of ozone. Skinner picked himself off the floor, feeling wobbly. He rubbed his aching forehead, fixing the Wolfcane with a curious stare.

What the hell was all that about?

The Wolfcane remained mute.

Rosie moaned again, drawing his attention away from the totem. He had to get her out of the lodge. He glanced back at the Wolfcane.

What the hell.

The moment his hand closed on the staff's polished ebony shaft, his fur prickled. Whatever the Wolfcane might be, it was a focal point for some form of energy. The sensation it sparked in him was weird, but not unpleasantly so.

He returned to where Rosie lay and picked her up, tossing her over his right shoulder so that he held the Uzi in one hand, the Wolfcane in the other.

"C'mon, girl. Let's blow this popsicle stand."

They managed to get as far as the parking lot before being spotted. Skinner was moving fast and low, doing his best to keep to the deep shadows, when he was hit from behind by what felt like a Mack truck.

The force of the blow knocked him off his feet, sending Rosie and the gun flying. Instinctively, he used the blunt end of the Wolfcane to strike back at his attacker.

The *vargr* grunted and staggered backward when the blow landed on his temple. Skinner felt his guts clench as he saw the mohawk crest starting between the werewolf's ears and running down its back. It was Hew.

The hulking werewolf snarled when he saw who he was facing. "*You*! I thought it was some fuckin' *coyotero*. But it's *you*! Jag was right! You *aren't* one of us! You're a fuckin' *traitor*!"

"Hew . . . I don't want to hurt you. . . ."

"I'm shaking." The bigger werewolf snorted. His eyes suddenly widened as he saw what Skinner held in his hands. "The Wolfcane! You're trying to steal the Wolfcane!"

Before he could move to protect himself, Skinner found Hew's taloned fingers curled around his throat, fangs snapping shut a millimeter in front of his nose. He dropped the Wolfcane, digging his own fingers into Hew's thick, muscle-corded neck, doing his best to force Hew's slavering jaws back.

The struggling werewolves fell to the ground, rolling around in the loose gravel of the parking lot, growling and snarling like rabid dogs. Skinner fought like a mad thing, but it was no use. Hew was nearly twice his size, outweighing him by a good fifty pounds. It was only a matter of time until he would get enough leverage to snap Skinner's neck like a dry twig.

Using his superior strength, Hew rolled his opponent onto his back, pinning his arms to his side. "You don't deserve to run with us," he hissed into Skinner's face. "You're nothing but a stinking, lousy traitor!" Hew reached out with and picked up the fallen Wolfcane, lifting it high to deliver a single, killing blow to Skinner's skull.

Something big and hairy blind-sided Hew in the chest, knocking him clear of Skinner. Hew yelped in alarmed confusion once, then there was the sound of massive, powerful jaws tearing into meat and bone.

Something warm and wet and sticky dripped into Skinner's face. He stared up at the creature crouching over him. At first he thought it was a wolf. It wasn't until it whined and licked his nose that he recognized the beast as the *ulfr* he had freed from the trap a few days earlier.

"Good boy," he rasped, getting to his feet.

Hew lay sprawled on his back, his throat torn out and his head hanging by a few shreds of muscle, his arms and legs spread akimbo. He looked like he was trying to make snow angels in a pool of his own blood.

The *ulfr* trotted over to Hew's corpse, sniffed it, then raised a leg and let loose with a steaming arc of piss.

"I like your style, fella." Skinner smiled crookedly, bending to retrieve the Wolfcane.

"You know they're not going to let you get away with this, pup."

The *ulfr* bared its teeth at the unseen newcomer, flattening its ears against its skull and lifting its tail in challenge.

Shaggybreeks stepped out of the shadows, clothed in his human skin. The *ulfr*, upon seeing him, lifted its ears and began wagging its tail.

Shaggybreeks pointed to Hew's body. There was a great sadness in the old Viking's voice. "They'll bring you down like a winded deer. You don't stand a chance, lad. Not on foot."

"Are you going to try and stop me?"

Shaggybreeks shrugged wearily. "Why should I? I have nothing in common with these inbred fools. The fact the *ulfr* has cast its lot with yours is a good sign, as far as I'm concerned." He pulled a keychain out of his vest pocket and tossed it to Skinner. "Here. Take this. It's the keys to the Hound's car. The '59 Caddy. It's yours—provided you do me a favor."

"Sure."

"Take the Hound with you."

"But—isn't he dead?"

"As he'll ever be. But that's not the point. I want you to take his body with you. All I ask is that once you've gotten as far as you can in the Caddy, you set both it—and the Hound—on fire. Ideally, I would have preferred to have set him adrift on a blazing funeral barge . . . but you can't have everything. Still, I think he would have approved."

Skinner and Shaggybreeks hurried to the waiting Caddy, Rosie suspended between them like a ragdoll. Skinner placed her carefully on the floor of the backseat, draping an old car rug and a pile of dirty laundry on top of her. He turned to face Shaggybreeks.

"The Hound's in the trunk. I already wrapped

him in his winding sheet and put the coin under his tongue. The rest is up to you."

"What about you? What will happen if they find out you helped us escape?"

The old Viking shrugged indifferently. "If it is my time to die, so be it. But they'll have to catch me first. Much has changed since I first came into this world, young Skinner. I have watched its boundaries grow until it became so big I no longer had a place in it. To hell with everything—both human and *vargr*!"

Skinner opened the driver's door. Before he could climb in, the *ulfr* bounded into the car ahead of him, positioning itself on the passenger's side of the front seat, wagging its tail. Skinner paused.

"Shaggybreeks—come with us. It's not too late. . . ."

The old Viking laughed and clapped him on the shoulder. "Don't worry about me, pup! I might be unafraid to die, but I'm far from digging my own grave! I think I'll drop my human skin, and run Wild once and for all. Who knows? Maybe I'll find myself a nice little she-wolf, just like Mama, to spend my declining years with! Now clear out of here, before the rest of the lodge finds out what you've been up to!"

Skinner slid behind the wheel of the vintage Cadillac and closed the door. The engine turned over immediately. Skinner was duly impressed. It might look like the Batmobile, but compared to his stepfather's old pickup, the Hound's Caddy was a mechanic's wet dream.

Skinner threw the Caddy into gear and headed away from the lodge. As he drew closer to the front gate, he could see two guards talking into their hand-held radios. Suddenly, one of them caught sight of the approaching vehicle and pointed. The second dropped his radio and reached for the Uzi slung across his back.

Skinner stuck the automatic weapon he'd lifted from Snuff out the driver's window, squeezing off bursts with one hand while keeping the other on the steering wheel as the Caddy bounced along the rutted dirt road.

The spray of silver bullets from his gun stitched across the ground and up the side of the second guard. The first guard let fly with his own barrage, taking out the passenger-side rearview mirror and blinding one of the highbeams before the Cadillac rolled over him. The *ulfr* stood with its front paws on the dashboard, barking enthusiastically and wagging its tail the whole time.

Skinner was so excited he didn't even realize he was still in his Wild skin until almost a half hour later, when a truck that had just passed him going the opposite direction nearly skidded off the highway.

Chapter Twenty-one

"I knew the cur was trouble from the start," growled Lord Feral.

"You should have let me kill him," snarled Jag, fingering the black satin patch covering his ruined eye.

"I heard you the first time, dear." Lady Erzule sighed. Patting her hair, she turned to fix Rend with a disapproving scowl. "I hold you personally responsible, Rend. After all, it was you who first brought this—this—*traître* into our midst!"

Rend lowered his eyes, unwilling to meet the gazes of those surrounding him. He had failed the pack.

Jez sat on the chaise lounge, sniffling into one of her dame's lace hankies. "But I don't *want* him dead! I want him *alive*!"

"Now, now, *cherie*. You can't have everything your way," clucked Erzule.

"Why *not*?" Jez sobbed.

Erzule sighed again and returned her attention to Rend. "As penance for your sin against the pack, you will track down the traitor and kill both him and the *coyotero* bitch. You will also secure the return of the Wolfcane to its rightful place.

Failure to do so will be punished by death. Is that understood?"

"Yes, milady."

"Very good. Now get out of my sight. I don't want to see you again unless you have the cur Skinner's head in one hand and the Wolfcane in the other."

Whatever the Hound might have been during his lifetime, he certainly hadn't been poor. A search of the cavernous glove compartment produced several credit cards bearing various different names, all of them Irish, and a roll of bills big enough to choke a pygmy hippo. Since Skinner had been forced to clothe himself in the Hound's dirty laundry, he was more than overjoyed by the discovery. He got off Highway 160 in Durango long enough to find a general store and buy himself some clothes that actually fit.

The store's owner had at first been suspicious of the barefoot young man with the silvery hair, dressed in a shirt three sizes too big and pair of pants so large they were held up by a length of cord. However, the minute the money came out, the shopkeeper's reservations vanished and he was more than happy to outfit Skinner with cowboy boots, jeans, flannel shirts, and a denim jacket. While he was at it, Skinner also bought Rosie some clothes, although he was forced to guess her size, since she was still unconscious in the back of the car.

A few miles out of Durango, Rosie finally started to wake up. The first thing she did upon coming to her senses was sit up, look around with a dazed expression on her face, and vomit copiously all over the backseat.

The *ulfr* leaned over the front seat and whined while Skinner watched Rosie in the rearview mirror.

"Wh—where am I?" she groaned.

"You're in a 1959 Cadillac, headed west on Highway 160."

She rubbed at her puffy, swollen eyes and frowned at the back of Skinner's head. "Who are you?"

"Don't you remember?"

Rosie bit her lower lip and looked out the window at the passing scenery. "All too much. But I don't recall you."

"You met me at your grandmother's house in Arizona."

She jerked her head back in his direction. He could see her looking into the mirror, and for a fleeting second their reflected gazes met and held.

"I *thought* you looked familiar. I'm sorry I pointed that rifle at you back then. For all I knew, you were just another *vargr* trying to get Root Woman to tell you where my people are hiding."

"Then she's not really your grandmother?"

"If you mean is she my mother's mother—no, she's not. Root Woman is human. But she *did* raise me."

Skinner wanted to ask her some more questions, but she was already turning green around the mouth again. This time she managed to roll down the window and stick her head outside. The *ulfr* thought this was an excellent idea and used its prehensile thumb to roll down *its* window as well.

It was going to be one hell of a road trip.

Skinner pulled into a tiny off-brand motel just off the highway in Tuba City, Arizona, later that night. He registered under the name Cormac O'Herlihy, using one of the Hound's myriad credit cards to pay for the room.

As he signed the register, the motel manager squinted in the direction of the Caddy, parked just outside the office door.

"You're going to have to put your dog in our kennel overnight, Mr. O'Herlihy. It's a state rule."

"Dog?" Skinner turned around to see what the hell the desk clerk was talking about. The *ulfr* was sitting in the front seat next to Rosie. In the poor light and with its tongue hanging from the corner of its mouth, it could almost pass for a particularly large German shepherd or Husky.

"Oh! The *dog*! I almost forgot about him! He's so much a part of the family I tend to forget he's, uh, you know—not human."

The desk clerk smiled and nodded. "My wife's the same way with her Chihuahua. The kennel is located next to the swimming pool area. Here's the master key. It will unlock any of the three pens. I hope you and your wife will have a pleasant stay."

"Look, I don't like this any more than you do," Skinner whispered to the *ulfr*. They were standing in front of the kennel, which consisted of a bare poured-concrete slab surrounded by a six-foot high hurricane fence and subdivided into three individual pens about three feet wide and eight feet deep.

Skinner squatted so that he was eye level with the *ulfr*, ruffling its thick neck-ruff. "Until we reach Rosie's people, we're all going to have to pretend we're something we're not. We can't draw any attention to ourselves—do you understand me?"

The *ulfr* whined and tried to tug its head free of Skinner's grip. He touched the half-wolf's muzzle, forcing it to look him directly in the eye.

"C'mon, fella. It's *important*. Do you understand?"

The *ulfr* whined again, licked Skinner's face, and walked into the pen.

"That's a good boy!" Skinner closed the door of the pen, smiling at his friend. "I'll buy you a nice fresh t-bone tomorrow, okay? How's that sound?"

As he walked across the recreation green, Skinner noticed a middle-aged man lounging in an open doorway a couple of units down from the one he was sharing with Rosie. His suit was rumpled and his tie askew, a cigarette pinched between his fingers. He looked like the stereotypical traveling salesman.

"You really got that dog of yours trained, buddy!" the salesman commented. "I wish I could get my beagle to behave like that."

"Yeah—well, he's a really smart dog."

"What's his name?"

"Uh—Fella."

"Fella, huh? That's a good, solid name for a dog that size. I can't stand it when people name their dogs shit like 'Brittany' and 'Loverboy.' What kinda name is that for a big dog, huh? So—what is he? Some kind of mix? I've never seen a dog that large before."

"He's, uh, half-wolf."

The salesman raised an eyebrow. "Really? Wow! Is he dangerous?"

"Not to me."

Rosie was sitting cross-legged on the double bed nearest the wall watching the television when he came in. She was dressed in the loose-fitting flannel shirt and jeans he'd bought for her earlier. Her hair was freshly washed and fanned across her shoulders to dry. The bruises had vanished from her face, but she still looked pale, despite her natural complexion.

"You feeling okay?"

"I feel a lot better than I did. Thanks for buying me these clothes."

"Don't thank me. Thank the Hound."

She frowned in puzzlement "Who's the Hound?"

"He's the *vargr* who used to own the car we're driving. Not to mention the credit cards we're using."

"Does he know this?"

"He doesn't know much of anything anymore. He's dead and packed in the trunk. I promised a friend I'd, uh, see to his funeral arrangements."

She seemed to take it all in stride. "I see. And what about the *ulfr*? Where'd he come from?"

"I helped him free himself from a trap on the

lodge grounds. He saved my bacon when I was trying to rescue you."

Rosie tilted her head and smiled with the corner of her mouth. "Do you always go out of your way to help others?"

Skinner felt his cheeks color. He shrugged and sat down in the room's solitary chair. "That's the way I was raised. If someone's in trouble, you try to help them. . . ."

Rosie barked a tiny laugh. "You *are* a strange *vargr*!"

He fixed her with a golden stare that was a twin of her own. "Is it so strange for a *vargr* to show compassion?"

"You mean to something besides a fellow *vargr*? I don't think you need me to answer that."

"Tell me about yourself, then. Tell me about your people. Why do the *vargr* hate you so?"

"They don't *hate* us, they *fear* us."

"Why are they afraid of your people, then?"

"Because we still have magic." When she saw the look of confusion on his face, she smiled apologetically. "There is a story among my people that claims there was a time, long ago, when all of the shifting kind possessed magic. The *coyotero* had coyote magic. The *kitsune* had fox magic. The *berskirs* had bear magic. The *selkie* had seal magic. And the *vargr* had wolf magic.

"But the *vargr* spent so much time imitating and infiltrating human society, they lost their magic, and with it their connection to the Wild. In the centuries since their self-imposed exile, they have grown increasingly jealous and resentful of those of us who can work magic. They still possess some artifacts from the time of the wolf-wizards—such as that cane you stole—but they are incapable of manipulating the power locked within it."

"Then it *wasn't* just my imagination! There really *is* some kind of weird power connected to that stick!"

Rosie narrowed her eyes. "You sensed magic?"

"Hell, I *saw* it!"

She leaned forward, her interest piqued. "What did it look like?"

"Like blue fire—the color of a butane flame. It snapped and crackled like static electricity, and I saw—naw, you'll think I'm nuts."

"No. Go on. Tell me what you saw."

"It was a giant wolf. Not like the ones alive now, but one of the prehistoric kind. Its eyes were full of fire and it *spoke* to me. . . ."

Rosie was visibly startled. "It *spoke*? What exactly did it say?"

"Something about the return of the Great Extinction. It didn't actually speak in words, but more in pictures. Do you know what it might have been?"

"I'm not sure—but from what you've described, you were given a vision by the totem-spirit of the *vargr*. Only shamans receive such visitations."

"What's a shaman?"

"They're a cross between wise men and wizards. The American Indians called them medicine men."

"Wise man? Wizard? That includes me out!" Skinner snorted.

"I wouldn't be so certain of that if I were you." Rosie was looking at him as if his flesh had suddenly turned to glass, exposing secrets within himself he was unaware of. Skinner shifted uncomfortably.

"Look, I'm just getting used to the idea of being a werewolf. Now you start talking about shamans and visions and totems. . . . Deep down I'm still a poor farm boy from Arkansas trying to make sense of the insanity that's taken over my life."

"Did you have strange dreams as a child? Dreams where you saw what would come to pass?"

"Sure, I had weird dreams as a kid. And I knew there was something different about me. But I had no idea I wasn't *human*, for the love of God! I'll admit that I've never really cared for the vast majority of people. But I don't *hate* humans! Most of the people I've really cared for were humans; the people who raised me—the ones I called mother and father—were generous and loving parents." His throat was suddenly very tight and he had to swallow in order to keep speaking. "My mother even continued to love and protect me after she had reason to condemn me as a monster. She allowed me to grow up innocent of my heritage— and my sin—without letting her knowledge taint how she felt about me."

Rosie uncoiled her legs and moved to turn off the television set. She smiled sadly for a long moment. "She sounds like an incredible woman."

"She was. And I miss her more than ever now. But what about the *coyotero*? How are they different from the *vargr*?"

"There are several differences, both cultural and physiological, between our races. While we are equally long-lived, the *coyotero* are, by nature, far smaller and more slender than *vargr*. And while *coyotero* have been known to dine on human flesh now and again, they prefer wild game. And, unlike the *vargr*, there are no elaborate—and uselessly bloody—rut melees. When a *coyotero* bitch mates, she mates for life. But perhaps our greatest difference is that we do not share the *vargr's* infamous allergy to silver."

She fell silent for a long moment. When she spoke again, her cheeks were flushed. "There is a ritual among the *coyotero*. When someone does us a great favor—such as you have done for me—it is traditional for the *coyotero* to tell that person its secret name. My name is Cactus Rose."

"It's a lovely name. Mine is Skinwalker."

"I think that's lovely, too."

She stepped forward hesitantly and he stood to meet her, each dropping their human skin.

She was much smaller and slighter than himself, her face and muzzle narrower than those of a *vargr*. Her pelt was silvery-gray, much like his own, off-setting her luminous eyes. Her three sets of teats were small and firm, the nipples already erect. She was beautiful.

She nuzzled his shoulder and he licked first her ear, then her muzzle. She felt so warm and fragile, he wanted to wrap his arms around her and protect her from everything cruel and harmful in the world. Her fur smelled of wilderness and open sky, and when he looked into her amber eyes, he saw desert sunsets and evening campfires. And he saw himself at her side. Forever.

When he mounted her, it was unlike anything

he had experienced during his brief sexual history. It wasn't rape or blind, instinctual rutting, but genuine lovemaking. Rosie whimpered like an un-weaned cub as she climaxed, chewing the pillow into styrofoam shreds.

When it was over they lay atop the covers, idly licking each other's fur and rubbing their muzzles together. They drifted off to sleep huddled together like sled dogs in high winter.

Later that night, William Cade came to Skinner in his dreams. He stepped from the empty motel closet and moved to the foot of the bed where his adopted son slept, wrapped in the arms of his lover.

Skinner sat up and stared at the man he had called father. At first it pained him to look at William Cade's wounds, knowing he was responsible for them, but there was no reproach in the dead man's eyes.

Without speaking, William Cade unbuttoned his blood-stained flannel shirt, exposing a gaping hole in his chest. He reached into the hole and removed his heart, holding it out toward Skinner, as if he was offering him a box of Valentine's Day choco-lates. The heart was still beating.

Skinner took his father's heart and held it in his hands. It was beating strongly, but he could only hear its pulsing inside his head. He looked up at his father, then swallowed the heart in one gulp. He felt it sliding down his throat, lodging in his chest. Where it belonged.

"My, aren't *we* cozy."
Skinner started awake to find himself unable to

breathe, looking into blood-red eyes suspended above his own face.

Rend was kneeling beside the bed, one hand clutching Skinner's throat. "I'm *very* disappointed in you, Skin," he hissed. "I take you in when you had nowhere and no one to turn to, and how do you repay me? Like *this*."

"Rend—it's not how it looks."

"Oh? That's interesting, cuz. Because it looks pretty damn *bad*!"

"Skinwalker?"

Rosie sat up, rubbing her eyes. "What is it—are you talking in your sleep?"

"Make one move, bitch, and I'll snap your boyfriend's head off and use it for a maraca!" Rend growled, showing his teeth. "Dig?"

Rosie's eyes widened in alarm, but she remained silent. Satisfied she was no immediate threat, Rend returned his attention to Skinner.

"You're dead meat, cuz. If I don't want to end up the same way, I've got to bring back your ears—with the rest of your head attached, of course. It was bad enough you put Jag's eye out and gave Jez the brush-off, but icing Hew and making off with the Wolfcane was just one step beyond, you know?"

"Rend—what they're doing isn't right! You know it, deep down, even if you won't come out and admit it! Treating humans like cattle . . . exterminating *esau* and *ulfr* like vermin . . . making war with our brothers . . ."

"It's the way of the pack, cuz."

"No it's *not*! It's the way of the *vargr*—or what the *vargr* have allowed themselves to become!"

Frustrated, Skinner moved to sit up and plead his case, but Rend growled and tightened his grip, forcing his head back into the pillow. Ignoring the constriction cutting off his air, Skinner surged upward, clawing at his friend's face. Rend yowled and fell back, pulling Skinner off the bed as he went.

The two werewolves rolled about on the floor between the double beds, snarling and ripping at one another with their feet and claws. Suddenly there was a third, smaller body included in the fray, snapping at Rend's exposed flank.

Rend shrieked as Rosie, her fore and hind claws dug deep into the muscles of his back, bit his right ear off. Staggering to his feet, he tried to free himself by smashing her against the room's sparse furnishings. It didn't work. As Rend lurched past, Skinner swiped at one of his calves, hamstringing him. Rend cried out again and collapsed to his knees, borne to the ground by Rosie's weight. Skinner knew the injury would not be permanent, but the damage was extensive enough that even Rend's *vargr* constitution would require time to recover.

Skinner got to his feet, shaking the blood from his coat. Rosie joined him, licking her paws. Rend lay sprawled on the carpet before them, clutching at his bleeding legs and glowering defiantly up at Skinner.

"Go ahead. Kill me. What are you waiting for?"

Skinner shook his head sadly. "I'm not going to kill you, Rend."

"Why not? It's what you want, isn't it?"

"I don't want to kill you, Rend. Despite what's just happened, you're my friend."

"Some friend!" he spat. "You're condemning me to death! If I return without your head and the Wolfcane, Erzule and Feral will see that I'm flayed alive and my raw flesh rubbed down with cayenne pepper, and *then* maybe I'll get lucky and they'll get around to killing me!"

"Come with us. You don't have to return to the lodge."

Rend barked a laugh, then looked at Skinner for a long moment. "You mean that, don't you?" he said, sounding genuinely amazed. "You really think I can turn my back on the pack and simply walk away...."

"You're not a dumb animal, Rend! You existed before you were a member of the pack."

"I existed—but as what? A serial rapist? A monster who preyed on junkies and closet queens looking for rough trade? Is that what I want to return to?"

"You don't *have* to be a monster—you have a choice, Rend!"

Rend looked at Skinner as if he was seeing him for the first time. "Do you honestly believe that something like myself can be redeemed? That I can tame the beast inside me?"

"I know it's not easy—especially when you possess the knowledge that you can commit any atrocity, endure the gravest injury, without suffering the consequences of your actions. It's always easier to be cruel than kind. To hurt rather than help. To think of yourself instead of others. But it *is* possible. If humans can conquer their baser instincts, why not *vargr*?"

Rend laughed and shook his head in disbelief. "You're a fool, Skinner. But a holy one."

"Then you'll come with us?"

"It's too late for me to try and change. It was too late for me from the moment my mother went into labor. As fucked up and imperfect as it may be, the pack is the only family I've ever known. The only place where I truly *belonged*. I can't abandon it."

"Damn it, Rend! They're going to *kill* you! Does that sound like a family to you?"

"I'm afraid so."

There was a pounding on the door of the motel room. *"Hey! What the fuck's goin' on in there? Don't-cha know it's fuckin' three in the morning here? I'm tryin' to get some sleep!"* Skinner recognized the irate voice as belonging to the salesman next door.

Taking advantage of the confusion, Rend got to his feet and pushed past Rosie. While his hamstrings weren't completely regenerated, he was still able to throw open the door and run past the salesman, clad in boxers and an undershirt, who turned to gape after the fleeing shape.

"Wha' the fuck—!"

Skinner quickly shifted back into his human skin, wrapping a towel around his waist and standing in the threshold, blocking the salesman's view of Rosie.

"I thought you only had the one dog?"

"I do."

"Then what the hell was that?"

"What was what?"

"That—that *thing* that damn near knocked me down!"

Rosie stepped out from behind the door, wearing nothing but Skinner's flannel shirt. "You did not see anything." Her voice was hard and sharp as struck flint.

The salesman blinked.

"You did not hear anything. You slept the whole night through. It was the deepest, soundest sleep you have ever known. There were no dreams. No sounds. No voices. Now go back to bed."

The salesman blinked again, suddenly looking very sleepy, and shuffled back to his room.

Skinner quickly shut the door. "How'd you manage that?"

"Like I said; the *coyotero* still have magic. We find it easier than killing witnesses, in the long run."

"You'll have to teach me that trick sometime. But first, we've got to get the hell out of here. If Rend found us this easily, the rest of the pack can't be far behind."

Chapter Twenty-two

Rend stopped running when he reached the stand of saguarro cacti, dropping onto his haunches and gasped for breath. He was still stunned that he had somehow survived his encounter with Skinner and the *coyotero*. Not that the renegade had done him any favors.

I should have killed him while he lay there sleeping. I had my hand on his throat. It would have been so easy to snap his neck and make off with the Wolfcane, but I didn't do it. Why?

Skinner's ideas concerning the capacity for humanity among the inhuman was brain-damaged twaddle, nothing more. If he closed his eyes he could still see Skinner, asleep on the bed, the *coyotero* female nestled against him, and he knew why he'd hesitated. He could have killed Skinner and raped the *coyotero* bitch alongside his cooling corpse, but he didn't.

Because when he saw the way they lay together, their limbs lazily intertwined, instead of feeling jealousy or lust, he'd experienced a twinge of happiness for his friend.

He'd been weak. He'd shown compassion toward an enemy. And now he was doomed.

"My, my, my! What have we here?"

The sound of Jag's voice made Rend's sphincter pucker.

"Looks like a sorry-ass fuck-up, if you ask me, boss." Ripper giggled.

The pack stepped out from behind the cacti, quiet as shadows. Jag was wearing a black velvet eye patch elaborately embroidered with a chinese dragon in red and gold thread. Ripper was rocking back and forth on the heels of his Doc Marten's, keeping time with drumsticks on his pants legs, his eyes fixed on Rend. Jez stood slightly behind her brother, nervously twisting a strand of her hair, while Sunder stood the furthest back, his eyes averted.

Jag casually lit a cigarette, cupping a match against the wind. "Ripper . . . ask him where's the renegade's head?"

"Jag wants to know where the renegade's head is, fuck-up."

"If he wants to know, he can ask me himself."

"Ripper, tell him I don't talk to dead meat."

"Jag says he don't talk to dead meat, dead meat."

Jag moved so fast all Rend's eye registered was an off-white blur. He leapt forward, snapping at Rend's flank. Rend lurched to his feet, but Ripper was already behind him, his claws grazing his buttocks, herding him forward.

"Where is he? Where is the renegade?" snarled Jag.

"I—I don't know! I haven't been able to locate him yet!"

"You're *lying*!" Jag grabbed Rend by the scruff of the neck, twisting his head to reveal what remained of his ear. "If you haven't made contact with the renegade, how did this happen? Did you cut yourself shaving?"

"I—I tangled with a true-coyote."

"Tell me *another* one, dead meat!" Jag snarled, cuffing him across the muzzle.

Jez pushed forward, her voice anxious. "What about the *coyotero* bitch? Is she traveling with him?"

"I told you—I haven't made contact with him—"

Sunder shook his head sadly. "Rend—don't lie to us. Don't lie to the pack. You're only making it worse."

Sunder was right. What was he hoping to accomplish, covering for Skinner? "Alright—I *did* see him. He's at the Westward-Ho Motel. Room 10."

"What about the *coyotero*? Is she still with him?" Jez asked again.

"They're—they're mated."

Jez' eyes narrowed and her mouth pulled itself into a tight bow. "Kill him and get it over with. Then we'll find the renegade and do the same thing to both him and his whore."

Rend shook his head, trembling like a malaria victim. "No. Jag—Jez—don't do this to me—please—"

They fell upon him as a group, burying their fangs and claws deep into his struggling flesh. Rend only had time for one yowl of pain. It was quick, but far from merciful.

Sunder squatted next to the empty kennel at the Westward-Ho Motel, his nostrils twitching. "I smell *ulfr.* Damn fresh, too."

Jag frowned. "*Ulfr*? Rend didn't say anything about Skinner traveling with an *ulfr*."

"Maybe it slipped his mind." Sunder grunted, dusting the palms of his hands on his buttocks as he stood up. "Getting killed tends to make folks forgetful."

"Don't give me that shit, Sunder!"

"I don't care! I still say it's not fair," Sunder snapped back. "So what if Skinner iced Snuff and Hew and hightailed it with the mojo stick? It wasn't Rend's fault!"

"He's the one who brought the renegade into the pack in the first place! Rend knew the rules!"

Sunder glowered at Jag for a second, then dropped his eyes and moved off. Jag let the breath he was holding escape. Things were turning to shit but fast. As much as he hated to admit it, he was already beginning to miss Rend's steward-ship. As his lieutenant, he had served as a buffer, counter-balancing and helping to control the per-sonal chemistries of the more unstable pack members.

While Ripper seemed eager to play the subservi-ent toady, he was a full-throttle psycho. The only member of the pack who had any influence over his manic mood swings had been Hew. Sunder had always been something of a cipher to Jag, preferring to hang with Rend, smoking dope in the back of the equipment van. And Jez—since the melee, she'd refused to let him so much as touch her.

The door to Room 10 was ajar when they ar-rived. Jag didn't need to look inside to know his prey had fled.

"What do we do now, Jag?" Ripper whined, bouncing on the balls of his feet.

The drummer's hyperactivity was starting to wear thin on Jag, and he had to restrain himself from nipping the bothersome youth. He couldn't afford to alienate Ripper, since his position as Alpha was far from secure.

"They can't be too far ahead. They're headed into *coyotero* territory, that much is certain. We'll keep following."

"What the hell's going on here?"

Jag and Ripper turned to stare at the traveling salesman standing in the door to Room 9. He was dressed in boxer shorts and an undershirt, knuckling sleep out of his eyes.

"Can't a guy get some simple shut-eye?"

Jag grinned at the salesman, exposing far too many teeth for a human mouth, and dropped his half-smoked cigarette. The salesman took a step backward into his room, slamming and locking the door on the menacing young man with the long white hair and nose ring and his equally unnerving bald companion.

They came in, anyway.

Four hundred miles and five hours later, Skinner and Rosie made Butter Junction, Arizona. Root Woman was in her front yard, tending her spirit traps, when they arrived. The old midwife watched the Caddy approach, puffing her briarwood pipe, her gnarled fingers tugging on the brim of her baseball cap.

Rosie jumped out of the car before it came to a full stop, running toward her grandmother. She swept Root Woman into her open arms, lifting the old lady off the ground in a bear hug.

Skinner threw the Caddy into park. "C'mon, Fella," he said to the *ulfr*, who was riding in the backseat. "Time to meet the in-laws. Oh, roll the window up before you get out, why don't you?"

Rosie was standing alongside Root Woman, one arm draped around her stooped shoulders, as Skinner approached. The old woman's smile faltered as he came close enough for her to recognize.

"Granny, this is the one who rescued me."

"Hello again. I don't know if you remember me, ma'am—"

"I remember you, Mr. Cade." Root Woman raised an eyebrow as she saw Fella trot up and position himself at Skinner's right hand. "It appears I misjudged you when you first came to me. I'm truly sorry. You have brought my grandchild back to me—I am an old woman, and far from rich. How can I ever repay you?"

"You know who my mother is, don't you?"

"Yes."

"Do you know where she is?"

"Yes."

"Take me to her."

"Are you sure this is what you want?"

"I'm as sure of it as I am of my love for your granddaughter."

Root Woman looked at Rosie, then Skinner, and nodded. "Very well. It's several hours' journey from here. When do you want to leave?"

"As soon as possible—but first, I have to honor a promise I made a friend."

*   *   *

Skinner drove the Caddy into the dry riverbed behind Root Woman's shack and got out carrying a five-gallon can of gasoline, Fella tagging along at his heels. He unlocked the car's trunk, holding a handkerchief to his face and breathing through his mouth. Fella reared up onto his hind legs and peered into the trunk, sniffing at the Hound's canvas-wrapped corpse.

"Get back, Fella," Skinner warned. "You don't want any of this stuff to get on you."

Fella whined and dropped back onto all fours, watching, his head cocked to one side, as Skinner showered the car with gasoline, starting with the trunk. Finished, Skinner hurled the empty canister aside and took a book of matches from his pants pocket.

"I don't know if you're in any position to appreciate it, Shaggybreeks, but I'm keeping my end of the bargain."

With that, he tossed the lit book into the open trunk and ran like hell, Fella at his side.

They left Root Woman's shack in a dilapidated pickup truck, all three of them wedged into the unair-conditioned cab, with Fella riding in the bed. Rosie was behind the wheel, steering the rusty old jalopy through dry washes and gullies that would have punctured the oil pan and broken the axle of most all-terrain vehicles.

The shocks on the truck were all but shot, and after a half hour Skinner's tailbone throbbed and his kidneys ached. Rosie and Root Woman, however, seemed completely at ease. No doubt they had made the trip so many times they no longer registered the discomfort. Fella seemed to be enjoying himself as well, spending most of the ride rushing from one side of the truck bed to the other to bark at jackrabbits startled from their cover by the vehicle's passage.

They were headed south, in the direction of the Coyote Mountains. After they reached the foothills, they could go no further in the truck. They would have to hike into the mountains themselves.

Skinner walked up to where Root Woman was squatting in the dirt, checking the contents of her backpack.

"Are you sure you can make it?" he asked solicitously.

Root Woman gave him a look so sharp it could cut glass. "I've been making my way through these mountains and back every month since I was old enough to take two steps, boy. I've walked along trails no wider than my foot in pitch dark, carrying babies in both arms and eight months gone with a child of my own. I figger I can make it just fine. How about you, tenderfoot?"

"Granny! Skinner was just trying to be nice!" Rosie chastised.

"Suggesting I'm feeble ain't my idea of being nice." She sniffed as she shouldered her backpack on. "Here's a good time for you to put that fancy conjuring staff you swiped from the *vargr* to some use. You're definitely going to need a walking stick from here on in."

* * *

"How does she do it?" Skinner wheezed two hours later. He was slumped against a cluster of boulders, gasping for air. He wiped at his brow with a bandanna and took another swig from his canteen. The water was warm, bordering on hot, and tasted of metal. He grimaced and screwed the cap back on. Rosie had stopped to join him.

"Do what?"

"You know—" Skinner nodded in the direction of Root Woman, a good hundred feet ahead of them. The old woman was making steady progress up a steep hill that would have made even the hardiest outdoor enthusiast balk, aided by nothing but a weathered piece of wood almost as tall as she was.

"Hurry up, you two! If we don't dawdle, we can make the encampment by dusk!" she called over her shoulder.

Skinner groaned and levered himself back on his feet, using the Wolfcane for support. He was all too aware that he had elected to undergo this excursion in brand-new cowboy boots.

"Where's Fella?"

"Last I saw of him, he was chasing a jackrabbit."

"Lucky him. I could go for one of those right about now."

"Come on, slow pokes! Time's a wastin'!" Root Woman shouted from above them.

"God, I hate colorful old geezers."

They reached the *coyotero* settlement just before sunset. Root Woman led them through a crevice so narrow they had to turn sideways to pass, which gradually widened until they found themselves in a small canyon. Tiny fires flickered above their heads from inside the caves—both natural and otherwise—that riddled the walls of the surrounding cliffs.

A shadowy figure emerged from behind an outcropping of rock. Although the guard spoke in a tongue Skinner had never heard before, it was clear they were being challenged. Root Woman held up her hand and gave the countersign in the same language. The guard—who was naked except for fringed buckskin chaps—waved them on, although he fixed Skinner with a blatantly suspicious glare.

Root Woman mounted a handmade ladder and began climbing toward the upper level of the *coyotero* cliff dwellings, Rosie and Skinner following behind her. Fella attempted to follow, but he could not manage more than a few rungs before losing his balance. He whined and barked in agitation from his place at the foot of the ladder.

"He'll be alright, won't he?" Skinner asked. "I mean—the *coyotero* won't do anything to him, will they?"

"Don't worry," Rosie reassured him. "My people have no quarrel with the *ulfr*."

They got off the ladder at the third level, facing a huge natural cave. An adobe brick wall had been built along the front margins and a young male *coyotero*, dressed in much-frayed denim jeans and an intricately beaded pectoral, sat cross-legged in the threshold, carving a kachina doll.

"She's expecting you," the craftsman said.

Root Woman nodded. She didn't seem surprised. "For how long?"

"She had a vision of the *vargr* renegade this afternoon."

Root Woman pushed aside the antelope hide that served as the front door and motioned for Skinner to enter. When Rosie moved to follow, the old woman stopped her. "Wait here, child. I'll let you know when it's time to come in."

Rosie began to protest, but the look Root Woman gave her kept her silent.

The interior of the cave was dark and close, smelling of woodsmoke and dried herbs. A woman dressed in the skin of a large coyote, the empty head resting atop her own, sat in front of a crude hearth, tending the fire with a long stick. The woman did not stop what she was doing nor did she look in their direction.

"Welcome, Skinwalker. I am Changing Woman, medicine woman of the *coyotero*. All who have questions they wish answered ask them of me."

"I want to know the name of my mother."

"That is not a question."

"I wasn't aware we were playing *Jeopardy*." After all he'd gone through in the last twenty-four hours, he wasn't in the mood to deal with an enigmatic mystic. Skinner took a deep breath, trying to control his impatience. "Very well—what is my mother's name?"

The shamanness stopped poking at the fire but remained silent. Skinner's patience, already worn thin, snapped completely.

"Well, do you know her name or *not*?"

The medicine woman turned to fix him with

eyes the color of freshly minted coins and pushed back the coyote's head, revealing hair that gleamed like silver threads in the dim light.

"Her name is Changing Woman."

There was an audible gasp from the direction of the doorway. Rosie was standing there, staring at Skinner with a look of stupefied shock on her face.

Root Woman shook her head in dismay, clucking her tongue. "Child, I thought I told you to wait outside!"

Skinner stepped toward his lover, one hand held out to her. "Rosie? What's wrong?"

Rosie shook her head violently, tears running down her cheeks. "You don't understand—"

"Don't understand what?"

"She's my mother, too."

Chapter Twenty-three

Choking back a sob, Rosie turned and fled the cliff dwelling. Skinner made to follow her, but Changing Woman raised a hand to stop him.

"Let her go, Skinwalker. Cactus Rose must deal with the truth in her own way, in her own time. There is nothing you can say or do that will change things."

Skinner turned back to face the woman who claimed to be his biological mother. When he first set out on his journey of self-discovery, weeks ago and a lifetime away, he had not foreseen it ending in such a way. But the one question he held deep inside was still waiting to be spoken, regardless of circumstance.

"Why?"

Changing Woman looked up at him, studying him silently. She motioned for him to be seated next to the hearth. When she next spoke, it was in the sing-song cadence of a tribal storyteller.

"What I am about to tell you is not the truth. Neither is it a lie. It is a legend. It is the story of the Pretending Kind; we who dwell between the cracks of human perception.

"There are many different breeds of Pretender—

some of which are more powerful—and dangerous—than others. And there are others not even the Pretending Kind have names for.

"The most powerful of the Pretenders are the *enkidu*—who the humans know as vampires. Just below them are those who Change. There are many shapeshifters, such as the legendary serpent-men of Eurasia, the *naga*, the *birskir* of the Arctic North, and the *bast*, the only breed to ever be worshipped as gods; but only the *vargr*, the *coyotero*, and the *kitsune*, the fox-people of the Orient, are still plentiful.

"There are others who masquerade as humans as well, such as the child-eating ogres; the *undine*, who appear in sailors' stories of merfolk and selkies; the *succubi* and *incubi*, who feed on human sexual energy ... to name the most common.

"Not unlike the humans they prey on, Pretenders do not know the secrets behind their origins. Some claim that we predated the humans. Others say that we arose from the oceans of creation concurrently, yet separately. And yet another school of thought holds that we were created from the fears, dreams, hopes, and nightmares of humankind; that we would not exist if there was not room for us within the hearts of man. Which is true? One or all?

"In any case, each of the Pretending Kind has its own magic of varying strength. Some—like the *seraphim*—are magic made manifest, while others—such as the ogres—have close to none at all. But only the *vargr* were foolish enough to *lose* their magic.

"In their bid to blend in with—and compete

against—human society, they turned their back on the Wild and became corrupt. They represent all that is bad in both man *and* beast. They are thoughtless, cruel, and rapacious. They are rapists, cannibals, and the most brutal of killers.

"Granted, many of the *coyotero* have been guilty of these deeds as well, but they acted out of the innocence of the beast. We have never *deliberately* preyed on humans for our food and sport. That is where the difference lies between us and our Old World cousins.

"The *vargr* are all belly and eyes. They desire all that they see. And that which they can not have—they destroy. Completely and utterly.

"The first time *coyotero* and *vargr* met in the New World, it was over four hundred years ago. A *vargr* had attached himself to a contingent of Spanish conquistadors in search of El Dorado, the fabled City of Gold. They attacked a peaceful village under the protection of the *coyotero*, raping the women and torturing the men in hopes of learning the whereabouts of this nonexistent city.

"The *coyotero* honored their pact, avenging the massacred tribe. But, in their innocence, they spared the *vargr*. The *vargr* lived among the *coyotero* for several seasons. While he was among them, he learned of their magic and tried to bend it to his will, but with no luck. Angered and jealous of the *coyotero*'s power, he returned to the land of his birth. Years later, he returned at the head of a pack of his fellows. They attacked the *coyotero* without warning, murdering their cubs and females, desecrating their most sacred totems and burial places in a vain attempt to destroy their

magic. The *vargr* and *coyotero* have been at war
with one another ever since.

"Over the last few centuries, fortune has not
smiled on the *coyotero*. Like the Native Americans,
we have found ourselves overwhelmed by our
enemy. What they lack in magic, the *vargr* have
more than made up for in other ways. They are
physically stronger than *coyotero*, and because of
their habit of raping human women, they far outnumber us. While there are a handful of *coyotero*
communities similar to this one scattered throughout the Southwest and the Dakotas, our numbers
continue to dwindle with each passing year.

"Like the far more powerful *enkidu*, the *vargr*
are obsessed with secretly shaping human society
to meet their own selfish ends, and they do not
suffer what they consider to be poachers on their
territory. Since they lack the *enkidu*'s psychic abilities, this is accomplished by a network of spies
and infiltrators. This, above all else, is what truly
separates the *vargr* from the other shifting races.
The *vargr* seek to bend nature and its ways to
meet their needs, thereby deluding themselves
into thinking they are lords of creation. This is a
deceit they acquired from breeding with humans.
In fact, they have become so like the humans they
seek dominion over they use firearms and silver
bullets in order to deal with enemies within their
group without having to engage in hand-to-hand
combat."

"But what does this have to do with me?"

"Be patient and allow me to continue my story.
All will be made clear in time. As I said, the *vargr*
and *coyotero* have been at war with one another

for centuries. Then, twenty years ago, we received news that the *vargr* wished to arrange a treaty of sorts. A nonaggression pact, as it were.

"The elders of the *coyotero* were hesitant at first. *Vargr* treachery is well known. But then they sent an emissary to convince us of their intent—a *vargr* noble named Feral."

"Feral?" Skinner was visibly shaken.

"I see you are familiar with his name. Do you know of him?"

"You could say that."

"Feral was quite eloquent and argued his people's position most persuasively. He claimed that the *vargr* had grown weary of wasting precious time that could be focused on other matters than battling the *coyotero*. There was more than enough room in the New World for both *vargr* and *coyotero* to live in harmony. And, given time, genuine friendship might blossom between our peoples, giving way to an exchange of cultures and ideologies.

"The elders were finally persuaded to attend a peace negotiation. Since I was the shamanness of the tribe, it was decided I would speak for the *coyotero*. We set out to the appointed place—there were a dozen of us, including my mate of many years, Standing Wolf.

"It was a trap.

"The *vargr* were waiting for us in greater numbers, and they fell upon our band like a pack of ravening wolves. All but two of the elders were killed. Feral took extreme pleasure in torturing my mate before my very eyes. He then raped me, inches away from Standing Wolf's peeled and vivisected body.

"I managed to escape—and I succeeded in reclaiming Standing Wolf's pelt as well." She gently stroked the coyote-skin draped about her, its forelegs knotted about her shoulders. "A few weeks later, I discovered I was with child.

"I was uncertain as to what I should do. My initial response when I learned of my pregnancy was to rid myself of it. There is a special herbal remedy Root Woman prepares for those clients of hers who wish to induce a miscarriage. It is a crude but effective abortifacient. Then it occurred to me—what if the cub I was carrying was fathered by Standing Wolf?

"We had whelped only once before—the cub dying shortly after birth. As I said, we *coyotero* are not a prolific race. So I elected to endure the pregnancy. When my time came, Root Woman served as my midwife, as have her mothers before her. I was delivered of twins. A boy and a girl.

"When Root Woman brought forth the cubs for me to lick clean—as is the custom—I saw that my worst fear, and wildest hope, had come true at the same time.

"The she-cub was pure *coyotero*. She was Standing Wolf's daughter, of that I had no doubt. I licked her clean, claiming her as my own. But the man-cub . . . the man-cub was *vargr*. Feral's get. In my anger, I bared my teeth. If Root Woman had not jerked you away at that instant, I would have torn your throat out before the birth fluids were dry.

"Root Woman asked me what she should do

with the man-cub. I told her to destroy it. She left the encampment with the baby and never spoke to me concerning it again. I assumed she had exposed it on a hillside somewhere. It wasn't until you came to her shack, seeking information concerning your origins, that she confessed to me what she'd done.

"Despite her bluster, Root Woman is kind-hearted, as were all those who carried her name before her. Taking pity on you, she handed you over to the white woman's foundling home, hoping you would find a place with human parents in another part of the country.

"So you see, Skinwalker, why I cast you aside when you were born. I had no way of knowing that you had inherited the shaman's inner eye. But even if I *had* known, the circumstances surrounding your birth were such that I could never be a real mother to you. Nor will I ever be. But I *can* be your teacher.

"You possess amazing wild talent. The power has been locked inside you since birth, but it was awakened upon your contact with the Wolfcane." She smiled when she saw the look of surprise on his face. "Yes, I know of your adventure with the Wolfcane. I had a vision that told me of it. Because of your unique heritage, you are the first *vargr* in centuries capable of working wolf-magic. That is why it spoke to you. Because you have ears that hear within, eyes that see beyond. Do you know what that means?"

Skinner shook his head.

"You are prophecy fulfilled." Changing Woman got to her feet and walked over to a wooden table laden with papers and books. She produced a bulky leather-bound volume and showed it to Skinner, her hands stroking its surface as if it was a sleeping animal. "This is the vision-journal of the *coyotero* shaman known as Broken Tooth. He served as the tribe's wise-man three hundred years ago—he was my grandfather, your great-grandfather."

Changing Woman opened the book, thumbing through the yellowed pages for a particular entry. "Ah, here it is: 'In my dream I saw a land where the fields were scorched and the forests reduced to charred stumps. The skies were full of ash and the rain fell like demon-tears, burning the flesh of those below. As I watched, a young warrior-wizard rose from the pool of blood that separates *coyotero* and *vargr*. The warrior-wizard rode on the back of a great wolf and carried the seal of the *vargr* in one hand. In his wake were *vargr*, *coyotero*, *ulfr*, humans, and true-beasts alike, following him wherever he might go. The dark skies rolled back and there was light and the earth blossomed once more.' "

Changing Woman closed the book and looked meaningfully at Skinner. "You are the messiah. The one prophesied who will heal the rift between *coyotero* and *vargr*. The one who will save the earth from ruin at the hands of the humans."

"Like hell!" Skinner snorted. "I may be a lot of things, but messiah ain't one of 'em!"

"Look at your hands."

"Huh?"

Changing Woman picked up a coup stick

wrapped in leather and decorated with eagle feathers and struck Skinner on the top of the head.

"Ow! What'd you do *that* for?" he yelped, rubbing his skull.

"If you are to survive the rigors of apprenticeship, Skinwalker, you must learn two things: believe in yourself, and do what you're told. Now look at your hands."

Skinner did as he was told. To his surprise, his hands and forearms were enveloped by a blue fire that flickered and flared like the nimbus of a small sun.

"What—?"

"Human scientists call it an aura. Lesser evolved humans call it witch-fire or a halo. The *kitsune* know it as foxfire. In each case, it is a manifestation of the psychic power that resides in those with a sympathy for magic. Look at me."

Skinner looked at Changing Woman and saw that she, too, was wrapped in blue fire. Her aura, however, seemed far more focused, with most of the energy centered around her head and hands.

"The reason I made this particular cave my home is because it is a place of power. It makes it easier for me to have my visions and work my spells. It amplifies what is invisible and renders it visible—for those who have eyes to see.

"We must work quickly. There is not much time. The *vargr* following on your trail are very close. If we are to avoid discovery, we must prepare you for your encounter with them. They plan to trick you, Skinwalker. They will try and appeal to the *vargr* within you and entice you back into the pack. They would have you betray the *coyotero* and still kill you for a Judas goat."

Root Woman found Rosie in one of the abandoned caves, huddled in the darkest corner. The old woman used the sounds of her sobs to pinpoint her exact location. She was sitting with her arms wrapped around her knees, her head bowed as she rocked back and forth.

"So there you are, child. I was beginning to think you'd left us and headed back to the truck."

Rosie lifted her face, the tears streaming down her face and dripping off the point of her chin. "Oh, Granny! What do I *do*?"

Root Woman knelt beside her and placed a thin arm around her shaking shoulders. "Do you love him?"

"He's my *brother*!"

Root Woman sighed and stroked her grandchild's hair. "Sometimes I think your mother did you a disservice handing you over to me to raise. I understand why she did—she wasn't fit to raise young 'uns, not after what the *vargr* did to her. But you came up with certain human preconceptions and taboos you wouldn't have had if you'd remained within the tribe. I reckon you don't know that your mama and daddy were uncle and niece, do you?"

Rosie stopped crying and looked at Root Woman. "No. Mother has never told me anything about Father, not even when I've asked."

"Not surprising. Standing Wolf is still a sore memory for her. She feels she's responsible for his death—not to mention those of the elders—

because Feral tricked her into believing him. The fact of the matter is incest isn't a sin among the *coyotero*. That's one of the things they share with the *vargr*. It's not compulsory, though.

"Besides, Skinner is a demi-brother. You may have shared the same mama, even the same womb, but you have different daddies. And it's hardly like you were raised under the same roof. But this is all window-dressing—the heart of the matter lies in whether or not you love him. Do you?"

"God help me, yes."

Rosie started to cry again. Root Woman pulled her into her arms, cradling her head between her flat, wrinkled breasts.

"Then that's all that matters."

Chapter Twenty-four

"You are certain this is where their trail leads?" Feral growled.

"Yes, milord," Jag replied.

They were crouched behind an outcropping of rock, hidden from the sole *coyotero* standing guard at the entrance of the settlement.

Feral stroked his chin. "This is proving to be quite advantageous. We have been trying to locate the *coyotero*'s base of operations for years! Now we can exterminate them like the vermin they are! It makes bringing the renegade to ground even more satisfying, don't you think, Jag?"

"Yes, my sire."

"How many do you think are holed up in there?" Sunder whispered.

"Hard to say. Maybe as many as twenty-five *coyotero*, both male and female."

"But there are only five of us! We'll be massacred!"

Feral opened the rucksack he'd brought with him, revealing a cache of 9mm semiautomatic weapons. "Never underestimate the effect of superior firepower."

"Cool!" Ripper snatched up one of the guns,

pointing it point-blank at Jag's head and dry-firing it several times in rapid succession.

"Stop that!" Jag snarled, slapping the weapon out of Ripper's hand.

The skinhead flashed his teeth and narrowed his eyes. "You shouldn't have done that, Jag."

Great! Of all the times for the little shit to pull a domination play! Well, he wasn't about to have the hairless bastard show him up in front of Feral. Jag slapped a magazine of silver-jacketed hollow-points into the breech of his 9mm and pressed the muzzle against Ripper's shaved temple.

"I shouldn't have done *what*, shit-for-brains?"

Sweat beaded on Ripper's upper lip and trickled down his exposed scalp. "Nu-nu-nuthin', Jag. I was just jivin' with you. You're the boss here, cuz. Everyone knows that."

"Fuckin' A." Jag cast a glance at Feral from the corner of his eye. If the older werewolf had noticed the little domination scuffle, he did not show it.

Sunder frowned. "But *coyotero* aren't allergic to silver, are they?"

Jez rolled her eyes in disgust. "If you get shot in the head, it doesn't matter if the bullets are silver or not, does it?"

"Guess not."

The guard didn't know what happened. One minute he was standing watch, the next his brains were exploding out the back of his head, taking with them two hundred and twenty-seven years of memory. Born ten years before the signing of the Declaration of Independence, the *coyotero* guard had fought alongside the Sioux at Little Big Horn. The *vargr* who killed him did not know this. And even if they had, it would not have mattered to them.

The raiders moved swiftly, strafing the walls of the canyon before their victims had a chance to react.

Changing Woman, hearing the gunfire, moved to the front of the cave. She looked over her shoulder at Skinner. "They've arrived."

"Changing Woman!"

Feral was standing on the floor of the canyon, surrounded by the younger *vargr*. Each held a gun at the ready, watching the cliffs for signs of movement.

"Changing Woman!"

The shamaness picked up her coup stick and replaced her husband's empty skull atop her head and prepared to step outside. Skinner scrambled to his feet, his eyes wide with alarm.

"You're not going out there to talk to him, are you?"

"He's calling my name. I must respond."

"He'll kill you!"

"He can try. Just as I will try and kill him."

"Changing Woman! Answer me, damn your eyes!"

Changing Woman shouldered aside Skinner and stood revealed on the ledge. Ripper lifted his weapon and took aim, but Jag swatted his hand down.

"I hear you, Feral. What is the reason for this attack on my people?"

"You know full well what it is we want! We

want the renegade called Skinner! Hand him over to us and we will leave without further incident!"

"I cannot do that, Feral. He is not mine to surrender."

"He is *vargr*. He has broken *vargr* rule! It is our right to claim him for punishment!"

"That's where you're wrong, Lord Feral. Skinwalker is not true *vargr*!"

"You lie! He's no *coyotero*."

"Did I say he was? Skinwalker is neither *vargr* nor *coyotero*. He is a race unto himself, bound by no law except that which his heart follows."

"You've been chewing too many psychedelic mushrooms, Changing Woman! The renegade is *vargr*. And he must pay the penalty of violating our most sacred of taboos!"

"I neither lie nor hallucinate, Feral. Don't you recognize your own seed?"

Feral fell silent as the younger werewolves began to buzz among themselves.

"That's right, Feral. The renegade is your son! I bore him twenty years ago, cursing your name with every contraction!"

"You think I would hesitate at killing one of my own? Woman, I've slain so many of my own children I could build a cathedral with their bones."

"Of that I have no doubt."

"Very well, if you will not surrender the renegade to us, we will take him by force."

Coyote Woman made a motion with her coup stick, and suddenly there was the sound of arrows being loosed into the air. The invading *vargr* looked confused as the first flight thunked into the dirt at their feet. Then Feral began to laugh.

"*Arrows?* You're going to try and stop us using bows and *arrows?* How pathetic!"

Ripper waved his arms at the *coyotero* archers, sticking out his tongue. "Hey, losers! We're not playin' fuckin' cowboys and Indians here!" He bent over and waved his ass back and forth, inviting another volley. "We're here to kick your mangy butts. Get it?" When his taunts failed to inspire another attack, he straightened up and smirked. "What a bunch of wusses!"

The arrow struck Ripper square in the chest, the feathered shaft jutting out of his sternum like a signpost. Ripper stared down at the arrow and sneered in disdain. "Is that the best you wimps can do—?" As he grasped the arrow by its shaft in preparation of yanking it free, his sneer disappeared into a grimace of immense pain. The bald werewolf screamed in agony and collapsed to his knees.

"*Burns!* It *burns!* Make it stop—*ahhhh!*" Ripper dropped his gun and clawed at his shirt, tearing it open to expose the entry wound. The pale, hairless flesh where the arrowhead was buried in his chest was swollen and black, oozing pus and lessidentifiable matter. It was as if within the span of seconds his wound had somehow reached the terminal stage of gangrene. The arrow came free from his chest with a wet, sucking sound. Ripper stared, horror-struck, at the gore-streaked arrowhead.

"*Silver!* They're using fuckin' *silver!*" he shrieked.

The remaining *vargr* quickly abandoned the center of the canyon, leaving Ripper to die of acute blood poisoning on his own.

As the *vargr* made their way toward the ladders that connected the canyon floor to the cliff dwellings above, a large, dark shadow positioned itself in front of them.

Fella growled, his raised hackles making him look bigger than he already was. Jag fired his gun at the *ulfr*, only to miss by inches. Fella turned and ran back into the shadows, drawing the *vargr*'s fire as he went.

"Don't waste your ammo on the damned *ulfr*!" Feral yelled.

A couple of *coyotero* ran from cover to try and pull up the ladder that connected the canyon floor to the cliff dwellings, but it was too late. Before they could reach the ladder, Jag was already at the top, emptying his clip into their skulls at point-blank range.

Feral was right behind him, followed by Jez and Sunder. A *coyotero* female, a child clutched in her arms, emerged at the mouth of one of the caves. When she saw the *vargr* standing over the bodies of her menfolk, she cried out in distress. Jag shot her through the head before she could turn to flee. The child, trapped in its dead mother's arms, cried in confusion and fear until Jag emptied a round into it. The baby's tiny skull disappeared in a cloud of blood and bone fragments.

"Enough!"

The *vargr* halted their slaughter, looking up in the direction of Skinner's voice. He stood at the very top of the cliff, leaning over its lip so they could get a good look at him.

"You want me? Okay, here I am!"

"The Wolfcane!" Feral called out. "Do you still have the Wolfcane?"

"I still have your damn stick!" Skinner held it up for them to see. "If you want me and the Wolfcane, you're going to have to come and get us!"

Jag lifted his 9 mm and squeezed off a shot in the direction of Skinner's head, but he ducked and the bullet ricocheted harmlessly off a rock. Feral spun on his heel and backhanded his son hard enough to draw blood.

"*Fool!*" he bellowed. "You might have struck the Wolfcane by mistake!"

Jag wiped the blood from his mouth and fixed Feral with a hot, angry glare with his remaining eye. Father and son were locked in a glowering match for a long moment until a sound from above distracted them. Someone from the top of the mesa was lowering a ladder to them.

Skinner stuck his head over the ledge again. "Like I said: if you want me, you gotta come get me!"

Growling under his breath, Feral shoved his gun into his coat pocket and clambered up the ladder, followed closely by the others.

The top of the mesa was relatively flat and barren, the wind whistling across its unsheltered expanse. The sky was filled with thousands upon thousands of stars shining brightly over the desert. There was no one in sight.

"Renegade! *Traitor!* Show yourself, coward!"

Feral yelled, firing his gun into the air for emphasis. "You can't hide from me!"

There was a gunshot behind him. Feral spun around in time to see Sunder standing on the edge of the mesa, swearing and firing a second round at the tier below.

"Lord Feral! They're taking away the ladder!"

"Great work, graybeard!" Jag snarled at Feral, getting so close his teeth were all the elder werewolf could see. "You maneuvered us into a trap!" Before his sire had a chance to react, Jag wrested his gun away from him. "You should have stayed home servicing Mother-dearest, grizzle-chin, and left the adventuring to me!"

"How dare you!" Feral shifted in response to his son's impudence, his expensive clothes ripping and tearing with the change into his Wild skin. "How dare you challenge *me*?"

Feral and Jag were on each other in a matter of seconds, snapping at each other's throats and flanks with foam-drenched fangs.

"Daddy! Jag! *Stop it!*" Jez screamed, her hands clamped against her ears to muffle the sounds of ripping fur and crunching bone. "This isn't the time for this! *Jag!*"

There was a sudden, pained yelp and the two disengaged. Feral lay huddled on the ground, clutching what was left of his right hand. Jag looked down at his father and spat out a mouthful of fingers. Grinning with blood-smeared teeth, Jag pissed on Feral, the stream striking him high on the chest and splashing in his face.

"You're past your prime, graybeard! You should never have come here!"

"I couldn't agree with you more."

Startled, Jag spun around to find Skinner standing behind him, the Wolfcane clutched in one hand like a battle-staff. Skinner's silvery pelt was covered in soot and grease from the chimney flue/emergency escape route he'd crawled through to reach the top of the mesa.

Jag lifted his gun to fire at Skinner's head, but Skinner used the butt of the Wolfcane to knock the weapon out of his hand. Jag lunged at Skinner's throat, but again Skinner was too quick for him, raising the Wolfcane to block the attack. Jag grabbed the hard ebony shaft and tried to wrest it from Skinner's grasp. They stood toe-to-toe, eyes locked, grimacing at each other.

"Jag—don't make me kill you—"

"Why—because we're brothers? I don't have any problem with fratricide, renegade. I'll kill you as easily as I murdered Bender—or Rend, for that matter."

"Rend?"

The mention of his friend's name distracted Skinner long enough for Jag to hook a leg around Skinner's calf and throw him off balance. Jag yanked the Wolfcane free of his demi-brother's grasp and, kneeling atop his chest, pressed it against his throat, forcing his chin up and back, exposing the soft meat over the jugular.

"Oh, yes. We mustn't forget dear Rend! He was another of Feral's by-blows, although we rarely mentioned it. That's why the fool was so loyal to me; he had a rather quaint sense of fraternal responsibility. Not that it helped him, in the end." Jag lowered his grinning face until his and Skinner's noses were almost touching. "Humans have a saying: 'Blood is thicker than water.' It is, you know. And it's *much* tastier, too!" The grin abruptly disappeared. "I bet you wish you'd bled to death in that alley in Albuquerque, brother-dearest. That way Rend would still be alive, not to mention your mother, the little *coyotero* bitch, and all their friends!"

Howling in rage, Skinner snapped his jaws shut on Jag's muzzle. He could feel the bridge of Jag's snout crack and splinter. Jag screamed in agony and let go of the Wolfcane, clamping his hands over his mutilated nose. He staggered backward, yowling as blood sprayed from his nostrils.

"*Jag!*" Jez screamed.

Jag turned to look at his twin sister, who was pointing behind him.

"Wha—?"

The silver head of the Wolfcane caught him in the back of his skull, crushing it like an eggshell. The force of the blow was so powerful that cranial fluid squirted from Jag's ears and eye sockets.

Skinner stood over Jag's body, his heart hammering in his chest. He knew he should feel exultation of some sort—he'd just killed his enemy, the murderer of his friend. But there was no joy in standing triumphant over the vanquished. He was alive. Jag was dead. That was it, nothing more.

He felt the bullet zip past his ear like an angry insect a second after hearing the shot. Jez, her face contorted by rage and grief, had her gun leveled at him.

"*Murderer!*"

Before she could squeeze off a second shot, a lithe, gray shadow emerged from the darkness behind Jez and grabbed her from behind. Shrieking invective, Jez fought for control of the weapon. Then another gray shadow appeared and another, finally disarming and wrestling her to the ground.

Suddenly the top of the mesa was swarming with slender gray shadows as the *coyotero* emerged from the network of holes that served as both ventilation and emergency evacuation systems for their community.

Sunder, finding himself surrounded by a dozen *coyotero* armed with silver-bladed knives and silver-tipped arrows, tossed down his gun and lifted his hands in surrender.

Changing Woman came forward and faced Feral, who stood nursing his mauled hand against his chest. Standing Wolf's empty skull snarled at his murderer from atop her head.

"You've grown careless in your old age, Lord Feral," she remarked acidly. "Living as Erzule's lapdog all these years has softened your wits."

"If you're going to kill me, bitch, get it over with," he growled.

"Who says we want to kill you? I was planning on sending you back to your queen with the heads of your wretched whelps."

Feral blanched. "Please—killing me would be better."

"For you, perhaps."

Changing Woman smiled. It was a cold and unnerving sight. "I shall be gracious. Far more gracious than you once were to me, twenty years ago, when you had the tables turned in your favor. If

you can take the Wolfcane away from your son,
then you and your companions get to leave unmo-
lested *with* the Wolfcane as the prize."

Feral looked from Changing Woman to Skinner
and back again. "It's some kind of trick. You're
going to use your damned coyote-magic to win."

Changing Woman raised her hands in denial. "I
give you my oath as a medicine woman there is
no *coyotero* magic involved."

Skinner gripped the Wolfcane between his
hands at waist level, his arms locked and rigid.
Following the instructions Changing Woman had
given him earlier, he tried to picture the energy
he sensed inside the staff. He glanced down and
was both surprised and elated to find the staff
wrapped in a nimbus of blue fire. He narrowed
his concentration, focusing the Wolfcane's fire into
his own hands and head.

"If you think I'm frightened by this mewling
pup of yours, Changing Woman, you're sadly
mistaken," sniffed Feral, squaring his shoulders.
He stepped forward and grabbed the Wolfcane's
haft with his good hand. "The Wolfcane is *vargr*!
It belongs with those who boast pure, undiluted
vargr blood! And no half-breed is going to keep
me from it!"

Feral pulled on the cane, trying to yank it free
of Skinner's grasp. Skinner dug his heels in and
struggled to keep both his grip and his balance.
Feral might have been old, but he was strong. The
blood from Feral's mangled right hand trickled
down the length of the polished shaft, making it
slippery. Father and son were snout-to-snout,
snarling into each other's faces. Every muscle in

their bodies stood out in full relief as they strained against one another.

After his battle with Jag, Skinner knew he was close—too close—to exhaustion. Should he falter even the slightest bit, everything would be over for him. He closed his eyes and focused his concentration even harder.

"Why do you close your eyes, traitor?" Feral snarled from between bared fangs. "Are you praying for help? From who? What god would look down on such as you with favor?"

Skinner's eyes reopened, but what looked out at Feral was far older, and far more terrible, than a teenaged boy.

"*I would*," said the Great Wolf.

Feral cried out as the ebony staff crackled at his touch. He felt his jaws snap shut and his muscles contract as an electrical charge surged up his arms. He tried to let go, but found his hands welded to the Wolfcane. The silver head pulsed with a strange light, the ruby eyes glowing like a campfire.

Feral stared in awestruck fear as the outline of a gigantic wolf made from witch-fire flickered into being above Skinner's head, superimposing its fearsome features over those of the young *vargr*. Feral knew he was facing the god-force of the *vargr*, the spirit of his race. He could feel its ancient eyes peering into the very depths of his soul. He had grown up within the pack, a *vargr* born and bred. And now, for the first time in his life, he knew what it was like to look into the eyes of a wolf and know fear.

The Great Wolf opened its jaws wide and closed

them about Feral's head and shoulders, shaking him as a she-wolf would a troublesome cub. There was the smell of ozone and frying flesh. Feral screamed once and was sent flying at least ten feet. He curled into a ball when he landed, his fur smoldering and eyes baked like egg custard. He shuddered and jerked like a cheaply made windup toy, whining like a kicked dog.

"*Daddy!*" Jez shrieked. Tearing herself free of her captors, she threw herself beside her father's steaming body. Sobbing hysterically, she cradled Feral's head in her lap. "Daddy, are you all right? Can you hear me?" Feral opened his mouth, as if to reply. His tongue had exploded and his teeth were reduced to little more than chalk. She looked up at Changing Woman, tears of hate rolling down her cheeks and matting the fur. "Damn you! You promised no coyote-magic!"

Changing Woman drew her ceremonial knife and knelt beside Feral. "And I kept my word," she said as she severed Feral's mutilated right hand and quickly wrapped it in a piece of cloth, tucking it inside a leather pouch at her side. "What you saw was wolf-magic."

"What about me? What are you going to do to me?" Jez sobbed.

Changing Woman shrugged. "That is up to Skinwalker to decide."

Jez jumped up, letting her father's head strike the ground, and ran to Skinner, throwing her arms around his neck. She buried her tear-wet face in his shoulder, babbling madly in his ear.

"Don't kill me, Skinner! I love you—! I'll be the queen soon, and you can help me get rid of

Mama! You can kill her and I'll take over and we can do as we like after that! It'll be wonderful, Skinner! I promise! I'm not mad at you for killing Jag and hurting Daddy. It's okay, I swear. . . ."

Skinner unwrapped her arms from around his neck, scowling at her in distaste.

"I don't think so."

Rosie and Changing Woman grabbed Jez, pinning her arms behind her. As they dragged her away, Jez yelled out, "Wait! There's something I must tell you!"

"What?"

"I'm pregnant."

Skinner looked her in the eye and knew she was telling him the truth.

"Let her go."

Changing Woman raised an eyebrow. "Are you certain that's wise?"

"I said let her go!"

Rosie and Changing Woman stepped away without further argument.

"Get out of here! Now! Before I change my mind!" Skinner barked.

"What about Daddy?"

Skinner stared at Feral, blinded and crippled by the very force that birthed his people countless millennia ago. This pathetic creature was his father—no. Not his father. His sire. He had provided the seed that Skinner grew from, nothing more. He looked over at Changing Woman, who merely shrugged.

Skinner turned back to Jez. "You can take him with you."

Jez didn't wait to be told twice. She quickly

shouldered what was left of her father onto her back and disappeared. Skinner turned his attention to the last of the *vargr*, Sunder.

"What about you? You can leave with Jez, if you like."

"That's the problem—I *don't* like Jez."

"You're welcome to stay then."

Sunder shook his head. "I'm a loner by nature. The only thing holding me to the pack was Rend. And now he's gone—"

"I understand."

As Sunder turned to leave, he fixed Skinner with a sideways grin and shook his head. "You a wolf-wizard. Who'd a thunk it?"

Chapter Twenty-five

One year later:

Skinner emerged from the sweat lodge and stood under the full moon that hung over the mesa, studying its dry ocean beds and dormant volcanoes as he wiped the perspiration from his body with a rough towel.

One year. So much had happened since he read the letter the day of his mother's funeral. He still considered Edna Cade his mother, although his relationship with Changing Woman had evolved since their initial reunion.

While she might be his mentor and friend, he knew Changing Woman could never be a mother to him. And he did not need her to be, for he had one already—one whose heritage lived in his heart and mind, if not his flesh. He still missed her, just as he missed Cheater and Rend.

After he let Jez go, they had relocated the settlement south, into Mexico, just to be on the safe side. Instead of living in caves and cliff-dwellings, this time the *coyotero* stayed atop the plateau in adobe buildings, rarely leaving the mesa. Skinner didn't regret the move, although Root Woman had complained mightily about being relocated from her familiar environs so late in life. But it was all for the best, really.

Rosie sat in front of their home, busy with the beadwork for the baby's ceremonial naming tunic, her swollen belly serving as a natural workbench. Fella dozed at her feet, sucking on his thumb. Changing Woman claimed that this rather undignified habit was a result of the *ulfr* being weaned too early.

Shortly after Rosie told him of her condition, Skinner had a vision claiming the child would be a boy. Changing Woman had one where it was a girl. Twins again, no doubt. He wondered if Jez had delivered twins, then dismissed the thought. He tried never to think of his demi-sister.

He had not been visited by the wolf-spirit since the night he battled Feral, but he could tell it was still there—buried inside the Wolfcane. If it had work for him to do, it was keeping it to itself. But then again, *vargr* live a very long time. It might be another century or two before the wolf-spirit set him on whatever path it had chosen for him.

Until then, he would continue studying magic under Changing Woman, love his mate and raise his cubs the best way he knew how. He could ask no more out of life. After all, in his heart of hearts, he was his father's son.

FANTASTICAL LANDS

SHROUD OF SHADOW by Gael Baudino. Natil is the last Elf—lone survivor in the Age of the Inquisition where there is no longer a place for her. Now, with her powers soon diminishing, she must slowly make her way to the final place where she will depart forever the world of mortals—but three things will intervene Natil from taking that final step. (452941—$4.99)

THE CATSWORLD PORTAL by Shirley Rousseau Murphy. Come to the land where an enchanting young woman will reclaim her rightful crown and liberate her people, where she will travel from the Hell Pit to the very heart of the sorceress queen's court, and where she will magically transform into the guise of a calico cat! "A captivating feline fantasy!"—*Booklist* (452755—$5.50)

RED BRIDE by Christopher Fowler. When John Chapel is offered a career change, his mundane life is transformed. He's drawn to Ixora, the woman of his dreams, and into a shadow realm—a place marked by murder and by the dark, unseen figure of a slayer who might reach out to claim not only their lives but their souls. (452933—$4.99)

BROTHERS OF THE DRAGON by Robin W. Bailey. Caught in a war between dragon-riders and bloodthirsty unicorns, two brothers trained in martial arts lead the forces of Light toward victory. (452518—$4.99)

UNDER THE THOUSAND STARS by John Deakins. Return to Barrow, a unique town in Elsewhen where even a worker of dark magic must sometimes work for the Light. (452534—$4.99)

HEART READERS by Kristine Kathryn Rusch. They are called heartreaders—magic-bonded pairs who can see into a person's very soul and read the nature of his or her heart—and through their strength, a kingdom might thrive or fall. (452828—$4.99)

Prices slightly higher in Canada.

Buy them at your local bookstore or use this convenient coupon for ordering.

PENGUIN USA
P.O. Box 999 – Dept. #17109
Bergenfield, New Jersey 07621

Please send me the books I have checked above.
I am enclosing $_____ (please add $2.00 to cover postage and handling). Send check or money order (no cash or C.O.D.'s) or charge by Mastercard or VISA (with a $15.00 minimum). Prices and numbers are subject to change without notice.

Card # _____ Exp. Date _____
Signature _____
Name _____
Address _____
City _____ State _____ Zip Code _____

For faster service when ordering by credit card call **1-800-253-6476**

Allow a minimum of 4-6 weeks for delivery. This offer is subject to change without notice.

If you and/or a friend would like to receive the *ROC Advance*, a bimonthly newsletter featuring all the newest and hottest ROC books and authors, on a complimentary basis, please fill out this form and return it to:

ROC Books/Penguin USA
375 Hudson Street
New York, NY 10014

Your Address
Name _____
Street _____ Apt. # _____
City _____ State _____ Zip _____

Friend's Address
Name _____
Street _____ Apt. # _____
City _____ State _____ Zip _____